TECHNOFARM

Other Books by Bob Biderman

A People's History of Coffee and Cafes
Eight Weeks in the Summer of Victoria's Jubilee
A Knight at Sea (as R.J. Raskin)
Sacha Dumont's Amsterdam
Strange Inheritance
Genesis Files
Judgement of Death
Paper Cuts
Mayan Strawberries
Letters to Nanette
Red Dreams
Moishe Kaplan and the SDS Murders
Anna and the Jewel Thieves (with David Kelley)
The Polka-Dotted Postman (with Cat Webb)
Further Education
Romancing Paris. Again.
Left-Handed Portuguese Zen

TECHNOFARM

Bob Biderman

First published in Great Britain by Black Apollo Press, 2015

HB - ISBN: 9781900355100
PB - ISBN: 9781900355810

A CIP catalogue record of this book is available at the British Library.

This is a work of fiction. Names, characters, businesses, places, events and incidents are used in a fictitious manner. Any resemblance to actual persons, living or dead, or actual businesses is purely coincidental.

Cover Design: Kevin Biderman

1994

CHAPTER 1

~ TUESDAY 21 JUNE 1994 ~

THE SUBTERRANEAN OFFICES in the great, red Victorian building, where darkness and gloom were built in like a moral prerogative, had once been used to hide the fresh corpses which had been offered to the medical school by the special procurers whose methods and supplies were rarely questioned by the college. They were hungry for cadavers to be butchered by clumsy students trying vainly to slice through the middle lamella of the lumbar fascia without botching up a kidney – or so the story was told to Grant when he first moved in several years before.

He had done what he could to brighten the place up, covering the walls with tapestries and masks from his time in Africa, Buddhist sculptures from his visits to the Far East, Mayan artefacts from trips to South America and other knickknacks from expeditions to the four corners of the globe when he had been on the payroll of the World Health Organisation. But, whatever he did, the dour air of the place, tinged with traces of formaldehyde, always seemed to filter through, staining his precious objects with a rather off-putting yellow so that in the end he took them back to his cramped apartment overlooking the British Museum.

It was a few minutes after he had come back to his office from the lecture. He was looking over a student paper, finding himself bored to tears, not so much from disinterest but from the sloppy workmanship. The paper had clearly been done in a rush, over a midnight bottle of plonk, he suspected – there were even a few reddish stains as evidence. No thought had been put into it, not even an attempt at analysis – just something dashed off in the wee hours of the morning and handed in like a bag of dirty socks.

He put the paper down in disgust. Why should he care? he wondered. And then he realised. He didn't anymore. It suddenly dawned on him – something he had known all the time. He hated teaching.

When he had left his job at the World Health Organisation, he had been suffering from what had been called fatigue. It wasn't an extraordinary diagnosis for someone who had travelled from disaster to disaster, from the latest drug-resistant strain of malaria in Burma to outbreaks of ancient bubonic plague in the highlands of Mexico. He could feel the gradual change coming over him long ago, from a youthful idealist on the front lines of the battle against pandemics to the mature pragmatist balancing the possible with the likely and making do with what he could get. Then came the accident at Seveso which put a mighty dent in his brightly polished armour – though he could have lived with that, since he was still convinced that he had acted properly.

But it was his time in Africa, two gruelling years in Kenya doing a study on the AIDS epidemic, that finally threw him over the brink. What he had witnessed there was, in terms of absolute horror, beyond anything he had ever seen.

Even now it continued to haunt him like an apocalyptic apparition. In his mind he would see that endless highway stretching from Nairobi to Mombassa. Along the road, all the truck stops, tiny villages with lean-to hovels, tin roofs baking in the blazing sun, heating up the stinking rooms like ovens; the ersatz beer halls, with slat wood benches and sticky tables; the tiny huts scattered in the back yards for the truckers. Dirty mattresses on the muddy ground, women with thin, dry lips and open sores on their arms and bony legs, so wasted they could hardly keep their stained skirts above their lanky hips. Every stop along the route had that same rank odour of beer and stale cum – the bodies, lifeless, gaunt, defiled as the land which stretched out flat and dry and grimy as far as he could see.

At the end of the road was the hospital, its wards overflowing with matchstick limbs, crammed into rooms without beds, naked in the damnable heat but too gaunt to sweat, faces with sunken eyes in lifeless heads, no longer black but an ashen shade of grey. They lingered on, half dead, clinging to a sort of zombie life that made living an obscenity.

That was the land he lived in now; not only at night when those terrible images would flood his mind, but sometimes, during lectures or meetings it would happen in an instant, like a black talon ripping through his head. And rather than fading quietly into the dark corners of his brain – as most obsessions do, given time – they seemed to be coming more frequently.

It was also why teaching had become such a burden to him. This morning, for example, when he had first come in and looked around at the students, quietly seated in the semicircular rows that ascended like the balcony of a miniature opera house in dizzying abruptness, he had hardly recognised a single one though this was the final lecture of term. Even as he spoke, he kept glancing, involuntarily, in the direction of a large, bald-headed man taking copious notes who stared at the lectern with grotesque eyes that seemed to bulge from his face. And he couldn't help thinking this person either had a thyroid condition or else was a serious lunatic.

His lecture had ended with his ideas on the general nature of poisons: "The first rule to remember is that everything is a poison. The second rule – seemingly a contradiction of the first – is that nothing is a poison. The third rule is that substances which are poisonous to one organism in the biological continuum are not necessarily poisonous to another. The fourth rule, a corollary of the third, is that substances toxic to one individual of a species are not necessarily toxic to another."

He looked up and noticed the expression of dismay on several youngish faces.

"If this sounds confusing," he went on, "we only have ourselves to blame. For 'poison' is one of those words that science could readily do without. Labelling some substance as a 'poison' is similar to labelling an individual as 'evil'. Whatever we say about that person in the future, the notion of evil remains like a bad taste overriding every other impression we might have had. The same is true with a substance labelled 'poison'. Whatever else it might be, once labelled it forever lingers in the mind.

"In fact, what we have seen is that any substance, any chemical or plant extract, can have either therapeutic or toxic effects on a particular organism. The equation will depend on two things – dosage and an individual's specific constitution at a certain point in time. All we can say with certainty is that the lesser quantity is curative while the greater is injurious. But the exact quantity is always relative.

"Rabbits can tolerate great amounts of atropine. They can be fed for weeks on the roots, berries and leaves of Atropa belladonna. They can also consume quantities of cocaine that would destroy most humans without showing signs of ill effects. Berries from the Deadly Nightshade plant can be eaten with seeming impunity by blackbirds but they are often fatal to pigs and sheep. Spotted Hemlock, disastrous to certain imbibing philosophers, can be easily tolerated by goats. Asperula odorata, on the other hand, can be eaten by humans but are often deadly to geese.

"For belladonna and hemlock, the toxic or therapeutic effects on humans are well-known. But how about other plants that we classify as foods? Take the mainstay of an ordinary stew, for example. How many of us know that the common potato can induce fits in some unlucky soul? Or that turnips can make some people suffer from breathlessness? Or that radishes in your salad can make someone extremely ill from its toxicological effects?

"None of us would have the audacity to call potatoes, turnips or radishes 'poisons', but that's exactly what they are to some..."

It was here that he stopped, focusing his eyes on a young woman in the third row who was waving her hand in the air. There was nothing more disturbing to him than losing his train of thought in mid-sentence.

Grant looked at the young woman dressed in black trousers and a black cardigan, her light brown hair pulled severely over her head and tied into an intricate knot.

He raised an eyebrow as a sign of impatience. "Is it urgent Miss..."

"Janet Haskel. Ms Janet Haskel," the woman, said, putting the emphasis on the titular designation.

"Is it urgent Ms Janet Haskel?" he repeated with a restrained sigh.

"I was wondering about your basic premise," she said, totally ignoring his question as well as his desire to move on. "If I did believe in evil, I suppose it follows that I would believe in poisons, too. Isn't that a semantic trap? I mean, doesn't the concept of 'poison' serve a useful purpose both in practice and in theory? That something can either be harmful or a remedy isn't really the issue. Aspirin can cure your headache or it can kill you. We don't call it a poison, though, since it's part of our basic arsenal of drugs. However, we do educate ourselves as to dosage and we make it clear that not following proscribed amounts can lead to disastrous results.

"On the other hand, we do call arsenic a poison because we don't want to encourage its use by patients even though it can and often is prescribed as a drug, under a different name, of course. I would think that toxicology is a useful branch of science only if we allow ourselves to call things by their proper names and establish definite parameters whereby we can determine cause and effect. That's what science is all about. The statement 'everything is relative' leaves it all up to

God. Frankly, I was hoping for a little more facts and figures. Looking down at my notes, I can find little I can use, except to be careful with radishes and potatoes."

"You have a question, I suppose?" Grant asked patiently, even though he felt his stomach churn.

"Well, I suppose my question is this – as future epidemiologists, how do we make sense of everything you said? I mean, how, for heaven's sake, would we use it?"

Part of him half admired her brashness. And maybe it was a fair question after all, he thought.

"From an epidemiological perspective," he replied, "we would like to know how a certain pollutant in the environment will affect the natural habitat or, more specifically, what its toxic effect will be on humans. Unfortunately, we cannot do this. We can only say that, from past experience a certain toxin released into the environment will be dangerous and probably will cause certain problems, but we can never be sure which individuals will be affected and what will be their reaction.

"For example, in July of 1976, an accident took place in the town of Seveso in Italy. A plant that manufactured trichlorophenol – a chemical used to make antiseptics – released a large amount of dibenzodioxins into the atmosphere contaminating an area of about 700 acres. Within a week, a number of children were hospitalised with chloracne and animals - sheep, dogs, cows, horses - began dying. The soil in an established radial area around the plant was analysed and was found to contain high levels of dioxin..."

Grant stopped for a moment and looked at the young woman who had challenged him. He could see she was concentrating on his words. "As the epidemiologist in charge, Ms Haskel, what would you have done?"

She didn't hesitate. Her response was immediate. "Because of the high levels of dioxin found in the soil, and since dioxin is known to be a teratogen in animals, all the women who were living in the exposure zones during their first trimester of pregnancy should have been offered therapeutic abortions."

"In fact, that is exactly what was done, Ms Haskel, on the advice of toxicologists who, as I said, had studied the effect of dioxin on animals. Of the 150 women contacted, thirty had abortions performed despite the resistance of the Catholic Church."

The young woman nodded her head in approval.

"However, of the 120 remaining women who gave birth, there were only two who bore children with anomalies – one with an intestinal obstruction, the other with a genital malformation, both of which were corrected by surgery."

"It still was the correct decision," said the woman.

"The advice on therapeutic abortions was given by toxicologists, one of whom was also an epidemiologist brought in to study the situation. It may have been proper advice based on the statistical data he had in hand, but I would be surprised if there wasn't some later doubt, some qualms..."

"Maybe that has more to say about the scientist than the science," Janet Haskel retorted, meeting his eye with a harsh, condemning look. "Without being able to make decisions based on statistical knowledge, what value is epidemiology?"

Grant felt extremely tired and his head hurt the way it did when he was coming down with the flu.

He was about to say something he would have regretted. But looking out at the younger students in the audience, he saw that they were fidgeting in their seats, seemingly embarrassed. So he ended by directing his final statement to them:

"Epidemiologists," he said, "are more like detectives than physicians. And like detectives, they can neither prevent a murder nor bring back the dead. But they can sometimes help to prevent more killings by finding the source of the gun and who it was that pulled the trigger. And in times like these, as keepers of a very troubled world, we need all the bloody help we can get..."

~

Recollecting the morning's disaster in his subterranean office, his thoughts were suddenly interrupted by a rapping sound. Looking up, he saw a silhouette of a young woman painted in profile on the opaque glass of his office door. He rubbed his eyes, trying to erase the images and then, clearing his throat, he said, loudly – perhaps louder than he had meant – "Come in!"

The door opened. He recognised her at once and it showed on his face. "Ms Haskel. Don't tell me you're still hungry for raw flesh..."

Her hair was down and hung loosely on her shoulders. She looked much less terrifying that way, he thought. In fact, close up, her face had an almost gentle look to it.

"I thought it was a fair question," she said. "It wasn't my purpose to antagonise you."

Grant looked down at the paper he had just been reading – attempting to read, that is – and then back up at her. "It was a fair question," he said. "I don't even mind being antagonised. At least you've given the issue some thought, which, I suspect is more than most of my students do..."

"You don't even know their names!" she blurted out. Then, closing her eyes, she said, "I'm sorry..."

"It's your manner I find a bit off-putting."

She opened her eyes again and looked at him squarely. "My manner? Oh, yes..."

"You're so combative, aren't you?"

"You'd rather have us pliant, I suppose."

"Pliant? No. Polite's more the word. It isn't such a bad trait."

"Except it doesn't get you anywhere." She gave him a questioning look. "What century are you living in?"

He chuckled. "Frankly, I don't know."

The corners of her mouth had worked their way into a frown. "I'm sorry I came," she said, turning on her heels.

Grant stood up. "Wait a minute..."

She turned back around and stared at him angrily.

"Why did you come to my office? Certainly not to apologise..."

"I wanted to tell you I'm dropping out of the course!"

"What for?"

"Financial reasons."

"Don't you have a grant?"

She gave him an ironic smile. "Hardly enough to pay my expenses."

"How about your parents? Can't they help you out?"

"They don't have much of an income. Besides, there are two more after me...and I'm the girl."

"I don't want you to leave the course," said Grant. He thought a moment and then wrote something down on a pad next to his telephone. "I've got some contacts at World Health," he said. "Let me find out what kind of funds they have for research assistants..."

"Why?" she asked. "You don't even like me. And I certainly don't like you."

"You've got a good mind," he said. "You're quick, you're bright, you're intelligent. And you're angry." He put his hand on her shoulder and looked into her eyes. "I'm not asking you to agree. Just think about it. You've got passion. What you need is a little compassion..."

"I could say the same thing about you," she replied, pulling herself away, "in reverse."

She stomped out of the office, nearly bumping into the figure who was standing in the doorway.

How long he had been standing there, Grant didn't know. But he recognised him at once. It was the man he had seen sitting in the lecture hall – the one with the bulging eyes.

There was a ridiculous smile on his face as he entered Grant's tiny office. The kind of oily smirk that might have been on a sleazy postcard captioned "Nudge, nudge. Wink, wink."

"You didn't see 'Oleana', did you?" he asked.

Grant looked at him quizzically. "I beg your pardon?"

"The play by Mamet. Really should, you know. It might have been written just for you."

"That's why I don't go to the theatre much," Grant responded. "Plays written for me are guaranteed to be boring." Then, narrowing his eyes, he said, "Who are you?"

The man was middle-aged and balding. But his face was pink like a baby's. Or a baboon's backside, Grant thought.

"Ruddle's the name," he said, holding out a curiously tiny hand. "T. S. Ruddle..."

Grant was surprised at the softness of the skin as he reluctantly shook the man's hand. It felt like a piece of refrigerated liver and it gave him the creeps.

Ruddle put down his black leather briefcase on Grant's desk, giving the hide a gentle caress before he opened it up, retrieving a manila folder from its contents. "I enjoyed your lecture," he continued. "Especially the bit about vegetables. I always wondered why turnips made me wheeze. My wife thinks it's self-induced..."

"What can I do for you, Ruddle," Grant asked impatiently, watching in dismay as the fat, little man colonised his desk.

Ruddle's bulging eyes had a bit of a twinkle. "It's not for me, Dr Grant. Oh, Gordon Bennett! Not me! Not at all!"

"It's just a phrase," said Grant, rubbing the back of his neck. "A manner of speaking."

"Oh, right! Of course!" He let out a strange little laugh. "My wife always says how literal I can be. 'Ruddle', she says, 'why are you always so literal?' 'Maybe it's my training,' I tell her. I trained as a chemist, you see. That was right before the war. Precision was the key. If you wanted a good titration, you had to follow the instruction manual to the letter. You had to be literal. But you're a scientist, Dr Grant. You know what I mean..."

"Listen," said Grant, losing his patience, " I've got quite a bit on my plate today..." He was convinced Ruddle was an insurance salesman.

The smile faded from Ruddle's lips. "Right you are, Dr Grant. I'll get to the point. It seems we need your services..."

"My services? What kind of services? What the blazes are you talking about?"

"I'm talking about past promissory notes. Bills of exchange. Obligations due." His narrow, almost hairless, eyebrows raised in a significant motion as he took out an ageing document from the folder and showed it to Grant. "That is your signature, isn't it? I'm afraid you've been seconded to us, Dr Grant."

He held the document in his hand, recalling a faint memory from the distant past and then looked up at Ruddle, at his hypnotically repellent eyes. His demeanour was no longer one of academic arrogance, but of tired resignation.

"What do you want from me?" he asked.

~

The 4:50 from King's Cross was a mixed assortment of early shift commuters, tourists, student types and other day-trippers catching the best light of a wonderful summer afternoon. The trip north, from London to East Anglia, so dark and bleak in winter, came into its own in the late spring and early summer. Outside, the yellow fields of rape covered the rolling hills like sun-drenched carpets. And where it wasn't gold, everything was moist and green and fertile.

To Grant, journeying by train was the most pleasant and civilised way to travel. There was none of the fuss and bother of traffic-jammed highways and one could sit back, relax and watch the world go by in relative luxury. Certainly the trains were a far cry from the carriages of his youth –

he still remembered with fondness the special smell of the upholstery and the quiet compartments that were so cosy and calm. But even now, even with the downgrading of service, the claw-back of little comforts like cushioned seats and writing tables, he still felt seduced by the special rhythm and the feel of great metal wheels gliding along iron rails.

The seats were nearly all filled as the train had left London. Twenty minutes later, they had reached Stevenage where many of the commuters got off. From there, the train sped on to Royston and, after off-loading more of the men in suits who neatly folded their broadsheets into their attachés, clicking them shut as they left, it proceeded on a leisurely milk run through village towns like Meldreth, Shepreth, Foxton and Whittlesford.

After Royston, those who remained seemed more casual and relaxed than the stiff, pasty-faced, bankers and accountants who used the outskirts of London as their bedrooms and nothing more. Instead of polished briefcases, brightly-coloured knapsacks now predominated. There was a wholesome and organic look about the remaining passengers, Grant thought – much more to his taste than the bloodless, pin-striped regiment who lived their life by mechanical precision and woke each morning to find the day a bland repeat of the one before and the one that would follow.

In the seat across from him, facing his way, was a young couple – a thin young man with a boyish face, thick hair swept back, un-parted, spectacles with circular black frames; and a young woman, dark eyes, long, dark hair, wearing a loose-fitting frock of pink and yellow.

He lay back against the headrest and wondered at the strange chain of circumstances that had brought him here.

The documents Ruddle had left him were of little help. A few extracts from hastily faxed medical records showing nothing more than several cases of some sort of pneumonic ailment. Too early for lab results on cultures. Nothing else significant except vague references to epidermal markings. Yet the whole thing was being taken seriously enough to have confidentiality stamps of the highest category on almost every page.

What was his mission? he had asked.

To find out if there was any cause for concern. To make sure all information was transmitted directly to the Agency. And to keep a lid on it should anything eventuate. That's all Ruddle would say.

"Ridiculous!" Grant had objected. "You claim there's a suspected environmental hazard, but you won't tell me what you suspect!"

"Information comes to us in various ways," Ruddle had said as he packed up his briefcase with the obsessive care of someone who brushes their dentures after every meal. "Like an elaborate puzzle, sometimes a piece is important because it has been given to you by someone who, for one reason or another, knows nothing else except that it is important."

Why him? he protested. Certainly there were plenty of competent people up there who could be relied upon?

But he had been requested especially by someone on the Cambridge team. Someone he knew, Ruddle had said. A GP named Pauline Quail.

~

He had phoned her right after Ruddle had left.

"It's good to hear your voice," he said. "I'm surprised you're still in Cambridge."

"How are you, Peter?" she asked. Her voice sounded genuinely concerned. But that was one of her talents, he remembered.

"Fine..." he replied.

There was a brief, awkward silence. Then she said, "Peter, I need your help... it's a professional problem," she hastened to add.

"I know. Environmental Health contacted me. What's going on up there?"

"There's some curious illnesses I've seen in the last few days. They've all been preliminarily diagnosed as mycoplasma infections but there's something about them that concerns me – the suddenness of the reaction, the severity..."

"We've been seeing new forms of mycoplasma with reactions like that," he said.

"Some of my patients are quite ill. And they don't seem to be responding to treatment..."

"It's a feature of these new bugs that they tend to be antibiotic resistant..."

"Yes, but there are other things. They all have a peculiar type of skin eruption. I've never seen one like that..."

"How many are in hospital?" he asked.

"I've sent five to Addenbrooke's so far...for respiratory insufficiency."

"What do they say up there?"

"They're still doing tests. But, I've seen several others this morning..."

"Well, it doesn't sound like there's much to go on. Until the hospital lab reports come in..."

Suddenly, her voice sounded ominous to him. "Peter, there's something else..."

"What?"

"Maybe it's better if we don't speak over the phone..." she said.

As he listened to that conversation again in his head, he thought of Pauline. He let his mind drift back to half-forgotten days.

The train jolted as it hit a bend in the track. He became aware that the young woman sitting across from him was looking in his direction. She was no more than twenty, he reckoned. Her smile, the unconscious bloom of youth, filled her face with a glowing radiance.

He closed his eyes and saw himself on a Burmese train, outside Rangoon. A sweet odour of orange blossoms and cinnamon filled his nostrils and he sensed the closeness of a warm, soft, fragrant woman. She was dressed in white linens which clung to her figure like silk. Her bare legs were tanned and the blush of her face mirrored the young woman who sat across from him.

They were in a hotel bedroom. Overhead, the propeller blades of the ceiling fan slowly stirred the humid air. The light, strained through the curtain's bamboo slats, fell on their naked bodies in concave stripes, twisting and bending and dancing to their motion.

He felt the cool sheets between their legs as he pressed his lips against hers, remembering the salty, erotic taste of her mouth.

Then everything started to change. All at once he was no longer a participant but staring down at her from above. He saw her colour was turning from flush to pink to grey before his eyes. The noise that emitted from her mouth wasn't desire but a mournful cry for help.

Suddenly his head was filled with a shrill, deafening sound and an explosion of hot red light, of fire...

"Are you all right?" The young man's hand was on his shoulder, gently shaking him. He opened his eyes and tried to orient himself, remembering where he was.

"You fell asleep," said the young man.

Grant got up from his seat. His body felt ungainly and clumsy. "I'm sorry..." he said.

"You must have had a nightmare," the young woman replied with a soft, understanding smile. "It happens to me..."

He made his way to the toilet and locked himself inside. He pressed down the tap, letting the water run into the sink until it flowed cold and then splashed it onto his face.

The train lurched. He felt his legs give way and he grabbed the toilet rail to steady himself. Then and only then did he notice his image in the mirror above the sink. It took a moment before he recognised who it was.

An instant later, he came to his senses. He shook it off as a passing attack, a slight nervous disorder. Nothing more.

At the same time, he felt the train grinding to a stop and he heard the driver's voice intoning over the speaker:

"Cambridge next. All passengers must alight..."

~

She was waiting for him at the station. When he first saw her standing there among the fresh-faced students rushing to get their bicycles from the tangled forest of rusty metal in the car park, he was struck by how much she had aged and how little. Her figure, still slim, seemed to carry extra weight, if not added poundage. And her eyes no longer had that unquenchable look of innocent adventure. But he thought there was something ageless about her welcoming smile as he made his way through the crush to greet her.

He gave her a kiss on her cheek as she held his hand and squeezed it gently. "It's so good to see you again, Peter," she said. And then, taking him by the arm, she led him outside to a Renault 2 CV, which would have been bright yellow if it hadn't been so dirty.

She opened the passenger door for him and, throwing some packages aside so he would have someplace to sit, she said, "I know a nice place where we can have a drink and talk..."

~

Brown's was one of those leafy cafés so much in vogue a few years before, spreading itself lightly over a massive area and achieving both a feel of space and intimacy by the use of ferns and potted plants. He ordered a whisky. She had a glass of Chablis instead of Glenlivet.

They caught up on old times as they drank.

"How is Hans?" he asked her.

"He's going through hard times, I expect just like the rest of the left oppositionists. They had such great hopes for the future, but instead they found themselves overwhelmed by the stampede to the free marketplace." She glanced down at her drink and ran her finger around the rim of the glass. "I haven't seen him for several years. I hear about him through Cicely..."

Then, looking up at Grant, she smiled in the manner of someone briefly recalling a past romance. "What about you, Peter? I heard you had taken a post at the university..."

"After I got back from Africa," he said. "I went through a pretty bad patch. The university job probably saved me from myself. But now it's starting to grow old..."

"Why's that?"

He shrugged. "I'm just not cut out to be a teacher, I suppose..."

"Of course not. You're a field epidemiologist. One of the best I've ever known..."

He cringed slightly and took a drink. "I'm not so sure," he said, putting down his glass. "Not after my experiences in Africa..." He looked at his watch and asked, "What time is the meeting?"

"We have a while yet," she replied.

"When did you and Hans split up?" he asked.

"Two – no, three years ago. But, really, we always had our separate worlds. After Cicely grew up, there was no need for pretence. Besides, he wanted to go back to Germany..."

"And you didn't?"

She laughed. "No. The German mind fascinates me, but in the end I find it incomprehensible. It's too precise. In many ways, I admire them their ability to achieve, to make things work. But when I'm there, after a while I find myself longing for the sweet disorder which is England. Yet once back home, this country drives me mad!

"Hans felt a duality, himself," she continued."He understood that aspect of the German nature, that rigidity. And he rebelled against it. He looked forward to the rebirth of a new Germany. He had great trust in the youth, in young people like Cicely..."

"How is Cicely?" he asked.

She thought a moment how best to put it. "She has fire in her eyes. She reminds me of Hans when he was young. She works as a freelance journalist. Just as he did..."

"Here or there?"

"Everywhere. She flits in and out, depending on her passion. I never know where she is or where she'll be. When she's on assignment, she simply disappears…"

Grant looked at his watch again.

"Yes, we should go," she said.

He motioned to the waiter and then turned back to her. "Just before I rang off this morning you were saying that something concerned you. Something you didn't want to speak about over the phone..."

"I don't know." She suddenly looked very glum, as if the whole thing might actually be a paranoid fantasy. "But I've been around for a while, Peter. I'm not the type who panics, easily..."

"I realise that," he said, "otherwise I wouldn't be up here now."

She let out a little sigh, as if what she had to say was so tenuous that it might fall apart if she breathed too hard. "When I was going through the records for the umpteenth time, I began to realise that someone in each of the households were related in a very curious way..."

"Not the patients themselves?" Grant asked.

"No. Just someone in the immediate family – the mother, perhaps, or a husband or a brother..." She stopped to take a sip of wine and then, as if trying to visualise something, she rolled the chilled glass against her cheek. "I used to be involved with an organisation, 'Physicians for Peace' – I think I might have sent you some literature..."

"I seem to remember something about that," he nodded, while thinking he probably filed it with the rest of his unwanted mail in the rubbish bin.

"It was an offshoot of the Campaign for Nuclear Disarmament. It originally started out as a way of sensitising people to the madness of atomic war, but it grew into a general critique of the nuclear industry. Now it's broadened even more, taking in a gamut of ecological problems – everything from toxic waste dumps to oil spills."

"A general purpose, one size fits all, do-good operation, I suppose." The look he gave her said everything.

"Crikey!" She let out a frustrated laugh. "What are you going to think of me now?"

"I'll think what I've always thought. That you're a good friend and a good physician who cares a hell of a lot more about her patients than most GPs and is currently under a lot of stress," he replied.

She looked up at him. Her eyes were wet and glistening. It was a different person. Someone he'd never seen before. Her voice was soft but the tone was almost pleading as she spoke: "Peter, I know something is wrong. I feel it."

It wasn't that he knew how to respond. On the one hand, he was struck by her open sincerity. On the other, he cringed at such a clichéd manipulation of logic. He wasn't one who easily fell for weepy protestations. But she wasn't someone who often wept.

He stood up. "Let's go," he said, taking some notes out of his wallet.

"Don't you dare," she said, taking money out of her purse at the same time. "You're my treat!"

~

The small conference room at Addenbrooke's was simmering. Not from extreme temperature, though the poor ventilation system contributed to the stuffy atmosphere, but from the agitated people inside.

Four men in suits were seated at a round table. From their tired expressions and manner of dress, Grant could tell they were administrators. Standing, clustered in the corners of the room were several knots of people – medical staff and technicians from the look of their outfits – engaged in animated discussions.

The contrast between the people seated at the table and those standing at the fringe was quite stark. It was as if two different nations on one ship were charting a course to opposing harbours.

A short grey man, with a face like a ferret, was making a very loud point and emphasising it with a gesticulating finger as Pauline Quail led Grant through the door. Even from across the room, his bright red cheeks, burning with indignation, made him stand out.

"That's Bernie Thompson," Pauline said, pointing to the ferret-faced man as she and Grant entered the conference room. "As you can see, he doesn't exactly exude patience."

"You'd better introduce me," said Grant. His voice was less than enthusiastic.

The intense verbosity seemed to ricochet off the walls as they walked over to the most heated corner.

"You have absolutely no authority to be doing this!" a man with a stethoscope hanging round his neck was arguing loudly. The listening device was bouncing wildly on his chest as he spoke.

"We have every authority!" shouted Thompson. "In a state of emergency we could take over the whole bloody hospital!"

"What emergency?" a woman medic shouted. "What emergency are you talking about? You should have been here last winter! Where the hell were you when we needed extra beds?"

"Excuse me," Pauline Quail said, pushing herself into the fray. "I hate to interrupt, but I need to speak with you, Bernie..." And saying that, she took him by the arm and guided him from the angry vortex like a vessel being towed from a whirlwind.

If Bernie Thompson was grateful, he didn't show it. "You were supposed to be here fifteen minutes ago," he hissed, glancing at his watch.

"I was delayed, Bernie," she said, moving quickly to the side of the room where Grant was waiting. It was as if the sooner she got there, the quicker she would be released of her charge.

"Bernie Thompson. Peter Grant." She introduced them succinctly and then stepped back.

"You're from CDSC?" asked Thompson, shaking hands.

"I work with them on a consultancy basis," said Grant.

Thompson lowered his voice. "I don't know what we've got ourselves into here. We've really stirred up a hornet's nest..."

"Well then maybe we better calm things down," said Grant, looking over at the table.

One of the administrators had stood up. He was a tall, angular man with silver streaks in his hair dressed in a well-cut suit that established him as management's top rung. Pulling out a watch from the pocket of his waistcoat, he said, "Gentlemen and ladies. I think it's time..."

The response wasn't immediate, but people did start drifting toward the table.

It took a few minutes before the room came to order.

"That's Netsworth," Pauline Quail whispered to Grant, as they sat down with Thompson, making their own little contingent at the round table. "He's Mr Big Wig here..."

Netsworth was one of those natural managers who had the personal presence which established some kind of discipline over chaotic situations without actually doing anything but being there. But today even Netsworth seemed unable to project a sense of calm.

"There seems to be a lot of confusion as to what actually is going on," Netsworth said, directing his statement to Bernie Thompson. "So maybe we could begin by discussing why a news quarantine was imposed..."

A number of heads around the table nodded in agreement.

"Suggested," Bernie Thompson put in.

"...suggested," Netsworth allowed. "But why even suggest a news blackout for something that essentially is a non-event?"

"What we have so far are twelve cases of atypical pneumonia," the senior consultant, a man named Browder, said.

"Fourteen," the matron, corrected. "Two more were admitted in the last hour."

"All right, fourteen," Browder went on, a little perturbed to have been contradicted by his own staff. "It may be a cause for concern, but how the blazes does it warrant this kind of intrusion?"

"They really are territorial little buggers, aren't they?" Pauline Quail whispered to Grant.

"Unless, of course, there's something those jolly little gentlemen at CDSC aren't telling us." The younger consultant, a pleasant looking man named Roger Cook, gave Grant a significant glance.

Grant suddenly realised that the other members of staff were staring at him too. He rubbed the top of his head, wondering how he got into this mess. But he had been used to dealing with impossible situations. So his response was automatic.

"There's nothing that the Communicable Disease Surveillance Centre could add to what you already know," said Grant. "It's true that we're taking any cluster of atypical pneumonitis very seriously now. The question of a voluntary embargo on news should be obvious. Scare stories of drug-resistant strains of mycoplasmas and mutant viruses create the kind of panic reactions that flood the surgeries and make it harder to weed out the 'sympathetic' cases from those that are real. Look what happened when the Indian Bubonic plague scare hit the headlines. Every Asian with a cough was suspect. At the outset, at least, until we can verify that there is no correctable environmental factor at work, we find it's best to keep a low profile."

Grant looked squarely at Netsworth. "However, we're here strictly on an advisory basis. No one's trying to tell you how to run your hospital."

"With all due respect, it still sounds to me as if you're being somewhat less than forthright," said Cook, the younger of the two consultants.

"I think we'll have to take the gentleman at his word," said Netsworth, somewhat mollified by Grant's approach. He looked over at an elderly man with a spotty complexion whose nose had the telltale signs of overindulgence. "Morton, what do we have from the lab?"

Morton Franks was the chief pathologist. He was due for retirement and was just coasting through his final months. "Nothing yet," he said in a bored tone of voice. "The early cultures show some possibility of mycoplasmas in several patients, but they could be false reads..."

There were so many mycoplasmas floating around hospital labs that it was easy to pick up false readings. This was why early cultures were never the best.

"I'll bet my boots it's not a mycoplasma," said Pauline Quail.

"Have we ruled out Legionella?" asked Browder looking over at the pathologist. He was referring to the bacteria that caused Legionnaire's Disease.

"We can't rule out anything this early," said Franks.

"I think we'll be able to rule that out quite fast once the epidemiological survey gets started," said Grant.

"So we're agreed about the quarantine? And an isolation ward?" Netsworth asked.

"Temporarily," said Browder, with a mannered disdain. "I think we'll see this blow over in a day or so."

"I'd like to point out that there's some difference between us," said Cook. His face appeared tense and angry. "From the patients I've examined, I believe we should be taking this very seriously indeed! The X-rays I've seen conform much more to a severe pulmonary oedema than to atypical pneumonia. That and the very peculiar exanthema lead me to suspect a possible toxic-allergic syndrome."

"What's your response to that, Carl?" Netsworth asked, turning to Browder.

"I'll wait for the lab reports," Browder mumbled. There was clearly no love lost between the two consultants.

"Have you tested for eosinophilia?" asked Grant, looking at the younger consultant.

"It's on order," Cook replied. "When can you get us your epidemiological data?"

"Set a meeting for tomorrow afternoon," said Grant. "I'll give you a report on my findings."

~

"Where are you staying?" Bernie Thompson asked Grant as they headed out of the conference room. "If you don't have a place, we could see about hospital quarters."

"I've got plenty of room in my house," Pauline said. She was walking between the two men. "You'd be a lot more comfortable there. You're also welcome to use my car – though you might find things more accessible on bicycle."

"Then I'll be off," said Thompson, "We'll meet at my office at nine." He left, mumbling, "Don't expect you'll find there's much to it."

"I just want to look in on a patient," Pauline said to Grant when Thompson had departed. "Why don't you come along?"

~

The open wards stretching out from the central corridor were antiseptic clean but the colour scheme and the plainness of the architecture made everything seem dreary. Only the occasional vase of flowers or the cheery clothes of a carefree visitor gave hope to the notion that somewhere outside those halls might be a world brighter than this.

It was one of Pauline's gripes. "I'm not saying everything has to be brilliant orange or there should be great smiling faces painted on the walls to elevate the mood. But that infernal shade of green!" Pauline shook her head. "Why do hospitals have to look so much like hospitals?"

"At least this one has beds and cleans the blood off the floor," Grant replied, following her down a corridor that jutted left and then seemed to go on forever. He felt that compared to what he saw on his travels, the English didn't know how lucky they were.

"I hope you can say that next year," she answered back.

Addenbrooke's had a fine reputation and, regardless of Pauline's critique, he was struck by its apparent efficiency. He sensed it in the demeanour of the staff, especially the nurses and orderlies, who didn't have that haggard, almost desperate look so often seen among institutional employees who felt themselves aboard a floundering boat, bailing out just enough water to keep it afloat.

A sign over the doorway indicated the children's ward was off to the right, down an adjoining corridor. However, Pauline continued straight along till she reached another set of doors marked 'Infectious Wards – Restricted Access'.

"She's being kept in isolation until the lab results come in," Pauline explained.

Entering the area, she went immediately to the nurses' station and chatted briefly with the young woman on duty. She was given two gauze masks, one of which she gave to Grant. Then, tying the flimsy mask over her nose and mouth she walked over to the room pointed out by the nurse.

She gave a quick, perfunctory tap at the door before opening it. Grant, tying his mask on, followed her inside and closed the door behind him.

The dimmer switch connected to the overhead light had been turned halfway, so that the bed with the plastic canopy, set in the middle of the room, was mercifully free from the overlit glare other wards had to suffer.

The first thing that struck him was the almost reverential stillness which centred all attention on the shallow, rasping sounds emanating from the bed. It was only when his eyes adjusted to the diminished light that he saw the couple sitting quietly at the side.

There was always something curiously surreal about the wearing of veils, Grant thought to himself. With the lower half of the face swathed in gauze, the focus of expression was the eyes. And, even if the eyes weren't the gateway to the soul, they said a lot about the heart. In the case of the two figures sitting there so still, they spoke of misery.

The couple stood up as Pauline came over to them. She hugged the woman and took the man's hand as warmly and easily as she had taken Grant's when she had met him at the railway station.

They spoke in whispers.

"How is she?"

"She seems to be resting easily now."

"Has the consultant been by to see her recently?" Pauline glanced at the chart. "Ah, yes. I see he has..."

She introduced Grant to Eduardo and Maria Rojas, telling them he was a specialist in communicable diseases.

"Isn't there some antibiotic that can help her?" Eduardo asked Grant. "In Chile they would have tried many antibiotics by now." His voice was beseeching, yet dignified. He had the forceful impatience of a man fighting for his daughter's well-being but, at the same time, realising he would gain nothing by antagonising those who held the child's life in their hands.

Grant replied that they were still awaiting the lab report and that he was there only as an advisor. However, if it wasn't a bacterial infection then antibiotics wouldn't work.

"But you will be able to do something, won't you doctor?" Maria asked. Her enormous eyes were great, moist pools of desperate supplication. Unlike her husband, she would make no pretence about pleading for her daughter as a woman, as a mother or as a Catholic who would willingly give her soul back to the Church; whatever it took to save her child.

It was at times like these that Grant remembered why he gave up practising medicine. He was ill-disposed to play the role of God especially when it was thrust on him by those who asked nothing more than to give them back their child's life.

Pauline, on the other hand, was secure in her role as healer. She knew her limitations. But as a woman, she had no qualms about sharing pain and sorrow and could do so without the threat to her professional standing often felt by her male counterparts.

"Believe me, Maria," said Pauline, looking at the grief-stricken woman with honest sympathy, "we'll do all we can. I asked Dr. Grant to come along so we could have his opinion. But it takes time to do the tests and we need to find the source of Felicia's illness before we can effectively treat it."

While Pauline was speaking, Grant had gone up to the child's bed and looked through the plastic oxygen tent at the girl who lay there so still. It was like seeing a figure shrouded in fog. The details were blurred and softened as if envisioned through a hazy lens – like a figure in a dream.

He lifted up the plastic tent and took the child's arm. It was limp and quite warm to the touch. He examined the skin which was blotchy and rough.

"Has your daughter ever suffered from psoriasis?" he asked, turning to the parents. "Does she often get rashes on her body on her arms?"

"Sometimes but not rough and flaky like that," said the father.

Feeling her pulse, he observed her colouring, the glazed look of her eyes and the shallowness of her breath. Then he let the side of the tent back down.

"She will be OK, doctor?" asked Maria, pressing once more for confirmation that everything would turn out well in the end.

"She's very ill," said Grant, "but the consultants here are some of the finest in the country."

Maria looked with alarm toward Dr. Quail. "What does he mean?" she asked in a fearful tone of voice.

"Felicia is very ill – you can see that yourself – but she's receiving the best care available." Pauline gave Maria another hug. "Trust us," she whispered in her ear. "We won't let her down."

~

It was a quiet, tree-lined street of Edwardian houses tucked in a little cul-de-sac off Chesterton Road. Each house, except for one, had a manicured garden. The one exception had a tangle of woody shrubs and wild plants that set it apart from its more genteel neighbours – like an ageing bohemian, sorely in need of a haircut.

"Home," she said, looking at him with a sad, sweet smile.

She got out.

He followed her as she opened the metal gate, rusty at the hinges, through the jungle of untamed shrubs and up the uneven path of paving stones which had begun to buckle from the menagerie of roots that had worked their way underneath them.

Standing next to her by the door as she fished through her purse for her key, he sensed the unpleasant odour of mildew.

"I'm always misplacing it," she said with a tinge of embarrassment. And then, smiling coyly like an errant school child, she breathed a sigh of relief. "I've found it!"

Pushing open the door, they walked into a dark hallway. She felt around for the light switch and, finding it, turned on the overhead bulb. The lighted hallway, rather bleak up till then, now appeared inviting and warm. The walls were papered with a pleasant, unobtrusive flowery design and were covered with pictures in various sized frames – original watercolours, it seemed to him, of landscapes that looked to be of the North, most likely Scotland. Perhaps the Western Isles, he thought.

She led him to the first room branching off the hall.

"This was Hans's study. I think you'll find it comfortable," she said.

It looked satisfactory enough, with a divan at one end and a desk set by the front window. The walls were lined with sagging shelves, heavily laden with books. And leafy plants were everywhere between the books, on the desk and covering the side tables which were thick with ceramic pots containing colourful and exotic species he would have been at pains to identify.

Leaving his valise by the divan, he followed her into the hall, passing the stairs which went to the upper floor, and down its length to the room at the back which turned out to be the kitchen.

The kitchen was a long, galley affair with French doors at the far side. There was a small dining table which looked out onto a pleasant rear garden. On the table, the raw components of a salad lay lifeless on a long wooden cutting board – a tomato, a piece of celery and a carrot. The luxuriously curly leaves of some expensive lettuce lay temptingly on a brightly coloured plate of Italian design. Standing by, ready to be mixed, was a bottle of extra-virgin olive oil and some Balsamic vinegar.

The tomato was one of the most luscious he had ever seen. Deep red and meaty, it reminded him of a French Pomme d'Amour rather than something found wasting away in a British supermarket.

"I was thinking of having something simple tonight," she said, looking wistfully at the vegetables. She glanced over at him.

"I'm not sure I'm hungry. But I could do with a drink," he suggested.

"Good idea!" She sounded relieved at not having to deal with food quite yet.

They left the kitchen for the adjoining room.

It was a cosy space with many more plants this time of the fern variety – a small piano, some well-used furniture topped with Madras throw-covers, probably from an Oxfam catalogue, freestanding shelves holding books (but, unlike the scientific tomes in the study, these seemed to be novels, biographies and books about faraway places).

She went over to the shelving unit at the side of the fireplace and turned on the stereo. Selecting a tape from a pile, she placed it in the playback unit and pressed a button. What came out of the speakers was the seductive, melancholy sound of Billie Holiday's 'Lady Sings the Blues'.

The music had a strange effect, transporting him someplace in his mind – someplace hazy, he wasn't sure where. He suddenly felt disoriented and slightly dizzy. He made his way to the sofa and sat down.

"Are you all right?" she asked, giving him a look of concern.

"Just a bit queasy. I've been running all day..."

It was as if an image was trying to push its way into his consciousness as he sat there, listening to the melancholy song. It had a curious sense of both the foreign and familiar, like piecing together a picture puzzle and recognising bits without yet visualising the whole.

She poured a drink from a dusty bottle atop the oak sideboard and brought it over to him. "I can change the tape if you find it disturbing," she said.

"No." He shook his head as he took the drink from her hand. "Thanks..."

Sipping the amber liquid, he felt his body warm to its glow. It tasted rich and sweet and suddenly his head filled with the phantom odour of fresh ground coffee and strong black tobacco. "Calvados," he said, looking up at her. "Calvados and Billie Holiday. It reminds me of a very special evening a long time ago."

She smiled at his recollection. "I haven't forgotten either," she said, looking around, searching for a cigarette. And then, finding a pack, she took one out with a slightly trembling hand.

"You don't smoke any more, do you?" she asked, lighting up. She pulled a chair opposite to where he was sitting on the couch, sat down and put the pack of cigarettes on the low table that stood between them.

Reaching over, he took one for himself. "Only occasionally," he said.

"I'm sorry for tempting you." She gave him a conspiratorial smile. "I know it's a nasty habit but I guess I'm still something of an anarchist..."

"You always were," he replied. "A very caring one though." The cigarette tasted good. That and the whisky had seemed to soothe his senses.

Taking a long drag on the mild narcotic, she slowly let the pale smoke drift from her thin but delicately formed lips. "I'm really surprised they sent you," she said.

He knew what she meant. "I am as well."

"I suggested you, of course. But they never listen to anything I say..." She laughed as if she, herself, understood why they wouldn't.

"It's rather low priority, I guess. Maybe nobody else was available..."

She glanced down, considering what to say. In the end, she simply looked at him and said, "I'm frightened."

Her eyes were a mix of wonderful colours, he thought. They were gentle and innocent. He had dreamed of those eyes. It was hard to remember that he had once felt betrayed by her. Or, more precisely, betrayed by her youth. Perhaps they both were. So long ago. Anyway, it was water under the bridge now.

He reached over and took her hand. It was still surprisingly soft and warm to his touch. "This is England," he said. "Not Africa. Things aren't totally out of control."

"Not yet, perhaps..."

"What is it?" He looked at her, searchingly, trying to make out what she was really saying.

"I wish I knew." She drew her hand away, stubbed out her cigarette and immediately lit up another. "If I were my own patient, I'd have diagnosed something vague, like free-floating anxiety. I'd have popped myself a valium and that would have been that. Except..."

"Except?"

"I don't like tranquillisers. I don't like being tranquillised."

"You never did. Though tranquillity has its place. It's not to be sneered at."

"This is different. I want to be alert."

"But what are you frightened of?" he asked again.

"Remember when I told you that I thought something was curious about the patients I had diagnosed with respiratory insufficiency?" She sighed. Her expression asked him please not to think of her as a fool.

"Yes..."

"You said I was under stress. But I've been working with people who've been predicting something like this was going to happen..."

Grant stubbed out his cigarette, feeling the downside the harshness in his lungs, the weakness in his chest. "We haven't found out what this is yet," he said.

"Of course." She tried to smile. "Maybe I have been acting ridiculous. Cambridge can be very provincial. If you stay here long enough, it gets incestuous."

She got up and went over to fetch the bottle. "Care for another drink?" she offered, toting it back.

He held out his thumb and forefinger, indicating how much to fill the glass. "What do you think of that young consultant – what's his name? – the one who spoke up at the meeting..."

"Roger Cook? He's OK. You can work with him. He doesn't seem to be power-tripping his way through life like most consultants – not like the Browders..."

"He and Browder seem to differ on the X-ray readings. Cook was convinced he saw pulmonary oedema..."

"Which confirms that it's not a mycoplasma..."

"Not necessarily," said Grant. "I've seen all kinds of curious responses to viruses and bacteria. But I'd agree that if the X-ray shows oedema, a toxic-allergic reaction is very likely." He thought a moment. Then he asked, "How about the other patients? The ones admitted from other surgeries? Do you know them?"

"I recognised a few names. Yes."

"But not everyone."

She shook her head.

"And as you said, Cambridge is a small town."

"I said it could be incestuous. I don't think you can call it small."

"I'd like to start going over the records tonight," said Grant, getting up and stretching his limbs. "It's going to be one hell of a job."

"I'll set you up in the study," she said. "Of course we've done our own initial assessments. There's nothing obvious. No commonality that hits you in the face. The addresses are all over the place. Various ages, class distinctions, jobs, states of health. Nobody was travelling..."

"Nothing but the vague relationships you've noted."

They were walking down the hallway, walking toward the study. "It sounds so silly when you say it," she replied.

He put his arm on her shoulder, as they stood outside the study door. "There probably is a relationship," he said. "But it might not mean exactly what you think."

CHAPTER 2

~WEDNESDAY 22 JUNE~

THE REGIONAL HEALTH Authority was just a short distance from Pauline Quail's house – ten minutes by car, five on bicycle. As she drove, she told Grant about the environmental health people she had worked with.

"Most of them have settled into a bureaucratic inertia," she said. "They see their job as rather routine and humdrum. Mainly statistical. How many cases of salmonella poisoning this week? That sort of thing. The water quality furore gave them a bit of a scare. They made a right balls-up of that one. But instead of becoming more alert, they just stuck their heads deeper into the mud."

"It's not only here," said Grant, as he watched her turn into a car park and zip the ageing Renault into a narrow space between two comparatively elephantine cars. "In a culture hooked on drugs, public health programmes don't seem to be relevant. If someone gets ill, they take a pill. So what difference does it make if there are a few more rats in the sewers? Or if people live in overcrowded hovels breeding lice and vermin? Preventive medicine today is essentially left to the vitamin companies."

"And Regional Health Departments are left in the hands of people like Thompson," she said, getting out without bothering to lock the door. "Bright young students certainly don't see it as a glowing career option."

He followed her into the vine-covered building that used to be a hospital. "I hope that's not a comment on the staff we'll be working with."

"Not totally," she said. "But wait till you meet Wanky Walter."

Thompson was already there when they came into the cluttered room filled with posters that somehow made Safe Sex seem tiresome and boring. His office was a glassed-in cubicle at the back with a small alcove that looked like a cage for a gerbil where his beleaguered secretary sat.

"I don't know where the others are," Thompson said, coming out of his office and glancing down at his watch with a practised annoyance.

"Why don't we take the opportunity to go over a few things before they arrive," said Grant, putting his briefcase down on an empty desk.

Thompson looked glum. Even more, he looked put-out – like someone whose authority was tenuous enough without having to contend with an interloper whose credentials were vague but who seemed to be bloody well taking the place over.

"I'm not sure where we're going to put you," he said, glancing down at the briefcase Grant had cavalierly dropped into his domain.

"It doesn't matter," Grant replied. "A cubbyhole will do. If we organise this properly, I should be out of your way in a matter of days..."

For the first time, Thompson's face held the barest trace of a smile.

"If not..." Grant gave him a significant look. "...we'll have trouble."

Thompson mechanically looked down at his watch again, mumbling something that sounded like, "Ratsbottom!"

"So who have we got?" asked Grant, raising his eyebrows.

"A field investigator and two statisticians."

"You just have one investigator on your staff?" Grant said with astonishment.

"We have three," said Thompson. "One's on holiday. Another is out of commission. Car accident. Broken collar bone or something."

Grant rubbed the back of his head. “Maybe we can get a secondment from another region,” he said.

“I’ve been phoning around,” said Thompson. “It won’t be easy. Not for today. There’s a lot of paperwork involved.”

“I could always fill in,” Pauline offered.

“I know,” said Grant, shaking his head. “But we need you to liaise with Addenbrooke’s.” He looked at Thompson. “We’ll have to put one of the statisticians in the field.”

“They’re not trained,” Thompson objected.

“It doesn’t matter. I’ve devised a simple questionnaire. I’ll tell them what to look for.”

“Maybe they could work off the phone.” Thompson seemed to be struggling to exert at least a modicum of control.

“Not for something like this,” said Grant. “There are several things that can only be indicated through first-hand observation.”

“But that still leaves only two field investigators,” Pauline pointed out.

“Three,” said Grant. “I’ll be doing some of the interviews myself.”

“Wanky” Walter Waldman came in wiggling the enormous eyebrows of his Groucho mask and smoking a pretend cigar. He sidled up to a young Asian woman who had arrived just a few seconds earlier, nursing a cup of tepid, muddy-looking brew.

“Hi, Toots!” he said. “Why don’t you and me run off to some deserted place?”

“Like the space in your head that used to hold your brain?” she replied, taking a step backward so as to avoid his clammy grasp.

Waldman let the corners of his mouth descend into a mock pout. “And after I said that I’d wait for you till the cows came home! Or was it that I’d wait for the cows till you came home?" He touched the tip of his index finger to his head, looked entreatingly upwards and kept the pose for a minute.

"Walter..." she started.

"Yes, my sweet?"

"Grow up!"

"You know I'd do anything for you, darling. Anything but that..."

"Hello, Tracy," Pauline came over to the exasperated woman and put a sympathetic hand on her shoulder.

The young woman looked up from her cup of sickly coffee and smiled bravely.

Bernie Thompson glanced at his watch and growled. "Ten after nine! We're late!"

"Better late than never," said Waldman.

"In your case," Thompson muttered, "I'm not so sure. But let's get on with it, shall we?" And motioning, without pleasure, at the man to his left, he said, "This is the consultant epidemiologist, Peter Grant."

Grant, who up till then was scanning through some papers Thompson had given him, looked up.

"Tracy Poon is our statistician," Thompson continued, by way of introduction. "And Walter Waldman is your field investigator."

"Hi," said Waldman, still sporting the Groucho mask. "Say the secret word and win the operation of your choice."

"Lobotomy," said Tracy Poon.

"Correct!" Waldman turned to her and wiggled his eyebrows.

"Waldman!" Bernie Thompson shouted. His face wore the pained expression of one whose lot in life was to endure minor torment. "If you'd be so kind, please take off that stupid mask!"

Waldman took off the mask. Without it, his face looked quite ordinary – a little sad, perhaps.

"Down to business!" Thompson said brusquely, seizing the opportunity of moving one step closer to tea break. "Let's keep the reports brief, shall we?" He turned to Pauline Quail. "How many admissions do we have so far?"

"As of this morning we have fifteen cases of what Addenbrookes is calling atypical pneumonitis. I've rung around to the surgeries and asked for an alert if any cases come in today."

"What's the breakdown?" asked Thompson.

Tracy took out some papers from a folder she had before her and passed them around. "I've done a spot map of the admissions," she said. "As you can see, they're dotted all over the place. I've found no immediate relationships."

"Have you checked with other local authorities?" asked Waldman. He looked at Pauline seriously. All trace of smugness had vanished from his face.

"I have. At present it seems to be confined to Cambridge."

"Let's review the clinical picture," said Thompson. He took one of the records and read from the chart. "Nausea, vomiting, headache, muscle pains, diarrhoea, shortness of breath..."

"Classic flu syndrome, isn't it?" said Waldman.

"Except for the curious nature of the rash, which seems to be a common element, and the severity of respiratory distress," said Pauline. "Also, initial X-rays are pointing to pulmonary oedema rather than a picture of atypical pneumonia."

"Have any other lab results come in yet?" asked Tracy.

"We're expecting them this morning," Pauline replied.

"Then there's no definite diagnosis as yet," said Waldman.

"That's right," Pauline confirmed.

"So what are we looking for?"

It was Grant who replied. "I examined one of the patients yesterday – an eight-year-old girl. From my experience, the type of rash I noted on her arms and torso is quite specific.

That and the pulmonary oedema lead me to believe that we're dealing with a severe toxic-allergic reaction."

Pauline nodded her head in agreement.

"But it still could be anything," Thompson put in. "Whatever the toxic agent, it could have entered through respiratory, digestive or dermal routes. Before we go any further, I think we're going to have to wait for the lab reports."

"I disagree," said Grant. "Until we know the toxic vector, we might just be seeing the tip of the iceberg. We don't want to be caught with our trousers down if this thing really explodes."

The last thing in the world Bernie Thompson wanted was to be caught with his trousers down. It happened to him once and it had caused him no end of grief. Which is why he grunted, "So what do you suggest?"

"What I propose," said Grant, "is that we do six detailed interviews this morning and reconvene this afternoon. Maybe by that time we'll have some of the lab reports."

"I wouldn't be able to do six interviews this morning," said Waldman.

"How many could you do?" asked Grant.

"Two or three at the most."

"If you do three and I do three, then we'll have six." Grant looked over at Tracy. "Could we have a copy of the patient list?"

Tracy took some sheets from her folder and passed them around. Grant had looked through the abstracts of the hospital records but he hadn't as yet seen it summarised in this form:

Patients Hospitalised at Addenbrookes on 20 June

Respiratory Insufficiency

Arbury

Arbury Ct - Rojas, Felicia, 8, primary school student,

Chesterton

De Fraville Ave. -Pink, Thomas, 15, secondary school student

Highfield Rd -Elton, Thomas, 41, lecturer, FE

Mulberry Close -Saunders, Anna, 52, teacher secondary school

Victoria Park - O'Reilly, Martin, 34, taxi driver

O'Reilly, Janet, 34, musician

Leys Ave. - Rodriquez, Pancho 37, printer

Colleges

Kings - Battersea, Kathy, 23, Linguistics student

Newnham

West Road - Huff, Frank, 30, teacher 6th form college.

Sidgwick Ave. - Loomis, Sydney, 41, archaeologist.

Central

City Rd - Bault, Susan, 27, unemployed

Mill Road Area

Gwydir St - Walker, Jack, 29, Clerk

Walker, Virginia, 22, Clerk

Glisson Rd - Martinez, Jose, 41, Auto mechanic

Sturton St - Patel, Mr. M. S., 33, Cook

Romsey Town

Perne Road - Perez, Beatrice, 65, retired seamstress

This time something curious struck him as he glanced down the list of names. "Anyone notice something peculiar?" he asked.

"You mean the Spanish surnames?" said Tracy.

Grant nodded.

"I noticed but it didn't seem significant."

"There's only four anyway," said Waldman. "Lots of English have names that are either French or Spanish origin. Look at Portillo..."

"That's four out of fifteen," said Grant. "Nearly 25%. I bet if you went through the phone directory you wouldn't find more than 2% of the names were Spanish." He looked over at Pauline. "There isn't a large Spanish population in Cambridge, is there?"

"They're not Spanish," Pauline said. "They're Chilean."

~

They went over the patient list, dividing it up into interview groups. Using the River Cam as a line of demarcation, Grant concentrated on the addresses to the north leaving Waldman to schedule meetings with someone in the household of the patients to the south.

For his first set of interviews Grant selected the two youngest patients and the two eldest, thinking that the contrasts between age and youth could possibly highlight certain commonalties. Each appointment was set one hour apart so that they could be completed that morning. One hour was hardly enough to go into great detail, but he saw the morning interviews as a fishing expedition. With any luck, the afternoon interviews could be made with a hypothesis in mind. Maybe then they'd have something to go on, rather than what they had now – which was nothing at all, except instinct and experience.

The questionnaire he had worked up was a general survey meant to rule out various possibilities such as waterborne disease, rodent-spread bacteria, fungal problems, typical virus nests, chemical spills or other specific environmental problems while concentrating on communal gathering points and links somewhere along the food chain.

He took Tracy Poon along with him to show her the ropes and give her some idea of how an epidemiological survey was conducted before sending her out on her own. Even though the questionnaire was well structured, the interview had to remain loose enough so that curiosities could be followed up. That required technique and it was something that took years of experience to accomplish even slightly well. But, as an American friend from the Center for Disease Control never tired of saying, "When time is of the essence, you make do with what you got!"

There was something about Tracy, however, that Grant thought might make the grade. It was more than her love of numbers. He was impressed with her immediate recognition of the Spanish surname curiosity – something Waldman hadn't seen at all. He sensed she was interested in puzzles. And solving puzzles was what epidemiology was all about.

"How long have you been working for the Department?" he asked as she drove him to their first appointment of the morning. They were in her little red Austin Metro – a perfect fit for her tiny figure but a little cramped for his long legs.

"Just six months," she said.

"What made you become a statistician?"

"I like numbers," she grinned. "But I didn't start out that way..."

"No?"

"My father wanted me to become a doctor. That was his dream when he came to England..."

"From Hong Kong?"

"No. But I know why you asked. Most of the Chinese here are from Hong Kong. Like my mother. She was from Hong Kong. Not my dad, though. He was from Malaysia. He came here in 1967. "

"It's a beautiful country. I spent some time there when I was stationed in Rangoon," said Grant.

"During the war?"

"It depends on which war you mean. I was there in the early 60s. A young doctor just out of medical school. That's where I met Pauline..."

"Dr Quail?" She glanced at him in surprise and then quickly turned her eyes back to the road. "I didn't think she was that old!"

He let out a little chuckle.

"I didn't mean it that way," she said, keeping one hand on the wheel while the other quickly covered her mouth.

"I guess we do go back a bit," he said.

"What was she like then?"

"Pauline? Pretty much the same. Only younger."

"I bet she was really beautiful!"

"She still is."

"Sure! But I mean in a girlish way." She hesitated a moment. Then she asked, "Were you..."

"Was I?"

"You know..."

"Oh. For a while." Then, looking at her youthful profile, he asked, "How about yourself. How come you didn't become a doctor?"

"Me? I can't stand the sight of blood!"

"That's reason enough," said Grant.

She pulled over to the side of the road. "Here we are. Leys Avenue."

Grant looked down at the clipboard which was resting on his lap. "Janet Styles. Housewife. Age 76." Then pointing to a small house fronted by a manicured garden, he said, "We're interviewing the husband...."

~

Morton Styles was a retired maths teacher who reeked of tobacco smoke. His teeth were pre-national health and the ones that remained had a patina of nicotine which matched his complexion. He wore a wool cardigan with several moth holes over a plaid shirt with purple stains that were probably a cheap brand of port. Around his neck was a bow tie that was a bit too loose but allowed him to breathe without causing serious distress.

Grant recognised the problem right away as Styles opened the door. Rheumatoid arthritis. Thick, lumpy swelling of the joints. Probably endemic in Cambridge with its cold, damp climate oozing out of the fens, he thought.

"Janet's ten years my junior," Styles said, leading Grant and the young woman he had introduced as his associate to the sitting room while shuffling behind. "Spry as a woodchuck. Looked after me the past five years without so much as a whimper."

He motioned for Grant and Tracy to sit on the sofa while he pulled up one of a pair of easy chairs with a matching paisley design which sat opposite each other like twin spinsters who still wore the same outfit.

"It happened that fast," he said, trying to snap his swollen fingers. "One day she was fit; then she went flat on her back. We thought it was just a bad case of influenza. She had influenza before, but never like this."

"It hits us harder as we get older," said Grant, making a notation on his clipboard.

"This wasn't the flu," he said. "It came on too quickly. Muscular tremors, palsy, weakness of the limbs. She couldn't even lift a plate. And then the psoriasis. She never had psoriasis."

"Viruses sometimes cause lesions of the skin," said Grant. "New viruses bring new symptoms..."

"So you think it's a mysterious virus," he said, slowly making his way to a tall cabinet with smoked glass doors. "I thought you people had abolished new diseases like politicians abolished war and starvation."

"It may be a virus and it may not," said Grant.

Styles opened the cabinet and brought out a bottle of French brandy. "I suppose it's always good to keep your options open. Care for a tipple?"

"It's a bit early," Grant said with a little smile.

He looked at Tracy. She shook her head.

"Purely medicinal," Styles assured her, opening the bottle and pouring an ounce into a brandy snifter. "Helps the catarrh, you know."

"I'd like to ask you a few questions," said Grant, trying to get the interview in gear. "Some of them might seem irrelevant or even quite personal, but your response might help us narrow down the possible cause or causes of your wife's illness."

"Rather like looking for the flea that stung the nag after she's gone and bolted," said Styles as he shuffled over to the chair across from Grant and eased himself down into it. "But don't mind me. Retirement's made me into a bit of a crank."

"When did you first notice the onset of the your wife's illness?"

"Three days ago now. Or was it four? Sunday night she woke up in fever and a great deal of pain..."

"And you noticed the psoriasis as you say from the very beginning?"

"Yes. It was quite a distinctive rash over her arms and midriff."

Grant made a notation about the rash and then began going through a series of questions, such as: Have you travelled recently? Have you had any visitors? Do you have any pets and, if so, have they been acting strangely? Have you had any problems with the heating system or the gas supplies? Have you noticed any change in the colour or taste of your water? Have you had any problem with machinery of any sort? Have you done any painting or decorating recently? Have you noticed any fungus growing on the walls? Have you seen any rodent droppings recently? To which Styles could think of nothing out of the ordinary.

After that Grant focused on questions concerning food. "Can you recall what you had to eat the evening your wife became ill?" he asked.

"What we have every weekend. Sunday roast, potatoes, sprouts. I ate it too. Didn't do me any harm."

"And earlier that day?"

"Just some soup from a tin. Bread and butter as I recall. A boiled egg for breakfast."

"It might seem a bit tedious, but I'm going to have to ask you to account for all your meals and snacks going back an entire week. I'd be especially interested in any foods your wife ate that you didn't. I also need to know the ingredients of any combined dishes, how they were cooked – boiled, baked or fried – whether there were any sauces used and so on."

"That's a tall order. I'd have to think..."

"Don't concern yourself at the moment. You can write it up after I leave and I'll ring back. But do give it some thought. Remember to include any snacks. Did either of you have any food outside of the house?

"You mean did we go out visiting that week? No, we haven't been out for a while. It's my arthritis..."

"Any cooked food brought in from a takeaway? Or did anyone bring a meal around?"

Styles shook his head.

"Could I take a look through the house?" asked Grant, getting up from his chair.

"I suppose," Styles answered. He didn't seem thrilled at the idea.

It was a quick tour. Grant had a keen eye and it didn't take him long to rule out the obvious. The house was well-kept. The kitchen was immaculate. The foods preserved at their proper temperatures, sealed in airtight containers. The dates on the tins he looked at were well within their life span and none of them were severely dented. There were no "exotic" foods. No pungent herbs that could set off unforeseen reactions. No spices that in combination would commonly elicit allergic attacks in people who unwittingly tried them.

Also, the drains smelled fresh. There was no sign of moulds or rising damp other than what would be expected in an elderly house located so close to the fens. Pushing his head through the trap door that led up to the attic, he saw no rodent droppings or other telltale signs of infestation.

Outside, the garden seemed well managed. There were only the most common varieties of shrubs and flowers and, quickly inspecting the supplies kept in the shed, he noticed nothing out of the ordinary. Styles assured him that his wife hadn't fertilised or sprayed the plants within the month.

He would have liked to have taken soil and water samples and even samples of the air from various rooms in the house. But it was impossible and besides, what he was looking for was a connection that would link a patient here with others scattered over the entire town.

"You will get that food list together, won't you?" Grant said, as he prepared to leave. "It's quite important."

"Going back a week, you say?"

"That's right. And one other thing..." Grant hesitated, trying to think how to phrase the question. "Was your wife politically active?"

"I beg your pardon?"

"Your wife. Was she politically involved at all?"

"Is that a cause for disease now days?"

"According to Dr Quail, there seems to be a connection amongst the people who came down with an illness similar to your wife's at about the same time. She thought they all had some vague political relationship. Did either you or your wife know Dr Quail socially?"

"That's a rather odd question," said Styles. "We're just long-standing patients of hers."

"You never met her outside the surgery?"

"No. But I would think a question like that was one more likely asked by a police detective," Styles said.

"I'm sorry, but we need to look into the vaguest connections," Grant said, thinking the old geezer wasn't far from the mark. He showed him the list of names and address of the other patients. "Do you know any of these people, even casually?" he asked.

Styles reached for his specs, his stiff joints trying to perform a task that once was as simple as standing up. The process seemed to take ages.

When the wire-rim glasses were finally in place, he studied the list. Then, after a few minutes thought, he slid the specs down on his nose till he could look at Grant over the top and said, "Can't say I know a single one."

~

"What did you make of that?"

They were sitting in the Metro. Grant had just finished scribbling the last of his notes when he asked the question.

It was as if he had read her mind. Tracy had been wondering what, indeed, to make of that interview. And how in heaven's name he could have found so much to write. Unless he wasn't writing about the interview at all, but simply thoughts that it engendered.

"I'm not sure," she said, hesitantly. "It doesn't seem as if we learned much. We kept drawing blanks, didn't we?"

He looked up from his writing. Perhaps he was slightly disappointed in her. Or maybe that was his manner. Anyway, his reply was somewhat curt and brusque.

"You can learn as much from negatives as positives," he said. "As much from what isn't as is."

"Are you saying that there's a lot of things we can rule out?"

It seemed to her that he was annoyed.

"We can't rule out anything based on a single interview. Especially an interview like that..."

"Because he's old?"

"Not because he's old, especially. But because he's rigid. It's like trying to find out what's happening on the periphery by interviewing someone who has tunnel vision."

She nodded even though she wasn't exactly sure what he was getting at.

"If you want to get to the truth, you can't just listen to people's words. You have to understand where they're coming from – what motivates them, what they're trying to achieve. Then you have to consider how they're building up their defences."

"Defences? Why would someone like him want to stop you from learning what caused his wife's illness? After all, it's in his interest..."

"Of course it's in his interest if he cares for her. And I expect he does. But I'm speaking of patterns of behaviour and ways of seeing. Sometimes people don't act entirely in their own self-interest. Therefore, anything anyone says has to be taken for what it is – a type of fabrication – and tested against other phenomena that have a more objective determination."

"I'm not sure what you mean," she said.

"Take a simple question that we've put in the questionnaire – 'Have you noticed any rodent droppings anywhere in the house recently?' For someone who is a very fastidious housekeeper, the mere idea of having mice, let alone rats in their home, is a shameful notion. Of course, it's absurd. Mice can go anywhere. But the idea of mice in one's house is connected to the notion of filth and poverty. Sometimes people are so convinced that mice would never enter their homes that the droppings they sweep up are seen as 'crumbs' or dirt trampled in from the street. They might even see a mouse dash by and pretend they're seeing spots..."

She gave him a curious look. "Did you see any mouse droppings in his house?"

"No. It's just an example..."

It seemed to her that he was upset and perhaps he was. But his annoyance was derived out of frustration, having to do these quickie interviews without the luxury of progressive refinement. For, unlike most kind of data retrieval, epidemiological interviewing was an art that demanded time and patience. Often he had only the vaguest idea of what he was looking for and so depended on his experience and intuition to modify questions and follow up leads that came to light perhaps on the third go-around.

A lot also had to do with the curiosities of memory.

What someone recalled was both random and selective. Recovering the past, no matter how recent, was a constant process of revision and embellishment; each successive rendering had new pieces added and certain bits left out.

The major stumbling block was what Grant called "selective misdirection". Often this involved a petty embarrassment or a misguided sense of protection. When it came down to it, people always felt they had something to cover-up, whether it was dust under the carpet or blood on the floor. The skill of interviewing came in sensing these little deceits, penetrating linguistic disguises, and unmasking them. Truth, he had decided, often came not as the opposite of lies but as establishing the reason for why someone would have lied at all.

But that took time. And time was one thing he didn't have.

He glanced down at the address of the next interview he had scheduled. "Aylestone Road," he said. "Is it far?"

"Not too far," she said, starting up the Metro. "No more than ten minutes..."

~

There was a sign on the door of Thomas Pink's house which said to come round the back. Grant took the path along the side of the house that led to a large glassed-in conservatory attached to the rear of the building. Tracy followed behind him.

"I wanted a geodesic dome," Pink explained when Grant wandered inside the open doorway and remarked on the enormity of the structure. "But Cambridge isn't Arizona when it comes to granting building permits. It's not even Croydon. Maybe more like Bromley or Bradford."

The conservatory looked as if it served both as a study and an arboretum. Exotic plants and vines twisted their way up the sides of the sun-drenched walls, as if struggling for a way out of their artificial habitat. Built into the circumference were several wooden worktables, retrieving the space where a swath of flowering creepers had been cut away, like a bit of jungle for someone to set up camp.

Grant recognised several rare varieties of plants and remarked on their fragility, complimenting Pink on his gardening acumen.

"You've seen them growing in Indonesia then?" Pink said, pouring some ruby-coloured liquid from a carafe into several tall glasses and handing one to Tracy and another to Grant.

"Several times," said Grant. "I remember being struck by their amazing translucence when they blossomed just after the rainy season. Quite spectacular!" he exclaimed, looking at the substance in the glass as he received it.

"Raspberry juice, if you're referring to the drink," he explained. "Freshly grown and freshly pressed."

Grant took an obliging sip and wished he had accepted a shot of brandy at Styles' house before. Then, putting down the glass, he watched Pink begin to fill little peat containers with mulch from the potting table at the other side of the room. Pink was one of those types always in motion, he guessed. It was an extraordinary kind of energy that probably had a chemical basis to it, but people like that had to be doing something – anything with a part of their anatomy whether the result was useful or not. They reminded him of toy aeroplanes with engines powered by rubber bands, flying like crazy until their energy was used up and then, without even a sputter, would nosedive down to earth and crash.

"How's your son?" asked Grant, taking his record from the clipboard.

Pink's manner began to change as soon as Grant got down to business. His movements, loose and limber, seemed to stiffen. "He's breathing is better, but he's still quite weak.

I suppose your being here means it's not a simple case of pneumonia."

"I'm looking into a series of cases that cropped up about the same time. We're trying to rule out environmental factors."

Pink continued to fill his little pots in a determined manner. "Don't you people ever consider ruling in environmental factors? Like the batches of leukaemia cases found in communities near nuclear reactors or the clusters of abnormal births in seacoast towns where toxic dumping occurred?"

It was the "you people" tone that got up Grant's nose. He'd heard it several times too often, and, even though he was usually quite detached during interviews, it made him react. "I don't think it's nuclear emissions or deep water dumping we have to worry about in this instance," he said, trying not to show his annoyance.

"I'm talking about an attitude," Pink went on. "How many people have to die before the medical profession stops talking about 'anecdotal' cases and realises that the earth is trying to tell us something about our way of existence?"

He really didn't want to get into this, he hadn't time. But Pink was the sort who would go on and on. "Whatever the earth is trying to tell us," he said, "we still have to interpret the sounds. I wouldn't want to defend the nuclear industry any more than I would have wanted to defend the coal industry a hundred years before. Nor would I care to get into the game of comparing one with the other by counting up victims. The consequence of economic decision-making is usually brutal. But blaming the cause of a disease on something just because it's there and is thought to be evil doesn't lead to any real solutions."

"I thought the link between low-level radiation and cancer had been pretty much established," said Pink, finally turning around. His hands were caked in dirt but his eyes were bright and alert. He seemed to be relishing this verbal fencing match but, what occurred to Grant, was that Pink needed to let off steam, like someone faced with personal sorrow who can hardly deal with the reality and finds themselves lashing out at the nearest windmill.

"I wouldn't argue with you," said Grant. "You might very well be right about the examples you mentioned. But I'd just caution you about cluster theories. If you took a handful of pennies and threw them up in the air, some would come down and roll into the far reaches of the room. Others would end up in clusters. Interpreting the pattern might lead you to looking for a hidden power or you might put it down to the nature of random factors – to chance or to chaos, take your choice. However, if I identified a nearby force, especially one that I considered malevolent, would I be justified in saying it caused the cluster?"

"You would if you saw it happen before," said Pink, getting back to his seeding job.

"What you're saying is that the truth and the obvious are always the same."

"Well, aren't they?"

"Then you might as well be dealing in witchcraft," said Grant.

"Witches might be more attuned to nature than the medical profession is," said Pink who had taken some dark specks from the inside of a folded paper towel with a pair of eyebrow tweezers and had begun to place them gently into little crevices in the soil of the pots.

Glancing over at Tracy and noticing her wide-eyed look of confusion, Grant suddenly became aware that the interview was getting out of hand. "Actually, we have more in common than you think," he said, using a gambit that got him out of tight corners more than once. "We're trying to explore the relationship, if there is one, between your son's illness and several others in the area who are showing the same symptoms. If you have any ideas of environmental factors which might be involved, I'd be interested in hearing them."

Pink seemed almost bewildered by Grant's sudden change of tone. The expression on his face became one of contemplation. His eyes had a distant look to them. Perhaps he had come to the realisation that there was nothing to be gained by alienating someone who had clearly come there to help solve the mystery that was tormenting him – why his son, a healthy, strapping lad of fifteen, had suddenly been turned into a weak, enfeebled child.

It wasn't an ordinary illness. Thomas had gone through all of them – measles, chickenpox, even the mumps. He had been nursed through severe bouts of influenza. And there had even been times when he was frighteningly close to the danger zone where a parent can feel a hint of that which is too terrifying to ponder.

But this was an illness altogether different. The symptoms, themselves – shortness of breath, fever, rash, muscular spasms – seemed so prosaic. But it wasn't the etiology of the disease that worried him so much as the feeling that his son was being devoured by something strange, something unknown, something evil.

"Frankly, I wish there was something easy I could blame it on," said Pink. "Maybe that would help."

Grant felt a wave of sympathy float over him and then disappear into the maze of hothouse flowers. "We could use your help," he said, taking out his pen and checking the questions he wanted to ask.

Pink never stopped puttering with his plants as Grant went through his list, giving a bit of water to one, pulling a few dried leaves from the next. He answered them as fully as he could, but, as with Styles, produced nothing of substance for Grant to chew on.

"Thomas is fifteen. But he's fairly independent. Maybe he eats half his meals at home, but he's out most of the time. Who knows what he came into contact with..."

"We can only do what we can," said Grant, starting his tour of the house with Pink showing him around. The difference between the managed order of the last place and here was as great as one could imagine. It would not have pleased the likes of Mrs Styles.

"My wife left me," Pink explained, as they wandered from one disaster area to the next. "That was five years ago. I haven't heard from her since."

It wasn't the mess as much as the disorder that Grant found difficult. In some rooms the walls had been stripped bare, with only the wooden lath between the beams and bits of plaster sticking through; others had been knocked down completely. In fact, the entire place looked as if it was in the throes of demolition.

"I've been in the process of redecorating for a while now," Pink said. "But I keep running out of cash."

"How many children do you have living with you?" asked Grant.

"Just Thomas. He spends a lot of time with his aunt. She lives just a quarter mile down the road. Mai has been a second mother to him. I don't know what I'd do without her."

They were standing by the entrance of what had been the sitting room. The floor had been torn up and planks had been laid over the joists. "I'm putting in parquet here," said Pink. "It's a bit costly, but it's bound to bring the asking price up."

"You're trying to sell?" asked Grant.

"As soon as I can. I've got a place in the country..."

That's three houses to inspect if he was going to do this right, Grant thought to himself. "Where would you say Thomas spent most of his time over the last few weeks?"

"At Mai's place. I was working out of town the week before last."

Grant took her address and then showed Pink the patient list, asking if he knew any of them.

"I don't socialise that much in Cambridge. I've got a woman friend in Norfolk so most often I'm there," he said. "But you could ask Mai. She knows everyone."

~

If the first interview confused her, the second one confounded her even more. Struggling to keep up with his long-legged stride as they walked from Pink's house to where the Metro was parked, she said, breathlessly, "I can't see how we'll ever get anywhere at this rate. An elderly couple who stayed at home and a teenage boy who was all over the place. Their house is antiseptic. His is a pigsty. I can't imagine where their paths could have crossed!"

"Maybe their paths didn't cross," Grant replied, slowing his pace slightly so that she could catch up. "I once had a case where a number of people came down with a rare infection. I eventually traced it to a fungus unearthed at a garden party. Everyone who had contracted this illness had been present at the party except for one old gentleman who had been bedridden for several years.

"He lived some miles away and had never left his house. It took days before I finally was able to connect him with the event ..."

"What was the connection?"

"Someone had been given a plant from the garden and had taken it home with them. The plant, and the fungal infection, was later passed on to the old man as a present. But he had no idea where it had come from."

They had reached the car. Tracy was considering his words as she opened the door. "So if you had asked the old gent whether he had been to the party or had known anyone who had been there, he would have answered 'no'."

"That's right." He opened the door on the passenger side and got in next to her. "And the other people who became ill didn't know him because the plant was passed on later by someone who didn't get an infection."

"How did you make the link then?"

"In the course of discussion, I found he had been a mountaineer before he had become bedridden. I asked him to tell me about his expeditions and it soon became clear that the reason he climbed mountains was to collect rare species of flowers that only grew at those heights. It turned out that he had been an avid horticulturist in his younger years. But that fact never came to light until he started talking about mountains. He had suppressed his memories of gardening like people sometimes do of great loves that no longer play a part in their lives. It becomes too painful to speak of them, so they lie buried in their subconscious. Even the plant that he had received was conveniently forgotten. He had tried to re-pot it and failed. I found it dying just three feet from his bed. The earth from the fungus-ridden garden was scattered on his floor along with all the other dirt and dust which had never been swept up."

"Something like that would never be picked up in a questionnaire."

"No it wouldn't," he agreed.

She started the car. "Where to next?"

"Metcalfe Road. We're meeting a woman named Hattie Burrows."

~

Hattie Burrows answered the door still holding her paintbrush. Her hands were speckled forest green and her face had a large mauve smudge which ran down from her temple to her chin, like the beginnings of a ceremonial makeup beseeching the gods to do what humans couldn't on their own.

"Sorry," she apologised. "I was painting. Time passed me by. When I finally get to work, I'm in another world."

She ushered them into the front parlour, softly lit and panelled in fine wood. There was a faint odour of linseed oil and musk and a curious stillness – not a natural silence but more like the absence of something that should have been.

Then Grant recognised what it was. The room was a museum, but a strange one, without a sense of time or place. It was like walking into a hall in the Victoria and Albert where samples of all the other exhibits had been brought in, leaving the viewers to decide for themselves whether they were in ancient Egypt or pre-Columbian Peru.

The walls were filled with tapestries and masks from the four corners of the world. The floors were covered with carpets from Ottoman Turkey and Persia coupled with throw rugs from Honduras and Guatemala. The furniture was an exhibit in itself, with 17th century England and 18th century France sharing space with a Japanese futon and Bauhaus chairs.

"Father was an anthropologist," she explained, seeing Grant's reaction. She took it as the kind of bewilderment that usually came over first-time guests. But, in fact, he was devouring this universal feast of artistry like an impoverished student suddenly thrown into a room with the world's greatest craftsmen.

"I'm a bit of an amateur anthropologist myself," said Grant, walking over to a mask he had once seen in the Ivory Coast and had wanted for himself. But the asking price had been too much. "It's a marvellous collection."

"Yes," she sighed. "He could never really decide which part of the earth he wanted to be in. So he took all of it."

What Grant found so amazing was how well it all fit together. The styles were outlandishly diverse but somehow, instead of being in opposition, they seemed to embellish one another like a multicultural choir.

"Most people say this room gives them the creeps," she went on. "I rather like it myself."

Grant looked back at her. Hattie Burrows was a middle-aged woman, in her early fifties, who wore her great mass of hair piled loosely atop her head, fixed with a large whalebone comb and a pair of long, ivory chopsticks. Her figure was full, rather than cumbersome, like someone who truly enjoyed eating and, unlike most English, found erotic pleasure in what to others was mere subsistence. Therefore she wore her weight differently from those women who grew to detest their bodies.

It was more a tribute to his perceptive observation than coincidence that she went on to suggest they adjourn to the kitchen for something to nibble.

The front room might have been her father's but the kitchen was clearly hers, he thought, as they concluded their walk down the long, narrow hallway by entering a large, rectangular space painted a brilliant shade of yellow.

But she was also her father's child, for even here the tribute was to ethnic diversity. Rather than masks, pots and pans and cooking utensils of various origins and dispositions hung from the wall in celebration of cultural diversity. The shelves next to the great, hot Aga cooker were laden with exotic spices and herbs neatly arranged in alphabetical order (the shelf marked "M" contained earthen flasks of fermented fish sauce from Mongolia and gaily labelled jars of spicy chocolate molé from Mexico).

She took a pan of lentils from the stove and stirred in some coconut milk. Then, placing it back on the cooker, she said, "They've been simmering since the morning. It's a wonderful dish from Sri Lanka, made with onions, garlic and fresh ginger and, of course, coconut cream. They love coconut cream in that part of the world and seem to thrive on it even though we've been told it's a deadly form of cholesterol. But I'm not sure how much I believe in all those dietary constraints, do you?" she asked as she served a great scoop into a clay bowl of an attractive Mayan design.

"Not if it smells as good as this," Grant said, accepting the bowl with the eagerness of someone who hadn't eaten since yesterday.

Tracy dug in as well, nodding her head appreciatively. "They use a lot of coconut cream in Malaysia," she said. "I never liked it much. But this is superb!"

Hattie Burrows smiled as all good cooks do when someone swallows something they have made and reacts as if they had been caressed by the gentle hand of a lover. "There's a marvellous little Californian wine that goes so well with that," she said, bringing a tapered green bottle from the fridge. She poured out several glasses and passed them to her guests.

Grant took a sip and checked his watch and realised he hadn't time to be seduced, even though he wouldn't have minded. Always another time, he thought.

"How's your father?" he asked.

"Gordon's doing as well as a man of seventy-five can expect," she replied. "He's quite frail. But he's been around the world twenty times and it's more than masks and artefacts he's brought back. He had everything there was to be had – malaria, encephalitis, amoebic dysentery. Even cholera. And he always snapped back..."

"Have you looked in on him yet today?"

"I phoned Addenbrooke's this morning. He seemed better than yesterday. But yesterday he was in terrible shape."

He took another glance around the kitchen. There were at least a hundred different spices in fancy little containers sitting on the shelves as well as herbs and other curious garnishes. If he allowed himself to look into the labyrinth of different combinations and their possible effects, he would be here for years, he thought to himself.

And then there was the comment that she dropped about her father – certainly it was more than artefacts he brought back. Grant could have written a thesis on the kind of viral stowaways these educated grave diggers brought with them, not to mention exotic bacteria, fungi and other nameless spores.

"When was the last time your father went on a dig?" he asked.

"Gordon?" She let out a little chuckle. "He's been retired for years, but all you have to do is mention that something older than a digital watch has been unearthed and he'll be on the phone trying to find out how he can get on the crew. The University made him an emeritus a while back and every so often they invite him along to add some prestige to a tedious Roman dig, I suppose. The last time..." She hesitated. "Let me see, I suppose it was March."

"Three months ago?"

"Yes."

Grant was beginning to feel it was hardly worth pursuing, but he brought out his questionnaire. More because he felt obliged to follow through once he put something in motion than thinking he had any chance of success.

"I suppose you do most of the cooking," he said, flipping through the sheets of his scribbles.

"Gordon used to cook quite a lot. But now it's mainly me. Yes, I do most of the cooking. Other than the occasional omelette."

"He's not on any special diet?"

"Well, he doesn't drink as much as he did..."

"I meant food."

"We tend not to eat things that are very, very spicy. It gives him wind."

"But other than that?"

She shook her head.

"Do you think you could remember back and tell me the menu for the previous seven days?"

"Oh, dear!" she said, putting a hand over her mouth. "I'm not that well organised..."

"Of course you are!" He pointed to the shelves. "You've put everything into alphabetical order! How much more organised can you get?"

"That's Gordon's doing. My mind really doesn't work that way. I'm not sure I could tell you what I had last night for dinner. And if I did, I wouldn't be sure exactly what I put in it. I'm always changing recipes around, you see..."

He did see. That was the problem. And he was beginning to feel the depressingly bleak futility of it all.

"For instance, last week we had some of those marvellous empanadas I brought home from the Chilean festival. I tried recreating the recipe substituting a little of this for a little of that but I doubt if now I could tell you everything I put in them."

His nostrils seemed to twitch like a tired hound that had suddenly been offered a scent. "Tell me about the Chilean festival," he said. "When was it?"

"Last week," she said. "There's a rather large Chilean community here in Cambridge, you know. There was, I should say. A lot of them have trickled back home since the end of Pinochet's government."

"Could you be more precise about the date?" he urged.

"It was the end of the week." She thought a moment. "Friday, I think. Yes, it was Friday."

"Both you and your father went?"

"Yes, for a bit. Gordon tires easily at these events. But he likes to show his support."

"Do you remember what kind of food they served?"

"Let's see. The empanadas of course. And a lovely rice salad. That was it, I think."

"And both you and your father ate there, you say?"

"No. Actually, we had eaten before we left. We didn't realise they were serving food and, anyway, Gordon tends to eat quite early."

"But the empanadas..." He looked almost disappointed.

"Yes. I brought a couple home with me. We had them for evening tea the next day."

"I'd like you to look at something," he said, fumbled around for his list of names and then showing it to her. "Do you know any of these people? Did you see any of them at the Chilean event?"

She spent a moment glancing through. "Well, Maria Rojas, of course. She was one of the organisers. And her..." She pointed to the name that Grant had recently pencilled in. "Mai Cunningham was there with her charming young nephew."

~

"We're on to something!"

The delight in Tracy's eyes was infectious. But he had seen too many leads go sour than to get euphoric over the first hit they had made all morning.

"Maybe," said Grant.

"Don't you think it's significant? I mean, here it is. Handed to us on a plate. The Chilean connection!"

"It's a connection. I'll grant you that. But let's hold off on the champagne."

She pressed her lips together. "Sorry," she said, in a lower voice. "Anyway, I don't drink champagne..."

He had her drop him off in the Arbury. She was to hunt up Waldman and get him to direct his interviews toward the event and, especially, the empanadas. After that she was to head for Addenbrooke's and question as many of the patients as she could. Meanwhile, he would focus his attention on Maria Rojas. Then they were to meet up at the Regional Office in the early afternoon.

~

The contrast between the Chesterton homes he had just visited and the Arbury Estate was striking. Here the quiet, tree-lined drives and manicured gardens were exchanged for gut-wrenching music, graffiti and dirty concrete.

It wasn't so much the noise as the numbing, ceaseless monotony of the drums that echoed through the open stairwell as he made his way up past the litter of Styrofoam containers smelling of rancid animal fat and candy wrappers that had left smears of chocolate on the steps.

The rear balcony that linked the entrances of the third floor apartments overlooked a children's playground where he could see two older boys shaking down a child half their size. It happened in an instant: first, a warning shove; next, the younger one emptied his pockets; then the two older boys took their receipts and left. It was such a well-practised manoeuvre that he hardly had time to shout before the incident was complete. What struck him was the absence of drama. Not even the pigeons eating the mouldering remains of a discarded tin of cat food gave a flutter.

He looked out toward the horizon and saw, in the distance, the tranquil college spires and wondered, for a moment, on the normality of it all. But his thoughts were almost immediately distracted by a stocky young man who was coming his way along the narrow balcony.

The young man was wearing a brown leather bomber jacket and his coarse black hair was slicked down on his head with a scented pomade. His face was round and nearly boyish and his features, Grant thought, were a mix of Spanish and New World Indian.

Grant checked the number of the flat from the list he carried in his hand and then greeted the young man as he came up to him. "I'm looking for Maria Rojas," he said. "Is that her apartment?" He pointed to the only door painted turquoise in the long row of dirty white ones he had passed.

The young man looked at Grant suspiciously. "Are you a cop?" he asked.

"No. I'm a doctor," Grant replied.

That designation seemed no better to him.

"Is that her door?" Grant asked again.

The boy nodded his head, reluctantly, and pushed his way past while Grant moved forward to the turquoise door. When he reached it he gave a knock.

He recognised the woman who answered but she hardly looked the same as when he saw her at the hospital. Then she had appeared pale and wane, in the half-light of her daughter's room. Now her face was radiant.

Her eyes lit up when she saw him. "Oh, Doctor. It's good of you to come. Felicia is so much better. It's a miracle!" She folded her hands together as if making a little prayer.

Grant came inside the apartment and followed her into the tiny living room which overlooked the courtyard. "I'm very glad to hear your daughter's feeling better," he said, though he suspected it might not be the miracle she thought it was.

Her broad smile reached across her face. "I went to her this morning and it was if she had woken from a dream. She was sitting up. The nurse was feeding her breakfast. I was so happy! I went to call Dr Quail. She's been so very good to us, I wanted to tell her the news right away!"

"There's a few questions I wanted to ask you that might help us find the cause of your daughter's illness..."

"Of course," she said. "But, please, Doctor, sit down." She pointed to the couch with the Mayan cover as it was their most comfortable piece of furniture. "Do you drink coffee? I was just about to make some..."

"Thank you," he said. "I take it black."

"Just like we do in Chile," she said with a melancholy smile. "Except the men, they sometimes like to add a little something we call it Aguardiente. Would you like I should put in a little drop?"

He had tasted Aguardiente when he had travelled in South America. It was a distillation of grapes that had the kick of a mule. So he politely refused.

The kitchen was just an alcove adjoining the main room. He could see her through the partition making proper coffee in a cafetiere by pouring steaming water into the glass pot to heat it up before putting in the grounds.

"Please, Doctor, make yourself comfortable. I won't be a minute," she was saying as she spooned some beans into an antique coffee grinder – one of the few relics she thought important enough to have brought with her when she had left her native home.

He was inspecting the frayed picture that was slowly decaying on the wall like a once sacred icon, when she came back into the room carrying a tray with the cafetiere and some little demitasse cups, which she placed on the table in front of the couch.

"Do you know who that is?" she asked.

"Allende?" he replied, questioningly.

"Yes. The great martyr of the Chilean peoples. Eduardo cut it out of the newspaper a long time ago and pasted it there. So many years have passed. I have told him it's time to forget. But, Eduardo, he won't let me take it down."

"Maybe it reminds him of why he's come," Grant suggested.

"He doesn't need reminding," said Maria, pouring out the steaming liquid into the tiny cups. "The problem with Eduardo is he can't forget. And so he cannot let himself become English because if he did then he must forget. Do you know what I am trying to say, Doctor?"

"I think so," Grant replied, accepting a cup from her and taking a grateful sip. "Good coffee," he said.

"I am happy to serve it to you," she smiled. "I get the beans from a stall at the market square. The man there, he can find special beans from Colombia which I think are very good. Most coffee they serve in England – you will excuse me, Doctor – is very terrible." She made a sour face to show her displeasure.

It was time to get down to business, he thought, before he was barraged by another coffee discourse. His experiences in America had made him believe that coffee connoisseurs were – like the Seventh-Day Adventists of food and drink – unstoppable.

He put down his cup and made a show of taking out his papers. "I wanted to ask you about the Chilean event – last Friday, wasn't it?"

"Yes, last Friday." she said. "Maybe one day you will come. We have it every year. It is part of our celebration. When the Chilean community was bigger we used to have a parade from Arbury down to the colleges. We would dress in our national costumes and, afterwards, we would have a grand fiesta. But now, there aren't many of us left. Many have gone back to the new Chile. Still, we try – how do you say it? – to carry on."

"Perhaps you could give me the details – the times, the place, the refreshments you served."

The wrinkles on her forehead became more pronounced as she tried to make sense of his request. "I'm sorry, Doctor. Is there something wrong? Is there something you didn't say?"

He adopted a more reassuring tone. "No. It's as I said when I spoke to you on the phone. There are a number of patients who came down with a similar illness at the same time. We want to look into the common factors. It seems that several of these people came to the fête..."

"But there was nothing to make them ill," she said, looking ever more concerned. "We had a celebration the same as every year..."

"Who did the cooking?" he asked.

"I did," she replied. "And others came to help, of course."

"You made the empanadas here?"

"Yes. But they were good empanadas, Doctor. Everyone had them. I ate them. My husband he ate them. My son he ate them too. Everyone ate them. Just my daughter got ill. And I make her empanadas every week. She has never become ill before. My empanadas are very, very good."

The more she spoke, the more emotional she seemed to get.

"I'm sure they are, Maria," he said. "It's very likely no one got ill from anything at the celebration – least of all your empanadas. It's my job to look into every possibility. You can understand that, can't you?"

Her large, dark eyes had become swollen with tears. She nodded. But he could tell that the hurt hadn't disappeared. Even the slightest suggestion that her cooking might have brought this terrible disease upon her daughter was bound to have set her off. He understood that now, but the injury had already been done.

"I do need your help," he said. "Can you give me a list of ingredients you used to make the food for last Friday and explain to me exactly how you prepared it?"

Obligingly, though not happily, she gave him what he wanted. The vegetables, she said, came from the market in town at a particular stall across from the coffee vendor, she said. The meat was from a local butcher shop. All the ingredients had been purchased fresh on Thursday and prepared that afternoon. The empanadas were put in cold storage after preparation and then heated once again at the celebration.

After checking her kitchen and equipment, he was convinced that she was a careful cook. Everything was scrubbed and spotless. She understood the rules of safe food preparation and was conscious of techniques like using well-defined areas for meats, poultry, bread and cheese, washing up as you worked, and wrapping things separately to limit the spread of food-borne bacteria like salmonella.

Of course there were a million and one problems that could go wrong, even in the most careful restaurants. But, generally, he had no question with her methods and thought her kitchen was relatively safe though it was located in a housing block that was used as a rubbish tip and clearly had a severe rodent problem. In fact, because of that she was probably more careful since, as with any struggle with predators, the war was one of attrition. Once you let up, however briefly, the rats and roaches took over.

Rats were a definite problem. In London, for example, the population of rats had reached epidemic proportions. Not since the time of the Black Death and the heyday of Rattus rattus, the rodent that was responsible for killing over a third of the population of medieval England, had the population grown so fast.

In the 18th century they had been driven out by Rattus norvegicus, a much fiercer breed. Victorian public health policies did much to bring them under control. But, lately, as the urban infrastructure was allowed to fall into decay, the incidence of rats surfacing from sewers where they had taken refuge began to grow till it became impossible for pest controllers to cope.

The problem for epidemiologists, was that rats, along with their symbiotic parasite, the flea, were responsible for passing on a good many of the diseases that infected the human population. As animals that inhabited the faecal swamps underground and the decay-ridden rubbish tips above, they were host to the most severe illnesses – typhus, rabies, Chaga's disease, salmonellosis, leptospirosis, and a multitude of others.

It was with relief that Grant hadn't spotted the other factor in the rat-flea-food-human connection. In areas like this, with such a severe rodent problem, even the most sanitary, careful households sometimes had a Trojan horse in the guise of the family pet. Often given leave to roam the house, they harboured the very disease-ridden insects which people were otherwise so careful to guard against. It was the cuddly kitten or the family hamster, so loving and innocent, that carried toxic gifts from the rats.

He was thinking about this as he had finished giving a clean bill of health to Maria's kitchen. They had come back into the living room just as the young man he had seen on the balcony came in through the door.

Seeing the boy, whose face was so similar to hers, Maria introduced him to Grant. "Doctor," she said, "this is my son, Salvador."

"Yes," said Grant, "we met."

He went over to shake the boy's hand, but then saw he couldn't. In one of Salvador's hands was a bottle of milk. In the other, he held a cat.

~

It was already 2:30 PM by the time the afternoon meeting got started. Waldman, the last to trail in, claimed he had got stalled in traffic. But, from the smell of his breath, Grant suspected it had more to do with an extended liquid lunch at some pub. Tracy Poon, who had been sent to interview the Addenbrooke's patients, was still trying to get her report typed into the computer when Thompson called them to order.

"Could we have your attention, Dr Quail? Or are we not important enough to be privy to your information?"

It was a rather snide remark and why he directed it toward Pauline Quail who was quietly chatting with Grant, had more to do with Thompson's pettiness than anything else. There was something he detested about her. Maybe it was the perkiness of her manner or her irrepressible energy. Or perhaps it was simply the way her clothes always seemed to be wrinkle-free. Just her alone was enough to annoy the hell out of him. Combined with Grant – the big man from wherever – she was intolerable. And that was even before she said anything.

Pauline, however, was used to his nonsense. As someone whose job demanded that she put up with all kinds of ridiculous personalities, she had long ago decided not to participate in the more banal games that people play – especially those in management – if they could be avoided. This ability to pursue her own ends without getting sidetracked in trivial squabbles made Thompson despise her even more since it deprived him of a certain power.

"I'd be happy to give my report if that's what you're asking for, Bernie," she said, calmly, giving him a frosty smile.

"Then why don't you get on with it!" he snapped.

She took out some sheets of paper from a folder and passed them around.

"Some of the lab reports have come in. Most interesting is the eosinophile test that Peter had suggested. The count is much higher than would have been expected for a local infection and points more toward some systemic disorder. Also we have been getting consistently negative reports on the various cultures. These findings, along with the chest X-rays and liver function tests which have indicated some abnormality, have led us to a preliminary diagnosis of toxic-allergic syndrome without reference to any specific casual agent."

"How about organophosphates?" asked Thompson.

It was a sensible question as pesticide poisoning was probably the first of a long list of potential culprits to look for.

"Blood test results have so far been negative."

"How many new cases did we have this morning?"

"As of noon, there were six new admissions," she said, handing around another sheet of paper.

"Whatever it is, it's still around," said Waldman, glancing at the notations.

"Not necessarily," Grant replied. "It could be delayed reactions or people who were waiting for the symptoms to disappear on their own. We'll have more of an indication as the week goes on."

"Has Addenbrooke's been able to make any prognosis?" Tracy asked Pauline.

"Not at this stage. The consultants are understandably reluctant. There's been some improvement in most of the patients, but I suspect we'll find it's a temporary effect due to the steroids. It's given them a rather artificial vigour. Frankly, most of the patients are very ill indeed. It's crucial to find the causative agent for any treatment to stand a chance."

Thompson scribbled down a note on his pad and then, looking at Grant, said, "So what has your team come up with?"

"We've hit on a link with the Chilean festival that was held last Friday, the 17th," he said, passing around copies of a chart that Thompson's secretary had typed up for him. "The only food served there were empanadas – a sort of Chilean meat pie – rice salad and crisps. The refreshments included beer and bottled soft drinks. The chart I've passed around is a summary of the surveys done today with patients or other informants. As you can see, we've checked whether they were present at the event and, if so, what was consumed.

"Of the nine patients documented, six had definitely attended the Chilean fête and one may have done. Two patients definitely did not attend the gathering nor did they know of anyone who did. However, it's possible that something from the event may have been passed on to them."

"You're assuming, then, that it's a food allergy," said Thompson.

"I think at this time the most likely scenario is that something was ingested at or emanated from the Chilean fête that caused an acute toxic-allergic reaction."

"But you have three people who claim to have been at the event and ate nothing while they were there," said Thompson scanning the list.

"That's correct," Grant confirmed. "I'm especially interested in the young woman, Kathy Battersea. There's a notation next to her that says she was on a very strict diet." He looked at Tracy Poon. "She was one of the patients you interviewed at Addenbrooke's, wasn't she?"

Tracy nodded. "She was quite adamant about not having eaten anything that afternoon."

"Did you ask her anything specific about her diet?"

"She was very weak. I didn't feel I could pursue it just then," Tracy said nervously. The truth was, it hadn't seemed relevant at the time. She had wanted to speak to as many of the patients as she could before the afternoon meeting. Her focus was the event and what food, if any, was eaten there.

"Not to worry," Grant said. "You can try again this afternoon."

"So what now?" asked Thompson. "I assume there's nothing left of the Chilean food to analyse."

"The Burrow's family brought back some of the empanadas, but they've been eaten," Grant said. "It's possible one of the other participants took something home and stuck it in the freezer." He looked at Waldman. "You might make a note of that."

Waldman nodded and made the pretence of writing something down. He found the whole business somewhat tiresome. In his mind, it was one of those things that would probably blow over after whatever it was had run its course. They'd never find it like they never found half the things that caused mystery illnesses. But he'd go through the motions anyway. Because that's what he was paid for.

"Meanwhile," said Grant, "we'll keep doing interviews. And hope for a break." He looked at Waldman and narrowed his eyes. "If those unfortunate victims up at Addenbrooke's have any chance at all, it's pretty much up to us."

~

When the meeting broke up, Grant and Waldman went off to continue their in-home interviews while Tracy Poon went back to Addenbrooke's and Pauline Quail returned to her surgery.

After they had left, Thompson sent his secretary on her tea break and then typed up a report. Upon completion, he faxed it, along with the statistical materials given out at the meeting, to the private number that had been given to him before.

Thompson's report ended by saying:

"We have reason to believe that the vector of infection is somehow related to a gathering held on 17 June, organised by a group known as the Chilean Friendship Society. It is suspected that the toxic agent is a food that was consumed or distributed there. Hopefully, further interviews this afternoon will clarify situation..."

Twenty minutes later, Thompson received a telephone call instructing him to send all relevant records and the list...

"What list?" Thompson asked.

"The list of all those who attended that Chilean event!"

"Is there a list?"

"Good God, man! What the blazes have you been doing? Playing with your genitals? There has to be one floating around somewhere!"

"I suppose..."

"Well, get it then!"

~

Quayside was a redeveloped area near the centre of town which had opened up the river front, mostly for the benefit of tourists. Or, as the council had argued, for the benefit of the city if one went along with the standard equation: tourism equals prosperity. The question of who actually prospered was moot, however. The property was owned by the colleges. And the offices that were to bear the costs of construction mostly went vacant. But the esplanade which overlooked the gardens of Magdelene College on the opposite bank gave the town a little Mediterranean flair and the frequent visitors from Europe a place to linger and watch the straw-hatted boatmen, hawking their services like sideshow barkers, take the punters for a ride.

Peter Grant and Pauline Quail were sitting outside by the river's edge at Emmanuel's Choice Café. Pauline had taken him there for a quick coffee before going their separate ways.

"I really love it when the backs are in flower," she said, indicating the tulips and daffodils blazing in bright, primary colours on the opposite shore. "It's practically the only thing about the colleges I like."

"Feudalism had its good sides," Grant replied. "Gardens were one."

"They still pretty much control the city, you know – though I suppose it's more subtle than the days when they forced the train station to be built on the outskirts of town so as not to entice the students. But their bare-faced hubris!" she pointed to the college across the way. "Imagine naming it after the second most important woman in the New Testament and then forcing everyone to pronounce it like the word for lugubriously sentimental..."

"Language is power," said Grant. "And power is making people speak like you do. But if they spoke like you, it wouldn't be too bad."

She looked at him and smiled. Her eyes seemed especially bright. Like the flowers. "I didn't see it, but there you are. It took a methodological approach."

"What?"

"The Chilean connection. Of course I would have known a number of those people. I used to go to their events. In fact, I should have gone last Friday except something came up..."

Grant took a sip of the cappuccino he had ordered and thought thank God for the Italians. He put down the cup and stirred the foam, watching it swirl into the creamy distillation. "We might be making too much of it," he said.

Her face showed her puzzlement.

"It's happened before," he continued. "When the pressure is on, conclusions often become forced..."

"You're saying there might not be a connection after all?"

"Certainly there's a connection. Just like there was a connection with you and some of the names. It might not be *the* connection, though..."

She seemed almost relieved to hear him say that. "If I had my choice, of course, I'd rather not have the Chileans blamed for it."

"It's not a question of blame," he said. "Whatever it is, I'm sure we'll find it's not simply a case of bad housekeeping."

"What then? The fête was held at the hall in Alex Wood Road. That venue is in constant use. If it were environmental, certainly we'd have picked up on it before or afterwards."

"I did ask Thompson to have it checked it out. But I'm convinced we're dealing with something that was ingested. Anything else – a gas or an airborne toxin – would have manifested itself differently."

"It's the ferocity of the reaction that concerned me," she said. "It's eating them alive like triggering off some autoimmune factor..." Her face was serious now. "I've seen something like it before..."

"So have I."

"Thompson's a fool, but he did ask the right question..."

"Organophosphates. Highly toxic pesticides. I once saw a young man who had ingested about a tenth of a gram self-destruct right before my eyes.."

"But they've done the tests and it's coming up blanks..."

"Regardless. It might be good to do a spot check of the market stalls where they bought the ingredients."

"Also, we might do some tests on people who went but didn't come down ill to compare..."

"Good idea." His mind was starting to work now. "How did people come? Were they invited?"

"It's an open event. There were posters. But, in the main, it's word-of-mouth..."

"So there wouldn't be an invitation list?"

"I wouldn't think so."

"I wonder if there was a sign-up sheet or something..."

"I don't know," she said. "I could ask."

"It would be good to have."

"That might be a bit tricky," she said, finishing up her glass of sparkling water which, by now, had lost its fizz.

"Why?"

"It's not the kind of thing they'd want the authorities to have. Not that there's anything to it, but these were all supporters of the Allende regime. They're a bit sensitive. As are some of the people who support them..."

"They trust you, though."

"Yes," she said. "But even so..."

"Well, give it a try, why don't you?"

She handed him the keys to the Renault after stopping in front of her surgery.

"I can use one of the staff cars," Pauline said. "Besides, you'll need it if you're hopping around..."

Before he drove off, he showed her the address for his next appointment. "Where is it on the map?" he asked, giving her the street index he had taken from the Regional office.

"Mai Cunningham?" She looked a little surprised seeing his port of call. "I know her quite well. She isn't ill?"

"It's her nephew. It seems he was staying with her..."

"Yes. I know Thomas. I didn't notice him on the list before..."

"His surname is Pink, not Cunningham."

"That accounts for it then," she said. "He's not one of my patients and I haven't met his father. I've just seen him at Mai's on occasion."

"What can you tell me about her?"

"Mai? She's a fascinating character. Started out as an actress but ended up making her own films..."

"What kind of films?" he asked, suspiciously.

"She's done some excellent documentaries. Actually, I haven't seen her for some time. She rang me several weeks ago about a project she was working on. I meant to get back to her..." Pauline gave a little shrug and then, with a twinkle in her eye, she said, "I think you'll find her interesting."

~

Mai Cunningham lived in a splendid house on DeFreville Avenue, a street of large, detached homes occupied by people of the professional class who earned enough to have escaped the straightjacket of provincial conformity. They all had a well-heeled look but, at the same time, an ambience just this side of Bohemia. If it were London, it might have been Hampstead. But being Cambridge, it was simply DeFreville.

She was a small woman with dark hair that reached for her shoulders and a fringe that fell straight across her brow and shifted jauntily from one side of her face to the other as she walked. She wore a black polo shirt with a collar that was turned down in an arty fashion and slacks of a similar colour.

"Come in!" she said, as she opened the heavy, oak-panelled door with an inset of stained glass. "Make yourself a drink and rummage around, if you want. I'll be with you in a sec!" And then she disappeared. He had no idea where.

The inside of the house looked very much like he imagined the other one would if Pink ever got the cash to finish it. Most of the walls had been knocked down to open up the space, so rooms flowed one into another and were defined by their use rather than by artificial partitions. There was a good deal of wood trim, built-in shelving, parquet floors, many large windows to let in the light and an abundance of huge, leafy plants that gave the place a primordial feel, accentuated by an Henri Rousseau print of a tiger peeking through the tangled flora of a moonlit jungle that was displayed over the mantelpiece.

He wandered through the front room, library, dining room and kitchen till he reached the end of the building. And then, suddenly, she appeared again in a burst.

"I'm sorry. I was on the phone. You're Dr what's-his-name, aren't you? Did you fix yourself a drink? Would you like something hot or something cold? Tea? Beer? Perrier water?"

"A glass of water would be fine," said Grant, watching her movements as one might observe a human whirlwind.

She went over to the giant fridge and opened it up. "Bubbles or still? Perrier or Vitelle?"

"It makes no difference," he said.

Suddenly she stopped what she was doing and put her hands over her face. "You have to excuse me. I'm absolutely devastated about Thomas." Then, letting her hands drop back, she looked at him and said, "It's Thomas you wanted to speak to me about, isn't it?"

He nodded. "I understand you and your nephew attended an event a few days before he became ill..."

"You mean the Chilean shindig? What about it?"

"Can you tell me if either of you had anything to eat there?"

"We may have done," she said. Then, squinting her eyes, she asked, "You don't think this is food-related?"

"It's something I'd like to check out."

"But food poisoning doesn't happen like that. I've had food poisoning before. You suffer like hell for a day or so and vomit it out of your system. There was quite a time lag between the fiesta and Tom's illness. And he didn't throw up; he just seemed to grow weak and breathless."

"Food poisonings manifest themselves in different ways," he said, "depending on the toxins involved and the individual."

"There must have been a hundred people at the event. How many came down ill?"

"I don't know," he said. "So far we've been able to confirm five. Thomas makes six."

"How about the others?" she asked, as if this made no sense to her at all.

"I'm not saying there is a definite relationship. It's just interesting enough to explore."

He had expected her to make another argumentative comment, but she surprised him.

"Do you have a cigarette?" she asked.

He shook his head.

"It figures," she muttered, as she searched through an ashtray for a smokable remnant. And then, finding one, she smoothed it out between her thumb and forefinger before lighting up.

She took a long drag and then let the smoke run out of her mouth slowly. "There's something else you should consider..." she began.

"What's that?"

"I've been doing research on some university projects concerning genetic manipulation – the dangers and pitfalls of unrestricted practices, what the future holds in store from an ecological perspective. I'm interested in the medical implications, especially the problem of a new eugenics movement being given a backdoor entry through biotechnology..." She stopped and took another drag at her cigarette as if using the moment to collect her thoughts.

Grant had no idea where this was leading. "That territory has been well covered, I would think," he said, impatiently.

"Not well enough," she shot back. "Sure, it's been batted around by ethics committees and academics, but it's never got a proper hearing. A real national debate has never been established. Anyway, I've been working with some people on this. We began getting wind of an organisation that was trying to push biotechnology onto the political agenda. There seems to be a lot of big money involved..."

He sympathised with the argument of science and big money being a dangerous mix, but he had known her kind before and sooner or later they all began talking about conspiracies of thirteen people who were plotting to rule the world, if not the universe. And the problem with conspiracies was that they were based on the notion that secret societies could work smoothly and effectively, while all his experience led him to believe the opposite. In his mind the most organisations could ever hope to do – whether secret or not – was establish a temporary equilibrium between order and chaos.

"What exactly were they involved with?" he asked, even though he found the conversation tiresome.

"They seemed to be a centre for a number of diverse projects that had commercial and military potential. One of their major testing grounds was here in Cambridge. We were trying to find out as much as we could about it, but they kept a tight lid on everything they were doing. They had very heavy security..."

"Then it seems like you really don't know that much about them," said Grant., "or what they do..."

"We know there was a problem – a serious problem. Something happened..."

"What?"

"We're not sure yet..."

Grant nodded. "So, getting back to the Chilean fête, did you eat any of the empanadas?"

Her mouth dropped open. "You haven't heard a word I said!"

"Yes I did. But I'd still like you to answer the question."

"I not only ate some, I brought some home. In fact," she said, walking over to the kitchen window, "I would have even fed some to my dog." She looked outside where the Terrier used to stay. "Unfortunately, it disappeared."

~

The last rays of summer light were dipping into the horizon when Peter Grant drove the Renault 2CV into Pauline's street, parking it in front of the Ford Transit van just several yards from her door.

The afternoon session had been depressingly unproductive. The only piece of good news was that Addenbrooke's had admitted only three new toxic-allergic patients. However, this was coupled with a report that a number of the earlier admissions had taken a turn for the worse.

After an exhausting day of interviews, Grant felt he was no closer to finding the source of what the consultants were now calling TA Syndrome. Even the link to the Chilean affair seemed to be elusive. So far, the combined interviews that he, Tracy Poon and Waldman had completed came to fifteen. Of those, ten had a definite connection with the event, but five hadn't. Furthermore, a significant percentage of people who had gone to the fête had denied eating anything there.

Then there was the young woman, Kathy Battersea – the one who said she was on a 'strict diet'. Tracy Poon had interviewed her again and found that Battersea was under the supervision of a holistic medic who had limited her intake of solids to fruits, vegetables and nuts. She drank only bottled mineral water.

Grant thought that her severe regimen might be worth exploring further. In the past he had found that special cases, where people had a harsh order imposed on their lives, could help an investigation by serving as a backdrop for inconsistencies – like a cellular dye which made certain abnormalities stand out.

As he walked up to Pauline's door, he made a mental note to interview the Battersea woman himself.

He used the key she had given him to let himself in.

The hallway was dark. He felt for the light and turned it on.

"Pauline?" he called out.

There wasn't any answer.

"Pauline? Are you home?"

He was making his way toward the kitchen when the phone rang.

"Pauline?" he called.

He walked into the kitchen and noticed the phone hanging on the wall.

It rang again. He was about to pick it up when the answering machine clicked on.

~

The man in the windowless transit van parked across from Pauline Quail's house suddenly came alive as the alarm sounded on the monitor. Tossing down his copy of Wired Magazine, he reached for the headphones and put them on just as the answering machine received the call. Adjusting the dials on the tape deck, he watched the line on the oscilloscope frantically dance across the screen:

The voice was deep. The tone was one of concern. The accent was foreign. "Dr Quail. This is Eduardo Rojas. It is urgent that I speak with you immediately. I tried phoning the surgery but they said you were not in. I will try again later..."

A brief pause and then the message continued, "My wife knows nothing about this. I must speak with you alone..." There was a click and the line on the oscilloscope made one last, desperate lurch before flattening out.

The man took off the headphones, picked up his magazine and flicked through the pages to find where he left off. Then, leaning back in the chair that was bolted to the floor, he began reading again.

~

It was about eight PM when Grant heard Pauline come in. Looking up from the desk where he was going over some papers and glancing out the open study door, he saw her in the dim light of the corridor. Perhaps it was the shadows, but it seemed to him there was a change in her appearance. She appeared tired and weary, but even more – the way her shoulders sloped, the way she bowed her head – she seemed somewhat downcast.

"There's a message for you..." he said as she passed by the door.

She was startled by his voice at first. But then realising it was Grant, a contented look came over her face. "It's so nice to see you in the study," she said, her figure framed in the doorway. "It's been vacant so long..."

Suddenly he felt something warm and radiant about her presence. "I'm glad to put it to use," he said.

"I meant it suits you. It's as if you belong..."

The room was comfortable. Certainly, he had felt at home. There was a sense of belonging. If only she hadn't said it.

"The message is on the answer-phone," he said. "It's from Eduardo Rojas. He says it's urgent. About his daughter, I suppose..."

"That's strange," she said. "I was just at Addenbrooke's looking in on Felicia Rojas. Maria was there..."

"He said he'd ring again. Do you often give patients your home phone number?"

She looked down at the floor, apparently in thought. "Only if they're friends."

Getting up from the desk, he walked over to where she was standing. She looked up. He saw the moisture in her eyes.

"How is Felicia?" he asked, gently taking her hand.

"Not good," she replied.

He nodded.

He stood there for a moment. Then he put his arm around her. Her head nestled on his shoulder. He felt the dampness on his shirt.

"You need to keep a distance," he said, softly.

"They're friends," she whispered.

She looked up into his eyes. He felt himself sinking into the pool of brilliant waters. He smelled her fragrance. His head bent toward her. He tasted the warm, salty, moisture of her lips.

"I missed you," she said.

"I missed you, too."

The telephone rang. The shrillness of the sound jangled their senses.

Pauline closed her eyes and sighed. "I'd better answer it."

She took the call in the study as he waited by the door.

Then, looking back at him, she held out the receiver. "It's for you," she said.

~

The Plaza Hotel sat opposite the University Centre and commanded a view of the river – not with grace but the way something big and expensive dominates space with its bulk. It fit into the surrounding architecture like an oversized concrete bunker dropped into the middle of a time warp.

Grant parked the Renault in the adjoining lot and then walked over to the hotel. He entered through the door held open by a uniformed porter and made his way, swiftly, into the lobby.

The lobby extended into a bar and tea room which overlooked the water. Glancing around, he failed to see the man he was meeting, so Grant found himself an empty table and sat down. A waitress dressed in baby-pink approached. He ordered a whisky.

The phone call that brought him had been brief.

"Grant? Bates here. Simon Bates. I need to see you rather urgently. Can you meet me at the Plaza in half an hour?"

The call was so abrupt that he hadn't even asked how Bates had known where he was staying. But, thinking about it, he realised that Bates must have spoken first with Thompson.

Bates arrived, flushed and bothered and slightly out-of-sorts. He brushed back his hair, threw his portfolio on the table and forced a smile as Grant stood up to shake his outstretched hand.

"How long has it been since Atlanta?" he said, making a sign to the waitress to bring him a whisky as well. "Six years or more?"

They had met when they both had been attached to the Communicable Disease Center in Georgia. Grant had been working with a World Health research project on new strains of malaria that had been cropping up in Southeast Asia. Bates, who already was a rising star at that time, was the project coordinator.

"Atlanta was eight years ago," said Grant.

"Eight years?" Bates shook his head. "I've been on the move so much I can hardly keep track of the past anymore."

"So what brings you up here?" asked Grant, giving him a questioning look. "I thought you were in the Health Ministry now..."

"I am."

"So why the high level interest? What's so important that you had to come up personally?"

"Do you remember the Spanish Toxic Oil Case?" asked Bates.

It stopped him cold. Of course he remembered it. How could he not?

The incident had hit the World Health Organisation like an earthquake, destroying numerous reputations and casting doubt on the science of epidemiology itself.

On the first of May, 1981, an eight year old boy from Torrrejon de Ardoz, a suburb of Madrid, died from acute respiratory insufficiency. By the fourth of May a number of other cases with similar clinical abnormalities caused a group of medical technicians to carry out an investigation in Torrejon. At this time, 23 cases had been identified with the probable cause cited as Legionnaires' Disease, since legionella gormanii had been isolated from one of the patients.

However, as the cases began to multiply, this diagnosis was soon changed to atypical pneumonia, perhaps caused by a variant mycoplasma. But by the 11th of May, a huge number of cases were being identified each week, not only in the Madrid province, put also in the neighbouring provinces of Avila and Segovia.

From that time the rate of illness grew exponentially, spreading to the provinces of Salamanca, Leon, Soria, Burgos, Zamora, Toledo and Santander. The number of emergency cases had dramatically increased, with 341 admissions a day.

Evidence quickly accumulated to indicate that the disease was environmentally induced, but despite months of investigation, the cause lay undetermined until the explosive nature of the outbreak had pushed hospital resources to the limit.

By the time Toxic Oil Syndrome (TOS) had been identified as the cause, with 'Factor X' in adulterated rape seed oil as the agent, over 20,000 cases had been reported and 336 victims were dead.

It had left the World Health Organisation in tatters. In order to find the so-called 'Factor X', samples had been sent to research centres in various countries from the massive supply of suspected oil collected by the Spanish Government. And all these years later, work was still going on.

"Here's the situation," said Bates. "One of the university labs here in Cambridge has been involved in the research around TOS. A number of years ago they had been sent five hundred litres of the toxic oil from the supply that had been collected when the Spanish government offered that exchange..."

Over a half million litres of oil had been collected from a population in a state of panic, Grant remembered. Everything was turned in, from motor oil to furniture polish and exchanged for cooking oil the government had promised was good.

"The suspect oil was kept in its original five-litre plastic containers to prevent further contamination. The Cambridge lab was originally issued 100 containers under strict guidelines of control. Over the years they managed to use about 30 containers – about 150 litres. The average laboratory consumption is a little over one litre a month. As part of their control, inventories are taken once a fortnight.

"Two weeks ago, the inventory showed that twelve litres had been used up in the fourteen day period. After checking their records, they came to the conclusion that two 5-litre containers were missing."

"But who would steal something like that?" asked Grant. "Certainly the containers would have been well marked with the international symbol for poison!"

"Of course they were. But it's been more than ten years. What began as a highly disciplined project deteriorated somewhat. Over the years, resources had been cut. They used to have five assistants, now there's only one. And the oil itself was never classified as a controlled poison..."

"What you're saying is they were sloppy," said Grant.

"I'm afraid so. Labels fell off. Cabinets were left unlocked. It's understandable but unforgivable."

"And the missing toxic oil?" Grant gave him a questioning look.

"I was sent up here last week to lead a team to trace it down. Our first clue came from Dr Quail when she phoned the Environmental Health Officer..."

Grant looked at him, astounded. "You mean you didn't take her into your confidence?"

"How could I?" Bates responded. "You can appreciate how highly sensitive this is. Any kind of leak to the press or even rumours spread by word-of-mouth could have caused immense damage. You remember the panic in Spain and the enormous economic costs to the food industry..."

The more Bates rabbited on, the more disgusted Grant felt. And then he noticed something strange. "You're speaking in the past tense," he said.

"I'm glad you caught that," Bates replied. "Thanks to you, old boy, we've managed to trace the stolen oil. What supply that's left..."

~

The black Mercedes glided into the Arbury Estate and pulled up alongside three police cars, their top lights swirling, shooting electrical colours silently into the night air.

"We had some information of our own," said Bates, getting out of the car and holding the door open for Grant to follow. "I put it together with what you had discovered and it led us to the epicentre." He waved his hand in obvious disdain. "This Godforsaken rubble."

A young, fair-haired, police constable walked over to the Mercedes, taking off his cap as he approached. "They're waiting for you upstairs, sir," he said, addressing Bates.

They followed the constable as he guided them up to the third floor balcony, where Grant had been just hours before.

"The only people with access to the research labs besides the scientists and lab assistants are the cleaners," Bates explained as they walked up the stairs. "Of course, we decided to interview them first. It seems that the janitorial work is farmed out to a private service that contracts with a good number of institutions in Cambridge. It also turns out that there's an arrangement amongst the men to fill in for each other if one of them needs some time off. As it happened, a cleaner from the Tech filled in for the usual chap at the TOS labs several nights before the oil was found to be missing. We put that information together with what you had given us and came up with the most likely scenario."

They were standing on the third floor balcony with a phalanx of police in front of the turquoise door. Along the balcony heads poked curiously out of half-open windows to see what was going on.

"Why on earth would Rojas steal some cooking oil from a laboratory?" asked Grant. The whole thing sounded like a wild fantasy to him. Like a story you'd read on the front page of the tabloid press and then, the next day, finding a small disclaimer on page 32 saying the whole thing was a fabrication.

"Why does anyone steal anything?" Bates responded. "Some of the containers still had their original labels, claiming to be the finest olive oil. The label was in Spanish. Maybe it reminded him of home. Who's to say what motivates these sort of people?"

Bates took some documents from his jacket pocket and displayed them to the senior officer at the door who gave them a cursory glance and then, satisfied that proper procedure was being followed, gave a sharp rap at the turquoise door.

"Police!" he called out. "Open up!"

Down the length of the balcony, curious heads pressed against the safety of their windows, now firmly shut. Grant caught a glimpse of those who watched and guessed that most of them had probably heard that shout before and felt their stomach curdle at the fear and apprehension.

"I was here earlier," he told Bates. "I looked through their kitchen..."

"But you didn't know what you were looking for then," Bates replied.

There was no answer to the police demand. But through the window, Grant could see a light was on somewhere in the apartment.

The officer-in-charge nodded to several burly-looking men.

"Certainly you could wait till they get home," Grant objected. But it was like speaking to the wind. The process, once begun, created its own motion. It took a force equal or greater in opposition for it to stop. That was a simple law of physics. And law, thought Grant, natural or unnatural, was what it was all about.

One of the men tried fitting a skeleton key into the outside lock. The key seemed to unlock the latch, but a bolt and chain inside kept the door from opening up. The heftiest of the two constables now put his shoulder to the door, the anger and tension in his meaty arm transferring itself into brute force as he heaved his weight against it.

There was a loud, cracking sound – a sound that seemed to echo through the night. Grant felt the sound in his chest and it created a terrible pain inside of him.

The door swung open. The police moved in with torches ablaze. Bates followed. And Grant came in last.

He saw them grouped, silently around a figure huddled into the corner of the room, the light of the torches directed onto the young, round face. In his arms he held a cat, close to his chest, like a mother clinging to her child for safety. His eyes, like the eyes of a deer caught in the headlights of an oncoming car, were set in a fearful gaze.

Bates had found the switch for the overhead lights and had gone into the kitchen with one of the constables to search.

Grant remained, transfixed by the look in Salvador's eyes – a mixture of terror and intense hatred. He stepped up closer to him, wanting to say something, he didn't know what. The cat bared one of its claws and hissed, sending little bits of paper which had covered the boy's trousers fluttering into the air. And Grant, letting his shoulders drop, stepped back.

He heard a commotion in the kitchen and turned. A cabinet, underneath the sink, had been opened. Bates stood up, holding a large plastic container. There was a big label in red and green that showed a peasant woman kneeling underneath an olive tree, her basket overflowing. On top, in bold letters, was written "Aceite de Oliva Suprema."

Bates' face wore a triumphant smile. Like a young Etonian who had just scored a goal in a gentlemanly football game through some wily manoeuvre. He bent down and retrieved the other container and held it up for Grant to see.

Grant felt his heart sink. He closed his eyes. When he opened them again, he noticed that the ageing cutout of the man with the thick moustache and benevolent face was no longer on the wall.

~

The lights were off when he got back to Pauline's house. He let himself in and made his way to the front room.

He felt around for the pole lamp that stood by the settee. Turning it on, he located the liquor and fixed himself a drink.

In the background, he could hear the faint sounds of music.

He took his drink back into the hallway. The melody of a Mozart piano concerto trickled down the stairs. He glanced at his watch. It was a quarter past ten.

He took off his shoes and climbed the short flight to the second floor. Upstairs, the strains of music drifted from a room facing the garden. The door of the room was open just slightly and a narrow shaft of light poured through the crack In the plain of light, he could see little specks of dust which danced to the music as if they were living things rather than molecules of inert matter.

Gently, he tapped at the door. It slid open, quietly.

She was in bed. There was a look of weariness on her face. But there was also the calmness of her smile.

"I didn't want to disturb you," he said.

"You didn't. I was waiting up for you but then, suddenly, I got extraordinarily tired..."

He came over to the side of the bed and put his hand on her brow. It felt warm. "It's been a long day," he said. "Get some rest. You'll feel better in the morning."

She held out her hand. "Stay for a while."

He sat down on the edge. He took her hand and put it next to his cheek.

"There's something wrong, isn't there?" she said.

He didn't speak. He couldn't.

"Tell me."

Looking down at his shoes, he thought how much his feet hurt and how much his body ached. Then, finally, he said, "Do you remember the toxic oil case in Spain?"

"That was a long time ago," she said. "What does it have to do with us?"

"Do you remember how it came about?"

"The oil was polluted with some sort of toxic ingredient. But I don't recall the specifics..."

"Oil had become very expensive because of some protectionist legislation that had been passed. Spain was only allowing the importation of rapeseed oil for industrial purposes. In order to prevent it from being sold for human consumption, the oil had been mixed with an aniline dye. But because the industrial oil was so cheap to purchase, some merchants began refining it – distilling the oil in order to remove the aniline. Then the refined oil was mixed with small amounts of raw olive oil, which gave it its dominant taste. The mixture was distributed in the barrios through a chain of street merchants who went door-to-door selling this ersatz olive oil for about half the price people paid for low grade cooking oil in the shops."

"So what was the toxic ingredient?"

"That was the big question. They theorised that the problem was in the refining process itself. To remove the aniline, the oil was heated to very high temperatures. This caused a chemical change creating new molecules known as anilides which remained in the refined oil, though in very small quantities. Some people think it's these anilides that caused extreme physiological reactions in the victims. But nothing was proven for certain. That's why samples of the oil were allocated to a number of research labs."

"Including Cambridge, I guess..."

He nodded.

"So what are they saying? That some of this oil ended up in Maria's empanadas?"

"They're saying more than that. They're saying Eduardo stole it."

"That's ridiculous!" Pauline sat up. "I know him! I know her, for goodness sake! He wouldn't steal it and she wouldn't use it for her cooking!"

"But they found ten litres of the stuff underneath her sink."

"Then someone put it there!" she exclaimed, getting out of bed.

She seemed to him a bit wobbly as she bent down to put on her slippers.

"Where are you going?" he asked.

"I just want to hear for myself!" she said, putting on her robe and heading downstairs.

He waited for her in her room, laying his head on a pillow and staring up at the ceiling.

It wasn't long before she returned. She appeared even more frail and spent than before. "The police waited till Eduardo and Maria got back," she said. "Then they arrested him..."

"Eduardo? For stealing the oil?"

"They're charging him with manslaughter."

CHAPTER 3

THURSDAY 23 JUNE

HE HARDLY SLEPT that night. He kept waking up, stirring himself out of a very strange dream. Something was wrong, seriously wrong. But he didn't know what.

He phoned Thompson at Regional Health after he got up.

"You must be pleased with yourself," Thompson said when he got a hold of him. "I suppose you'll be going back to London now."

"There's a few loose ends I'd like to tie up," Grant replied. "I'd be a lot happier if we knew the vector of transmission."

"The important thing is the toxic element has been identified. That's all Addenbrooke's needs."

"You contacted them already?" And then it struck him. "How did you know?"

"The ministry kept me informed. When can I expect your report?"

"Just as soon as I'm satisfied that we're done."

Pauline joined him in the kitchen as he was making coffee. She looked dreadful.

"I think you ought to spend the day in bed," he advised.

"Too much to do," she said, running some tap water into a glass and then downing an aspirin and decongestant.

He poured some coffee made with a filter mechanism into a cup and handed it to her. She used it to warm her hands and then took a sip.

"Does Regional know?" she asked.

He nodded. "Bates must have been briefing him."

"And not you?"

"It's curious, isn't it?"

She glanced up at the clock on the wall. It was 9:30 AM. A worried look came over her face. "It's late," she said. "I told Maria I'd contact a solicitor for her."

He drank his coffee and observed her with concern. "Are you going to your surgery?"

"No," she said. "I cancelled my appointments. I planned on going to Addenbrooke's." Suddenly she sat down and put her hand on her temple, massaging it with her fingertips. "I've got such a bloody headache!"

"How about spending the morning here, at least?" he suggested, trying to carefully choose his words. "You can always go there in the afternoon."

"I suppose I could make some phone calls..."

"So you'll go back up to bed?"

"After my phone calls perhaps..."

He got up and walked over to the sink where he rinsed out his cup.

"You're not giving up?" she said, following his movements with her eyes.

"There are still a few questions I want to ask," he told her.

~

Roger Cook, the younger of the two senior consultants treating the TA Syndrome patients, had been making his morning rounds when the nurse called him to the phone.

"I wonder if we could have a chat," said Grant, who was on the other end of the line.

"It could be arranged," Cook replied. "When did you have in mind?"

"As soon as you can tear yourself away."

"Where are you?" asked Cook, raising his eyebrows. It was a habit of his, whenever his curiosity was aroused, to raise his eyebrows. It made his youthful face more austere.

"In the lobby downstairs..."

They met in the doctors' lounge. It was too early for drinks so Grant settled for a cup of gut-wrenching hospital coffee.

"You heard about the toxic oil hypothesis, I suppose," Grant began.

Cook's eyebrows leapt upwards. "Are you suggesting there's some disagreement?"

"I don't think Thompson would have put it in those words," said Grant.

"But you have your doubts?"

Grant shrugged.

"What's your alternative?"

"I don't have one..."

Cook looked at Grant intently, trying to size him up.

"...yet."

"I got the literature from our library," said Cook. "The pathology seems consistent."

"The pathology was all over the place," Grant replied. "I read several of the reports when I was working for World Health. But some of the symptoms are consistent, I'll give you that."

"Trouble is, you see, there isn't much of a cure. All we can do is try to see them through the critical stage.."

"Atropine?"

Cook nodded. "Sometimes it works. Sometimes it doesn't. We've already had one death..."

"Who?"

"The Styles woman."

"Sorry to hear that," said Grant. "I interviewed her husband. A crusty old bugger. He claims they lived a fairly isolated life. Never went out to eat. Never had food brought in..."

"Maybe his wife had a secret existence. It's happened more than once."

"Perhaps." Grant glanced down at the floor and rubbed his chin. "I'd like to interview one of your patients. A young woman Kathy Battersea."

"I don't have any objections," said Cook. "Just be advised that the girl's very ill."

~

The curtain around Kathy Battersea's bed was drawn, giving a sense of privacy even in the open ward. The nurse who brought him told Grant, "She's resting quietly now. But she had quite a bad night."

"I won't stay long," he assured her. "There's just a few questions I wanted to ask."

A strong scent of floral perfume mixed with the antiseptic flavoured air as he made his way through the soft divide. Two plastic pitchers were filled with a bright display of petunias, begonias and daisies in stark contrast to the otherwise insipid surroundings.

She was a lovely young woman – slim and blonde with great, wide, innocent eyes. It was hard to tell whether her facial pallor was her natural colouring. In a sad, almost melancholy way, it seemed to suit her.

"This is Dr Grant," the nurse said by way of introduction, "He'd like to speak with you, Kathy. If you feel up to it..."

The woman made a tired movement with her hand and tried to smile. She clearly had no objection. It was as if to say, one doctor more or less wasn't going to matter.

The nurse left them alone and Grant pulled up a chair. He glanced through her records and then, in a gentle tone of voice, he said, "You're a student at Trinity, I see. What are you reading?"

She tried clearing her throat before she began to speak. The sounds were hoarse, as if she hadn't much breath. "French literature. Nineteenth century..."

"Flaubert. Dumas. Proust. Stendhal. Wonderful writers," he said. "But my favourite is Zola. What do you think?"

She nodded, weakly. "Germinal..."

"A wonderful book," he said. "Gripping stuff. Unfortunately, I only read him in translation..."

"Better in the original..." she said.

"I don't doubt that at all. But..." he made a little movement of his shoulders. "...at least I managed a taste."

"A taste..." She ran a delicate finger over her bottom lip.

"Would you like some water?" he asked.

She tried to lift her head. He lent her a hand, bolstering the pillow behind her. Then, taking the container from the bedside table, he let her take a few sips through the straw.

"Do you remember your whereabouts last Friday?" asked Grant as he put the water bottle back on the shelf.

He watched as she ran her tongue over her lips as if to ingest the last trace of moisture. "My boyfriend..."

"You went someplace with your boyfriend?"

"To..."

"You went to your boyfriend's house."

She nodded.

"Did you go anywhere with him?"

She shook her head.

"You stayed there all day?"

She nodded.

"I understand you're on a rather strict diet."

She nodded.

"Just fruits, vegetables and nuts?"

She nodded.

"Nothing else?"

She shook her head.

"Nothing at all?"

She shook her head.

"What do you drink?"

She mouthed the word. "Water..."

"Nothing else? Not even fruit juice?"

"Fruit juice. Yes."

"Vegetable juice?"

"Sometimes."

"Milk?"

She shook her head.

"Herbal tea?"

"Sometimes."

"Beer or wine?"

She shook her head.

Grant made a notation and then he asked, "When you eat a salad, what do you have on it?"

"Lemon...sometimes."

"A little oil, perhaps?"

She shook her head.

"Sometimes?"

She shrugged.

"In the last two weeks, have you put any oil at all in your salad?"

She shook her head.

"Are you positive?"

She nodded.

"How can you be certain?" he asked.

She made a movement with her hand.

"I write..."

"You write?"

She cleared her throat. The words came out with great effort. "I write down everything I eat..."

"You keep a diary of everything you eat?"

She nodded. "My nutritionist..."

"Your nutritionist asked you to keep one."

She nodded.

"Do you have the diary with you?"

She motioned toward the cabinet where she kept her personal things.

"May I see it?"

She gave a little shrug and closed her eyes.

She lay there very still. With her eyes closed and the mask-like pallor of her ivory skin, she looked quite peaceful. Yet underneath that calm veneer, Grant knew that something insidious was going on. A reaction had been triggered where the chemistry of her body had turned itself against her. And he thought that despite her careful consumption of food, she was now in the process of quite literally devouring everything within her.

~

Grant used one of the hospital pay phones to ring Chapman, a colleague at World Health in London.

"The only research scientist doing work on anilines in Cambridge is Professor Malcolm Fraiser at Preston Labs," Chapman told him. "WHO gave him a grant of £50,000. But that was about nine years ago."

After hanging up, Grant dialled Directory Enquiries, got the number for Preston Labs and gave Professor Fraiser a call. Fraiser said he had a few minutes and if Grant was in town he could just drop by as the lab wasn't far from Lion Yard.

~

Preston Labs was part of a medieval complex that housed a variety of scientific projects behind a facade of grandiose splendour. The splendour, however, wasn't so grandiose once you walked inside the door.

He found Professor Fraiser in a dilapidated office on the third floor. Fraiser was a small man with a hawk nose and a batch of unruly hair that grew from the back of his head in dirty white tufts like unprocessed cotton. He was brewing himself a cup of tea in a flask set above a Bunsen burner when Grant came in.

"I can offer you some port if you don't want any of this rot," he said, indicating the sorrowful looking tea bag that appeared to be on its third go-around before it was plunked into the boiling pot. "Curiously, I have an easier time getting the college to supply me with fortified wine than tea. Does this say something about them or me?"

Grant accepted the port which was poured into a paper cup of dubious extraction. Fraiser offered him that and a chair with wobbly legs. "I'd be careful of sitting there," he warned him. "It's a relic of the Civil War so the college won't throw it out. However, they've kept me too, so I really can't complain."

The office looked to Grant like a treasure-trove of recycled artefacts. Even the paper clips had a rusty look to them. "This is Cambridge, isn't it?" he asked. "I thought you were exempt from the budget cuts up here."

"Welcome to the New Order," Fraiser said. "Take a stroll down the hall to poly-nucleaic acids. They've even got a new extractor fan. And an electric kettle. But, then again, they're fundable, aren't they?" A hint of jealous indignation spilled out along with the words.

"You should see the kind of facilities people ten years my junior have at American universities," he went on. "No wonder so many brains have been drained from here."

"Why have you stayed?" asked Grant.

"I know it might sound odd, but I quite enjoy the weather," he replied. Then, screwing up his eyes, he said, "Dr Peter Grant? Epidemiology? Didn't I speak with you before?"

"A colleague, perhaps," said Grant.

"Have you been able to trace that missing oil yet?" he asked.

"You haven't been informed?"

"No one informs me of anything," said Fraiser. "You know, there was a day when chemistry was king. Dye research was the top of the pops, as they say. Do they still use that expression? But then, Manchester was a thriving mill town once upon a time."

"You wouldn't mind if I took a look around your laboratory, do you?" asked Grant.

"Mind? Why should I mind?" asked Fraiser. "I only wish more people would come and see what we're doing here. Maybe then we'd get some funds!"

Grant followed him out of the office and down a narrow, faintly lit corridor.

"You were involved in the Spanish toxic oil research, I suppose," said Fraiser, as he hobbled down the hallway.

"Only peripherally. I'm quite familiar with it though."

"It put us on the map for a while. They knew that anilides were probably involved, but they couldn't figure out how. We had been doing research into free radical molecules for years. It started with work in the dye industry, trying to find out how certain dyes change after exposure to light. But it's only recently that biochemists have taken an interest, even though we've been warning them of the effect for years..."

"Free radicals – those are molecules with an unpaired electron that can trigger off a chain chemical reaction on its own, aren't they?"

"Yes. We've been trying to see how the process actually works in humans. There's some evidence that it can cause a reaction which eventually destroys the fats in cell membranes."

"I suppose that would account for the wasting effect in some of the patients."

"It very well could," said Fraiser, as they came to the end of the corridor. Fraiser opened the door with a key on the end of a chain which itself was connected to a belt loop on his trousers. He pushed open the door and turned on the lights.

It was a well-stocked lab with some specialised equipment like computerised spectrographs that probably ate nicely into the £50,000 grant Chapman had told him about.

"I could show you some of our cellular studies, if you're interested," said Fraiser, pointing to an electron microscope set up at the back of the room.

"I'm very interested," said Grant. "But I'd like to ask you a few questions about your supplies of oil first."

"Ah, yes," said Fraiser with a grimace. "The supposed theft..."

"Supposed? Are you saying it didn't happen?"

"Well, no. I'm not saying it didn't happen. Two of the five-litre containers are obviously missing. I just can't imagine how it happened."

"When did you first notice that some of the oil was missing?" asked Grant.

"I didn't notice it at all. It came out during the inspection the other day."

"What inspection?"

"The audit. At least that's what they said. Quite unusual though. Haven't had one in ten years and then suddenly..."

"The audit was by the funding agency?"

"No. It was a health and safety check. They were auditing reportable toxic substances..."

"But the cooking oil certainly wasn't a reportable substance."

"According to them it was. They went through my records with a fine-tooth comb."

Grant looked around. "Where do you keep your supplies of oil?"

"That's just it. I keep them in there," he said, pointing to a door behind the electron microscope. He walked over and opened the door with another key from his dangling chain. The closet was dark. He reached for the cord of an overhead light and turned it on.

"All the unused oil is still in its original boxes. We just take the containers out one at a time. The used container is kept there," he said, indicating a plastic bottle that rested alone on a wooden shelf above the cartons.

"Do you think your researchers could have used more oil than they said?" asked Grant, knowing all too well how clumsy students could be.

"Our work is very precise," Fraiser said. "We're very careful to note the lot number and the amount when we use the oil. Besides, there's only two of us left on the project –

myself and a mature PhD student who, if anything, is even more pernickety than I am."

"The police are claiming that it was stolen by the cleaner," said Grant.

"That's absurd," replied Fraiser. "Firstly, how would they get in? The closet lock wasn't broken and the cleaning staff don't have access to the key."

"Do you think it's possible you left the closet door open?" asked Grant.

"It's possible," said Fraiser. "But I didn't."

~

Leaving Preston Labs, Grant was unaware of the man sitting by the window of the small café, opposite, reading the Daily Mail.

Nor did Grant see him pocket the newspaper, toss down a handful of coins and head for the door just a moment after Grant turned the corner, making his way toward the Lion Yard.

Grant stopped at a phone box and dialled Pauline's number.

"Mai Cunningham rang," she said when he got through to her. "She wants to introduce me to someone who might have some useful information..."

"About genetic experimentation?" He made a face.

"I think it's worth looking into," she said. "It might be coincidental, but Mai claims there was some sort of problem at a Cambridge research centre right before the illnesses cropped up..."

"You're in no condition to go," said Grant.

"I was hoping that you'd meet her in my place..."

He agreed, despite his misgivings. Reluctantly, he dialled the number Pauline had read out to him.

~

The row of houseboats moored along the waterway might well have been travellers' encampments if they had wheels. Yet bobbing gently on the narrow river, these converted barges, once the mainstay of Cambridge commerce, had a look of quiet tranquillity despite or, perhaps, because of the sweet smell of cannabis that wafted through the air.

Gaia's Revenge was set somewhat apart from the others, further down the green of Stourbridge Common towards the fen. It was far enough away from the Pike & Eel, across the river, so as to enjoy the quiet, but close enough to catch the lights from the pub's garden.

Not being familiar with houseboat culture, Grant stood beside the long, narrow craft wondering how to accomplish his entrance. He ended up tapping on one of the curtained windows cut into the raised section of the cabin with a pen he took from his jacket pocket.

Moments later a man appeared from the inner depths of the hull. He dropped a small, aluminium ladder over the side, fixing the hooks at the top end to the boat's metal rail.

"You must be Dr. Grant," he said, guiding the older man's hesitant movements over the rail with an arm that was both strong and steady.

He had a slim, wiry build with sinews that tightened his near translucent skin, exhibiting veins like the see-through man leaning against the wall in one of the lecture rooms at Grant's college. His hair was light and close cut. His face, like his figure, was youthful. But his eyes – magnetic blue behind round, wire-rimmed spectacles – were the part of his anatomy that gave him depth.

"You have the advantage of me," said Grant.

"I suppose I do," said the young man. "You can call me Vermuden."

Ducking his head, he followed Vermuden through the undersized door into the cabin and at once felt himself entering another, unexpected world. From the outside, it had seemed the quarters of the narrow boat would be cramped and uncomfortable. But the space was quite deceptive. What it lost in width it made up in length which stretched out forty feet or so. And once he had oriented himself to see things long and narrow instead of short and wide, he understood what seamen always realised – that tight spaces don't necessarily have to be cramped. In fact, it can do much to simplify life.

The entrance led into the galley, with a fold-out table on one side and a kitchen arrangement on the other. A planter box with a herb garden rested on a window shelf on the kitchen side and the table, opposite, had cafe style seats which formed a little alcove.

Further along was a study area with rows of bookshelves and a wider shelf at the bottom which was used as a desk. At the very far end was a bedroom arrangement, partly curtained off. Through the sheer fabric Grant could see the shapely form of a woman getting dressed.

Looking back at Vermuden he noticed that the young man was doing up the last few buttons of his denim shirt that fit loosely over jeans which, themselves, hung ragged and cuffless over his bare feet.

A woman appeared from behind the bedroom curtains.

It was Mai. Her face was slightly flushed, though hardly from embarrassment, Grant thought. "You got any coffee?" she asked, smoothing down the wrinkles of her chartreuse blouse.

Vermuden went to the sink and retrieved a small espresso pot shaped like a modified hourglass, unscrewed the top, extracted the metal filter and rinsed it out.

"I understand Eduardo Rojas was arrested last night," Vermuden said as he dried the apparatus out and filled it with a couple of spoonfuls of grounds from a package of Lavazia which had been prominently displayed on the food shelf. "What were the charges?"

"Theft," said Grant. "And murder."

"That's ridiculous!" said Mai. "The cops are crazy! What's it about?"

"There's evidence that the people who came down had all ingested toxic cooking oil which was responsible for a major epidemic of food poisoning in Spain. The oil had been sent to a Cambridge lab some years ago for analysis. Eduardo was charged with taking some of the tainted oil from the lab which, they claim, was then somehow ingested by a few of the people who attended the Chilean event."

The fragrant aroma of the coffee bubbling through the spout of the espresso pot quickly filled the concentrated atmosphere. Vermuden took the pot by the handle and filled three tiny cups. He handed one to Mai and another to Grant.

"I know something about the so-called Toxic Oil scandal," he said, taking one of the tiny cups himself and sipping at the heated essence.

Grant wasn't surprised. The case had been highly publicised a decade ago, making garish headlines for a few days in the European press and then popping up periodically as the gruesome death toll rose throughout the year. The trial of the oil vendors, which took place with the atmosphere of a lynch-mob and the subsequent civil suits by the thousands of victims demanding compensation for the destruction of lives, families and careers would certainly have come to the attention of anyone concerned with the problems of food quality – let alone hard-core, earth-firsters like Vermuden – even though, judging from his appearance, he probably was a student back then.

"Certainly you, of all people, must know that the toxic oil scandal was a massive cover-up," said Vermuden with a look of smugness that made Grant's stomach turn.

"I know there were alternative theories, none of which were proven..."

"Come on, Doctor Grant!" Vermuden narrowed his eyes. Behind the circular glasses the gaze became even more accusatory. "Refined rapeseed oil was a massive industry. It had been going on for years. Over a million litres had been distributed all over the country. Yet the epidemic was limited to five or six provinces in Northern Spain."

"There are explanations for that," said Grant. "The most probable hypothesis is a particular batch of oil was more toxic than others, either through insufficient refinement, chemical change through overheating or through mixture with another element."

"But there were cases of people in the same family who consumed the oil in equal amounts. Only a relatively small number of them showed any sign of illness at all. In fact, one of the researchers tested a supply of oil taken from the homes of people who had come down with the illness. He fed a group of monkeys for weeks. Do you know what happened? The monkeys didn't get ill. They gained weight. They gained energy. They thrived!"

Grant took a sip of coffee. It tasted strong and the flavour was bitter. "Monkeys aren't humans," he said.

"What are you saying?" asked Mai. "That one step up on the evolutionary ladder we die from things that monkeys thrive on?"

What could he answer to that? It was all part of the mystery of life, he thought. Why does one species thrive on something that makes another ill? But he knew it happened not only between species but within the same family.

"The other explanation," said Grant, "has to do with the notion of a co-factor. Something can exist benignly in a latent state but turns toxic when combined with something else – a co-factor which triggers off a chemical change. This can have to do with the specific biological processes within an organism or it can be an external agent. In the case of toxic oil, the co-factor idea could help explain why two people could ingest the same oil while only one of them would come down with the illness."

"Isn't that the same idea being used to explain why out of millions of people with HIV, only a small percentage are coming down with full blown AIDS?" asked Vermuden.

"That's one of the theories being debated," said Grant. The idea was only slowly taking hold in the scientific community as predictions of massive infection within the general population failed to materialise.

"Of course there's another idea being broached by a few scientists who still have the courage to think for themselves..." Vermuden left his sentence dangling, took another sip of coffee and winked at Mai.

"Listen," said Grant, "we could stand around here all night debating the origins of the great diseases and whether God or the devil is at work, but I came here because you said you had some information about certain experimental work that might relate to this case. I'd like to hear what you have to say."

"This information will mean nothing," said Vermuden, "unless you have an open mind."

"My mind is open to all sorts of things," Grant responded.

"I'm talking about ways of seeing," Vermuden continued. "We've all been brought up to believe that in a free society science is morally correct. When we hear of medical experimentation like the kind that happened in German concentration camps during the war – the injection of diseases like typhus into healthy bodies; the brutal experimentation on pregnant women – we say, yes, that was the Nazis. German society was mad and German scientists, like Mengele, were little more than monsters. But we conveniently forget that the experiments in eugenics – the forced sterilisations, the terrorising of those thought to be subnormal – that research was begun in England and the United States. How do we explain the Tuskegee study of syphilis where poor Blacks were left untreated so the stages of the disease could be observed? That was supported with government funds from the United States Department of Public Health, not the German Gestapo. And how about the recent revelations in America where prisoners had their scrotums injected to see how radiation affected the reproductive process? How about the experiments sponsored by the Atomic Energy Commission where men, women and children were fed plutonium in order to better understand radiation disease? This wasn't Hitler's Germany or Stalin's Russia. Those experiments had been going on for three decades in democratic America."

"Thanks for the lecture," said Grant. "Now maybe you could tell me what you're getting at."

"I told you," said Vermuden. "It's ways of seeing. I don't believe the Tuskegee doctors saw themselves as evil monsters. They justified their work the way we all justify our lives. The reason they are being vilified is because syphilis is a particularly lurid disease and poor Black farmers aren't appropriate victims any more. But medical science experiments with people every day in prisons, in hospitals, in laboratories. Sometimes with their patient's so-called consent. Sometimes without. But it's all for the greater good of humanity."

"All right," said Grant, "so the world is a rotten place. So people are sometimes willing to do anything for their careers, for their jobs, for money. That isn't new and, until we get heaven on earth, that isn't going to change. But let's look at this particular situation. I came here in good faith because I am trying to find out why some people, in their prime of life, are lying desperately ill in a hospital ward. You said you had some information that might help. Instead what you've done is take up valuable time by giving me a lecture on scientific morality. Did it ever occur to you that you're being just a little self-righteous, Vermuden?"

"Anyone of us with a mission to perform can be accused of being self-righteous. I can. You can. Even our friend, Mai.

But I understand my mission and what it means for my life. Can you say the same, my good Doctor Grant?"

Part of him felt like getting up and leaving Gaia's Revenge right then. The gentle motion of the boat in the water coupled with the day's events had made him somewhat disoriented. And Vermuden's philosophical cant had gone straight to his stomach, making him so nauseous he wanted to retch. On the other hand, he hated to think this episode was going to be a total waste of time.

He turned to Mai, as a last resort. "Listen," he said, "I'm going to have to leave in a minute or so. I'm suspicious of the toxic oil theory for a number of reasons. And placing the blame on Eduardo and accusing him of murder seems precipitous to say the least. I assume that the information you're dangling before me has to do with some bio-genetic research going on here in Cambridge. I won't beat around the bush – I'd be somewhat suspicious about that, too. But I'd like to hear what you have to say if you or your friend want to say it."

~

Mai glanced over at Vermuden with a look that seemed to indicate that maybe enough was enough. She herself wasn't sure why Vermuden obviously distrusted Grant so much, though she suspected it had something to do with his relationship to the World Health Organisation.

"I was doing a documentary about the GATT conference in Uruguay," she said. "I met an Indian woman there who was part of Karnataka Farmers Union revolt against the seed copyright provision that had been forced through by the multinational biochemical companies..."

Grant was aware of the hotly debated provision in the General Agreement on Tariffs and Trade giving companies power to enforce copyright on scientifically produced seed. What that meant, in fact, was farmers would no longer be allowed to gather seeds from crops but would have to buy them from seed companies controlled by multinational chemical and pharmaceutical corporations. Though this was of little importance to large agricultural concerns, it was a disaster to small farmers who were being forced to spend heavily on compatible fertilisers and pesticides. In all the hoopla over the great victories of the trade millennium, this was one of the lesser publicised results which meant little to the Western consumers who applauded the chance to buy cheaper television sets but set off a fire storm of protest in the lesser developed states of the south.

"I decided to focus the film around that particular issue since it had so much to do with the covert ways western technology is controlling the economies of the Third World. I was also interested in the un-publicised struggle that's being waged against it. Recently there was a protest of 500,000 in Bangalore directed against the Cargill seed company which ended in the offices of Cargill being ransacked. But what I was trying to show in my film was how these concerns are global rather than local. How all the Free Trade rhetoric of GATT was really just a bunch of crap because it only represents the interests of the rich by promoting giant producers against the interests of the local farming communities. Far from creating diversity, they are forcing a monoculture which is in direct opposition to biological renewal and abundance."

He was more in tune with what Mai was saying than Vermuden's dour reproaches. His work in Africa had convinced him that the so-called Green Revolution policies being touted by the international agencies had been misguided at the very least and probably disastrous as it had so little to do with local farming conditions.

"I met Chris at the Uruguay conference," Mai said, motioning toward Vermuden. "He had been doing research on the bio-genetic side of the equation – the development of plants manufactured for the purposes of agribusiness. He showed me how bioengineering had become the twin brother to information technology as the most important economic force in the near future. Yet most of what was being done was secret because the products were patentable and so much money was at stake. Here was an industry that was becoming vital to our lives and it was understood by so few people. I was really astounded by the information and statistics as I started going through it."

"So you decided to research the Cambridge biotechnology connection," said Grant, summing it up for her.

"It turned out that one of the major research centres was here. An outfit called TechnoFarm. It was awfully hard to penetrate. There were lots of rumours in the scientific community of course. But we had trouble actually finding anyone who worked with them and was willing to talk."

"The research facilities are out on the old Girton highway," Vermuden said, finally deciding that he might as well join in. "People used to say there were two-headed goats out there and cross-bred animals like pigs with lamb's fur. But we weren't really interested in the tabloid stuff. We'd been keeping watch there for about a month..."

"Looking for what?" asked Grant.

"Anything," he said. "We logged in notes each day and kept a documentation of photographs."

Vermuden took a notebook from the shelf above his head, placed it on the table and opened it up. The first page had a diary account of the initial watch and a picture which had been taped onto the bottom.

Leaning forward to get a better look, Grant saw what appeared to be a thick row of bamboo behind a chain-link fence. The only thing unusual seemed to be the lushness of the growth.

"It looks fairly innocuous," said Grant. "What's the problem?"

"Well," Mai replied, turning the page, "one problem is this." She pointed to a feathery mound by the edge of the fence which Grant had trouble interpreting at first. Then he saw. It was a pile of dead birds.

"We were lucky to get this shot," said Vermuden. "In an hour they were gone."

"Pesticides," said Grant. "You'll find those bird mounds on every farm just after they've sprayed."

"But that's the curious thing," Mai responded. "We were there a month and never saw them spray. Not once."

"You probably weren't there when they did it," replied Grant.

"I took periodic soil samples," said Vermuden.

Grant looked at him in astonishment. "How could you do that?"

Vermuden's eyes twinkled. "I have my ways."

Except for the picture of the birds, there still seemed to be nothing exceptional. "How many acres does it cover?" Grant asked.

"Quite a few," Mai replied, turning the page of the notebook. "But the real work is done here, we suspect," she said, pointing to another photo. The picture had been taken from above and showed an immense structure, just two storeys high but extending out into the fields in six distinct wings, like tentacles reaching out into the grasslands. From this heightened perspective one could see the main facility, in fact, was reached by an access road which led from another highway some distance away.

"How did you get these shots?" asked Grant, with a certain admiration coming through in his voice. There were times he could have used skills like these in his investigatory work. "A sky-hook?"

"You're close," said Vermuden, who obviously took pride in his accomplishments. "I chartered a hot air balloon for a day. They're pretty common hereabouts. No one took any notice."

Mai turned the page of the notebook again. "Then, last Thursday, work started on an inner, electrified fence. By Friday it was complete."

"That's over one mile of perimeter they fenced in about thirty hours," said Vermuden. "They must have had about twenty men on the job."

"A rush order, I guess," said Grant, looking closely at the photo. The inner fence blocked out all view of the garden. The simple "No Trespass" warning signs had been replaced by ones that much more threatening "High Voltage Electrified Fence. Do Not Enter on Risk of Death!"

"So what did you make of it?" asked Grant.

"They were sure under pressure to keep something in – or to keep something out," said Mai.

"Or maybe it's a case of locking the lab after the virus has bolted," Vermuden added.

"Do you have any reason to think that?" asked Grant.

"I have reason to think many things," said Vermuden. "We know that TechnoFarm was involved in several aspects of applying biotechnology to commercial projects – medical and pharmaceutical as well as agricultural. They're on the cutting edge. They're also in a race with other world competitors in Europe, America and Japan. And it's winner take all where patent rights are concerned. So, like other R&D corporations, they need to come up with the goods pretty damn fast or else all those expensive projects become yesterday's trash. When you're in that kind of rough and tumble, you start bending rules and taking chances."

"That's all very speculative," said Grant.

"What we do know is that something did happen that scared the willies off them," said Mai.

Grant paged through the notebook. He saw the transformation into what looked to be an armed camp. He turned the pages back to the beginning again.

"Who else was involved in these observation besides you?" he asked.

"I don't think that's information you need to know," replied Vermuden.

~

Pauline somehow seemed perkier, more energetic and alert, when Grant came back to check on her. He told her about his meeting with Vermuden.

"TechnoFarm." She mulled the name over in her head. "I think I have some information on them in my files upstairs. "I'll give a look," she said. "Meanwhile, maybe you could give a call to Katz..."

"Who is Katz?" he asked.

She handed him a slip of paper with a name and number written on it. "He's a solicitor."

He watched her move across the room, perhaps not as lightly as her former self, but certainly with ease. And he found himself wondering what she might have taken from her medicine chest.

Going into the study, he dialled the number she had given him and was put straight through.

"I'm representing Eduardo Rojas," Katz told him. "I understand you were there when the police broke into his apartment. This whole thing smells like a tin of rancid fish to me, Grant. What the hell is going on?"

"I wish I knew," Grant replied.

"You wish you knew? Aren't you with Environmental Health?"

He found the man's blustering tone offensive. "I was drawn into the case. I didn't initiate it."

"Mrs Rojas claims you checked through her house just a day before the police came barging in."

"My visit had to do with her daughter's illness. I was doing an epidemiological investigation."

"You checked through her kitchen and saw nothing that led you to contact the police?"

"That's correct. But I did think that there were certain factors which made it probable the disease was somehow linked to the Chilean fiesta and, therefore, by implication..."

"That's no reason to send in the police on a search and seizure mission," Katz broke in.

"I didn't send in the police," Grant said, articulating each syllable so there could be no misunderstanding. "There was nothing I saw in her house that would merit a further search and certainly nothing illegal..."

"So you didn't see the suspected oil?"

"No. But then again I didn't look under the sink where the police eventually found it."

"Then who informed the police?"

"Someone from London. According to them, they were notified that some of the toxic oil was missing from a Cambridge lab. They claim that Eduardo worked there as a cleaner..."

"He didn't. He worked at the Tech miles away from where the oil was stashed."

"They say he exchanged jobs with someone there on the day the oil went missing," Grant said.

"Where are you getting this information?" asked Katz. "None of this is in the police report..."

"A man called Simon Bates – one of the higher ups in the Health Ministry. I don't know his exact position. He's the one who filled me in on the details. I'm surprised it wasn't in the report."

"I'm not," said Katz. "What information you get, you have to bully out of them. So how did they put Eduardo together with the missing oil? It sounds like quite a detective job without much to go on. How did they know when the oil went missing?"

"An audit had alerted them to the fact that some of the oil was missing. They claim they were on the lookout for any reported illness which fit the known etiology. They also claim that once the cases were discovered, it was a matter of working backwards to find a commonalty. They knew the agent – the toxic oil. I had hypothesised the commonalty – the Chilean event. They put it all in the hopper and came up with Eduardo."

"Excuse my language, doctor, but that's a bunch of cow droppings..."

"Well, you're his solicitor. If I were you, I'd point that out to the police. I'd also question the rather striking coincidence that the first audit held in years just happened to take place a few days before the so-called theft."

"It sounds like you have some rather strong doubts."

"Yes."

"Well, maybe you could help do something then. Can you come to my office?"

"I've got a pretty tight schedule..."

"Think of it as mutual support," said Katz. "There's probably a quid pro quo in it for you someplace."

~

The office of Morris Katz, Solicitor, was right above an Italian cafe called the Roma. The pungent aroma of freshly brewed espresso mixed with a thick gust of tobacco nearly overwhelmed anyone who entered.

"It comes up through the floorboards," he said as Grant sat down on one of the several rickety chairs set around a glass table which Katz referred to as his "conference area".

Katz, himself, was behind his desk, amidst dusty tomes and rolls of blue-ribboned briefs which were scattered hither and yon like unopened party favours. "I don't smoke or drink caffeine anymore," he said, patting his ample belly. "I've been told it's bad for the heart. But my idiot doctor didn't say anything about bathing myself in the odour."

He was a tall man with a long face, drooping jowls and a mass of wavy hair which would have been cut to a fashionable length if this were several decades before. He wasn't particularly obese – to Grant's eye, at least – but had enough extra meat on his bones to make him look slightly seedy in his three piece woollen herringbone that had stretched accordingly as his body had filled out.

"You're a doctor, aren't you?" he asked, giving Grant a challenging look. "What do you think about that?"

"As long as your blood pressure isn't soaring, I'd say you should do whatever makes you feel comfortable," Grant replied.

"Quite right," said Katz, pulling out a pack of Benson and Hedges from his jacket pocket, offering one to Grant who declined, and lighting up. Then, lifting the telephone extension from the table he punched out a number and said, "Carlo, could you have one of your charming daughters bring up a couple of espressos and some pastries? A nice selection. Thanks a lot."

There was a look of sublime satisfaction on his face as Katz put down the phone. "Good," he said. "I feel better already." And then he took a long and grateful puff on his cigarette.

Grant looked at his watch. "I don't have much time," he said.

"Neither do I," Katz said. "Neither does Rojas."

"What do you mean?" asked Grant, wondering if this cryptic remark wasn't just another lawyer's device to grab attention.

"If what you say is true, that toxic oil taken from a Cambridge laboratory was actually found in his apartment..."

"There's no 'if' about it," Grant cut in. "I was there when they found the stuff..."

"All right," said Katz. He seemed to be focusing his mind as he watched the thin swirls of smoke disperse in the air.

"Let me put it another way. If Eduardo didn't steal the oil which was found in his apartment, then it was planted there by persons unknown who want him to be what the Americans call 'a fall guy'. You've seen that film by Oliver Stone about the Kennedy murder, haven't you?"

"I don't think we're talking about political assassination here," said Grant. One thing he couldn't stand about lawyers was their penchant for hyperbole. On the other hand, the notion that Eduardo was possibly being setup had been put on the back burner of his consciousness not out of naiveté, but an intensity of purpose and a self-imposed discipline which forbade any rush to judgement.

"It might not be on a presidential level, but Eduardo Rojas is a political refugee who is being used as a scapegoat. Why?"

The question was left dangling in the smoky air as the door opened and a buxom young woman wearing a tight fitting apron walked in carrying a tray which she placed daintily on the table. She swept back some strands of her thick, black hair which fell over her large, mascaraed eyes and said, "Two days! I told you how bad to have been without coffee for too long a time. You get – how you say? – the jittering." She took the thin wrist of one hand by two fingers of the other and made a trembling movement. "Nervisimo..." She laughed. "Mama Mia!"

Katz gestured toward the young woman. "My dealer," he said. "Won't leave me alone."

Grant took a coffee as the young woman disappeared out the door, leaving a trail of Italian perfume. His mind was still fixed on the question Katz had brought up. "What makes you so certain that Eduardo Rojas didn't take the oil?" he asked.

"I've worked with these people for a number of years," said Katz. "I know them to be hard working and very moral. The women, especially, are all good Catholics. Even if you could convince me that Eduardo stole the oil – which would take some doing, I assure you – you'd never get me to believe that Maria would use it."

"Well, he is your client..." said Grant.

"You said yourself you had doubts when I spoke to you on the phone," Katz reminded him.

"Yes, I do. But doubt is any scientist's stock in trade."

"According to the police report, the cleaners from Central Janitorial Service sometimes stand in for one another. Eduardo was said to have taken over the shift at Preston Labs for a man named Solomon Ashu..." Getting up from his chair at the table, Katz went over to his desk and rummaged through some files.

"Most of my work is with immigration problems. Cambridge doesn't have that large of a refugee community, so there aren't that many problems. But those that happen usually end up on my desk..."

He stopped suddenly as he found the file he was after. He opened it and read. "Solomon Ashu. Picked up yesterday by immigration for unspecified violations. Taken to Blakenhurst..."

"Blakenhurst? Where's that?" asked Grant.

"It's a prison near Birmingham. They've taken a number of the asylum seekers there recently like the hunger strikers from Campsfield House. It's usually their last stop before deportation."

"Can they do that?" asked Grant. "Without a hearing?"

"They can and they do. Anybody who hasn't got their final confirmation of refugee status can be picked up for deportation. No reason need be given. No attorney need be present. They have no right of consul and limited right to appeal."

"And this man Ashu hadn't received refugee status yet? How could he have worked then?" asked Grant.

"He was given temporary leave to remain in the UK. Finding a job isn't that difficult provided you're willing to accept a pittance of a wage and no benefits. That's how a lot of dirty work is done in Europe these days. If you make a group of people illegal or quasi-legal you create a de facto underground labour force that can undercut any regulatory wage. The unions can't crack it since they've lost a large part of their membership and most of their clout. And legal workers are forced to eat shite because they know that a dozen others out there are just aching to do their job at half the cost. If you want to know the roots of immigrant bashing, there it is."

"It also seems that some people don't want Mr Ashu found."

"They didn't count on me, in that case," said Katz.

Grant drained his tiny cup of coffee. He got up and put out his hand. "We'll keep in touch," he said.

"We certainly will," said Katz, giving Grant's outstretched hand a firm but clammy shake. Then, squinting his eyes in such a way that furrowed his brow into a paradoxical expression, he said, "What the hell do you think is happening?"

Grant would have liked to answer that question. Unfortunately, he was still at the stage where he was chasing flies with a blindfold on. So, instead of giving a reply, he asked for a favour.

"There's something I'd like you to do," said Grant. "I understand that some sort of mailing list was gathered at the fiesta last week. I'd like you to get a copy for me."

Katz, looked at him suspiciously. "Why would you want it?"

"I still think there's a strong possibility that whatever was being passed around had something to do with the festival. That list seems to be the only source of locating the people who attended."

"The problem is that it's politically sensitive," said Katz. "It's not the kind of thing we'd want circulated."

"I'd treat it with discretion," said Grant. "You did say something about a quid pro quo..."

Katz rubbed the side of his nose as he thought it over. Then he said, "I'll see what I can do."

~

He rang the regional office from a phone box. Thompson wasn't there so he asked for Tracy Poon.

"Something strange is going on here," she told him when she came on the line. "Thompson's ordered us to drop everything related to TA Syndrome. He's put us on a salmonella case. What's more," she said in a lowered voice, "he told us not to speak with you! What's it about?"

"I'm not sure," said Grant, "except that London is putting pressure on him to bury it. There's something they don't want exposed. But there's no reason for you to get involved," he told her. "It wouldn't help your career..."

"If my career is to be stuck the rest of my life with those two slap-heads, then help is something I don't particularly want. Is there anything I can do for you?"

"Well," he said, clearing his throat, "in fact there is. When you interviewed that young student at Addenbrooke's – Kathy Battersea – did you happen to get the number of her boyfriend?"

"I think so," said Tracy. "Because she was staying with him right before she went to hospital. I thought you might need it."

"Tracy, you're a gem!" he said.

He could almost see her blush at the other end of the line as she read him off the phone number and address of Bill Pinter, Kathy Battersea's boyfriend.

She ended by saying, "Take care of yourself, Dr Grant. And thanks for trusting me."

~

He tried ringing the number several times from the phone box and then, again, when he got back to Pauline's. Each time he came up blank. But he persisted. His intuition told him that a piece of information was there which might be a key to understanding something which he now desperately needed to understand.

She suddenly appeared in the study just as he put down the phone. He was surprised to see her up and about. The sparkle was back in her eye. But in a very strange and disconcerting way it had lost its charm – almost as if it had been manufactured. As if she were a replicant.

"How do you feel?" he asked.

"Much better," she said. "I do think I might have it under control!" He sensed she wasn't talking to him but to herself. However, she was oblivious to his concern. And as she spoke he thought of a childhood story about a disabled steam engine, with all the energy it could muster, trying to climb an impossible mountain.

"I found a copy of an article that I cut out some months ago from the Economist. It's about the new technology in agriculture and the coming revolution in the way farming will be run. The article also talks about some of the main visionaries, the most important people in the field. One of them is a man named Blumgarten – a professor in plant biology at Cambridge. He's also on the board of one of the largest agricultural research facilities devoted to developing new bio-genetic techniques. Guess the name? TechnoFarm! And guess who's giving the prestigious Morton lecture on New Paths in the Integration of Technology and Science?" She picked up a copy of the Cambridge Evening News and waved it at him. "Blumgarten! Today at 3 PM!"

~

Jeremiah Blumgarten was a visionary. A brilliant scientist, he was one of the early researchers in the relatively new field of biochemistry back in the 50s when high-flyers opted for quantum physics. Blumgarten foresaw the glowing future of applied genetics before most of his contemporaries understood the technological implications of Wilson and Crick's crudely drawn little diagram or had given much thought to that curious shape, the double helix which came to symbolise the biological revolution just as the stylised atom had symbolised the revolution in physics a generation before.

But it was only in 1973, when Cohen and Boyer managed to extract a bit of DNA from an African frog and splice it into a bacterium, that Blumgarten suddenly realised a new industry was about to be launched that would change the world. If the model of DNA had given him a dream, the Cohen-Boyer experiment gave him a tool. For the first time scientists like Blumgarten had a way of moving genes from one organism to another and the mechanism to redesign nature however they wished. To Blumgarten, it was the birth of the new era for humankind. The ancient dream of alchemy – the transformation of base metal into gold – paled in the face of those wonders yet to behold.

His approach was quite different from most of his colleagues in the field of biochemistry who stuck to high profile research trying to create new, genetically engineered drugs and chimeras for medical experiments. Instead, Blumgarten focused his energies on the potentials these new techniques held for agriculture. He soon became a leading consultant in plant biotechnology, one of the first to use Agrobacterium tumafaciens – a soil bacterium that caused crowngall tumour in plants – to manipulate botanic chromosomes.

Within a few years, several American universities were offering him endowed professorships, with guaranteed funding for his projects along with a six-figure salary. He turned these offers down, however, to set up his own genetic engineering research company, modelled on the new, by-the-seat-of-your-pants biotech organisations like Genetech that were becoming overnight success stories. Blumgarten had sensed correctly that the time was right to turn his vision from a dream into reality. But it took over a decade of hard work convincing wary investors that the fantastic pictures he drew for them were actually feasible and then forming the all-important corporate alliances that could provide the structure to implement his ideas.

But it finally came to pass. TechnoFarm had become a reality. The new world had been born. And the Cambridge Senate had invited him to give the laudatory Morton lecture so he could tell about it.

Standing there on stage, before his peers, Blumgarten looked anything but the high-powered corporate impresario. Short and stocky, with a mass of unkempt grey-speckled hair, he appeared almost a caricature of the eccentric scientist. On closer inspection, however, it seemed to some – especially his detractors – that this was a look tailored to reap a desired effect. It pushed the subliminal message of the dotty professor, whose head was in the clouds, but who was worthy of trust. Like Einstein, he had eyes that were wide, innocent and lugubrious. But Blumgarten was commercially shrewd in the ways Einstein wasn't. And as he stood quietly on stage, one could feel the power of his presence as he brought the audience to a hush.

It was only when the hall was finally quiet and the audience had focused its collective attention, like a beast made meek by the gaze of its master, that Blumgarten finally spoke. Running his hand through the air, as if clearing away the fog, he said:

"Imagine a world without hunger."

He stopped and let the words hang in the atmosphere like a single, lingering chord struck on a piano. The room became heavy with silence, then he continued:

"Imagine the deserts made fertile and the scrub-lands made green. Imagine the Arctic in flower and the Sahara in bloom. Imagine a country like Britain with four harvests a year, with open fields of citrus and exotic vegetation. Imagine a world without pesticides, yet able to feed its billions."

He lifted a finger and waited so his next words would have their optimum effect.

"I want you to imagine one thing more. I want you to imagine an organic farm of bountiful produce – firm, tasty and succulent as your last trip to Provence. A farm that is more cost effective than the most efficient American agribusiness. I want you to imagine a farm so environmentally symbiotic that it essentially runs itself. A farm that frees humankind from its most enduring burden – the eternal quest for food."

Again he stopped.

"Incredible? Unbelievable? Lest this sound like just another fairy-tale, let me assure you that I am not speaking of the next century. Not the next decade. I am speaking of today..."

He held out his hands and cupped them.

"Ladies and gentlemen. The future is here! The future is now!"

Suddenly, the lights in the hall went off. The curtain opened. A rear projector lit up and huge words appeared on a gigantic screen.

TechnoFarm

The Future is here! The Future is now!

An unseen stereophonic music system struck up the chords appropriate for the preview of a Hollywood extravaganza.

Then Blumgarten's voice came over the speakers, in tones both dulcet and professorial. On screen, the Great Barrier Reef and the magnificence of the surrounding sea came into view:

"It is one of the great ironies of nature that terrestrial life is bathed in an atmosphere of chemically inert nitrogen which, though vital to life, our organic systems cannot use. Humans must get their nitrogen from plants. And plants must get it from the soil or the oceans..."

An ugly industrial behemoth, belching forth black smoke, came on screen.

"... or through the costly process of manufacturing fertiliser."

The image on the screen quickly changed to tiny turquoise-coloured plankton swimming in tropical waters.

"Life, at the beginning of the food chain is able to siphon inert nitrogen and use it by making it chemically reactive. This fixation is accomplished through intermediary workings of algae in the oceans and bacteria in the atmosphere."

The scene was now a research laboratory. The camera focused in on an electron microscope and then faded into an animated rendition of the bacterial world – the amoeboid body dissolving into the nucleus and then the chromosomes themselves.

"For many years, scientists have attempted to learn the technique of how bacteria can achieve nitrogen fixation."

The chromosomes dissolved into the double helix of the bacterial genome.

"We have finally been able to trace this process to a family of bacterial genes known as nif genes..."

The image faded out and then reformed itself into a schematic diagram with a representation of a bacteria next to a plant cell.

"With the proper technique, through genetic manipulation we are now able to insert these nif genes into plants..."

The diagram showed a cleaved bacterial plasmid combining with the plant DNA to form a recombinant plasmid.

"...thus allowing plants to manufacture their own fertiliser."

The image of a lone seedling becoming a full-fledged plant took over the screen. Its history from seed to maturity, compressed by time-lapse techniques, played out in just several seconds.

"If we can manipulate plants to create their own fertiliser we have already cut the costs of farming by thirty percent. But what else do plants need to survive?"

The giant words came on the screen:

Fertilisation

Irrigation

Protection

Adaptation

"Plants are perhaps the most misunderstood of God's creatures. We see them as the background to our life, like the sky or the water. But few of us realise that plants possess an amazing intelligence. Plants have senses just as animals. They can taste, hear, smell, feel and some can even detect with sensory apparatus akin to sight. They have the ability to compute, to measure and to analyse. Plants already provide us with our oxygenated air, our food, our major source of energy, our clothing, our medicine and our shelter. But we have just begun to bring plants into the service of mankind."

Irrigation

On the screen now was a weedy, scruffy little plant. In the background, a clicking sound could be heard which got progressively louder.

"Behold the tuber. Listen carefully and you can hear it talk. What is it saying?"

Drops of rain appeared and began to fall onto the plant. The rain, soft at first, fell harder. As it did, the clicking began to die down.

"It is asking for water."

A field, vast acres of corn, took over the screen.

"We have been able to breed plant sensors which can send out electrical impulses when their roots are dry..."

The field suddenly became awash as great sprays of water shot into the air.

"...triggering off an underground sprinkler system. The plants tell the system when they are thirsty. When they are quenched, the system automatically shuts off..."

Protection

A picture of a small plot of mixed vegetation now appeared.

Around the periphery of the garden was a row of curious looking flowers.

"Most plants have a self-protecting apparatus built in to their biology. Many have a natural pesticide specifically formulated to deter their primary predators. With slight alterations we can maximise their effect..."

The screen showed an invasion of field mice, voraciously eating their way up to the field.

"However, some predators are harder to stop..."

The focus now was on the strange-looking flowers.

"Some plants have the ability to digest protein..."

The inner workings of the Venus Fly Trap came into view. Inside the open flower, a fly buzzed around until, quite suddenly, the trap snapped shut. A tiny camera picked up the digestive process as the plant enzymes made the fly dissolve.

"We have been able to combine certain qualities from various species of plants to create a very interesting hybrid..."

The foraging mice appeared again, about to invade the garden. But suddenly, their movements slowed. They seemed groggy, almost drunk.

"Chemical changes to the perfume of certain flowers can produce a tranquillising effect on predators..."

The mice, lured to the flowers on their periphery, began to stumble and fall. As they did, the flowers bent over the bodies.

"We can also adapt carnivorous plants to digest the bodies of small rodents..."

The flowers seemed to change colour. There was a pulsating fluorescence. And then, slowly, they began to straighten their stems, leaving behind the undigested skeleton.

"Changes to the perfumes attract a variety of other predators such as locusts and grasshoppers..."

A plague of locusts seemed to fall from the sky and lay in heaps by the garden.

"The odour can have a deadly effect on their central nervous system..."

Adaptation

A wide-angled picture taken from a flying plane passed with dizzying speed through the rainforests of the Amazon.

"Plants need certain essentials to survive. Variations in light, temperature or soil determine whether a specific species or variety will thrive..."

The picture now hurtled across the wastelands of Southwestern America. The ground below looked monotonously barren.

"But even in the most austere conditions, certain plants have been able to adapt and survive..."

The picture was of the frozen tundra in the Arctic. Out of the frozen ground a flowering grass emerged.

"Can we adapt plants to flourish where none have grown before?"

An image came on the screen of a dark-skinned man wearing a serape, picking red berries from a tree.

"Can we grow coffee outside of the tropics?"

An orchard came into view. Ripe oranges, plums and peaches were hanging lushly from the boughs.

"Can citrus grow in colder climes?"

An Indian market with piles of brightly coloured spices filled the screen.

"Can we transplant the precious condiments from the Orient?"

Suddenly the image of Blumgarten, himself, came into view.

"Come with me, ladies and gentleman, as I take you on a brief tour of TechnoFarm!"

Blumgarten pushed open a gate and entered a garden of earthy delights. The colours were so rich and tactile, the vegetation so lush and ripe, that one could almost smell the odour of bountiful harvest in heaven, itself.

A unified gasp could almost be heard from the audience at the spectacle on the screen, as they followed Blumgarten with hungry eyes.

And when the lights came on again, the sophisticated ladies and gentlemen, the jaded dons and the intelligentsia of Cambridge, still stared in disbelief. Gone was the feeling of annoyance at his patronising tone. Gone was the embarrassment at his outlandish, almost simpleminded discourse.

Perhaps Blumgarten knew them better than they knew themselves. Perhaps he had reached the child inside them that so desperately wanted to believe again.

In the end, they rose and gave him a standing ovation. All except one man in the back who seemed to have been taking copious notes.

It wasn't notes, however. On his pad was a sketch which could have been taken as a reasonable likeness of the man who had been speaking.

As the audience rose to applaud, his facial muscles tensed. He took his pen and across the drawing he carved a jagged "X" ripping through the image of Blumgarten. Then, tearing out the sheet of paper and wadding it into his pocket, he got up and left.

~

It was late afternoon when Vermuden returned to his houseboat. Opening the hatch and making his way down into the hold, he was greeted by a dense cloud of smoke.

"I really wish you wouldn't light up in the cabin," he said, focusing his displeasure on the woman who was sitting at the galley table, nervously puffing on her cigarette.

"Why not?" she asked. "You do it all the time."

"Not tobacco."

Mai shrugged, took a long and satisfying drag and then stubbed the cigarette out. "Did you get a chance to question him?" she asked, watching Vermuden as he made his way to the curtained off section.

"It wasn't that kind of meeting. No one questions God."

"They used to." She watched his silhouette behind the curtain, as he took off his suit, exposing the contours of his lean, tight, muscular figure. She lit up another cigarette and blew out the match. "They used to say God was dead when I was younger."

"He's been resurrected. With a vengeance. How long have you been waiting here?" He poked his head out from the curtains and looked at her, questioningly and then disappeared behind the screen again.

"Not long. I was with Thomas..."

"How is he?"

"Not well. Getting worse, I suspect..." There was silence. Then she said, "I want to tell Grant..."

He came out from the curtained area looking more himself in form-fitting jeans and an extra-tight tee shirt. "Then tell him..." The statement was completed by his look of disdain.

"Why don't you want me to?"

"Because I don't trust the good doctor," he said, filling the espresso pot with water.

"You don't trust anybody..."

"Very few people are worthy of trust."

"Do you trust me?"

He put the coffee grounds in the top compartment, screwed it to the base and then lit the fire on the stove. "Sometimes."

"Do you trust yourself?"

"Always." He turned to her and grinned.

She hated that grin. She thought it was smug and self-righteous. Stubbing out the cigarette she had just lit, she got up.

"Where are you going?" he asked.

"Out," she said. "I'll see you later...perhaps..."

~

Pauline looked pale and haggard as she got off the phone with Addenbrooke's. "All the TA Syndrome patients have taken a turn for the worse. Several are now on life support. Cook doesn't hold out much hope. He's still trying to research the treatments used in Spain..."

"Until we know the source, what else can he do?" said Grant.

It was one thing to reject a likely hypotheses. It was quite another to find a better replacement. And they had nothing but a ragged trail to follow. A trail without signposts or even continuity. Trails like that he knew all too well. They were the kind you follow only as a last resort.

But he had nothing else. And time was running short.

Then the telephone rang.

"I'll get it," said Grant, reaching for the receiver.

It was Mai Cunningham. "I'd like to show you something," she said. "It might help with your research..."

"It was when I was looking through the sequence of shots of the perimeter fence that I noticed something curious..." Mai told him when he got there.

She had brought him into her lab and had found the envelope of negatives in her file. Placing the strip of negatives on a light box, she examined them through an eyepiece magnifier.

"I remember the ones you're talking about," said Grant. "Why did he take them?"

"It wasn't the fence he was interested in but the sky above it. Vermuden was trying to keep track of the bird formations to see if he could detect any peculiarities. He suspected that something from TechnoFarm was causing them to die."

She handed him the eyepiece. "Take a look for yourself. If you want, I can put them in the enlarger and blow them up."

Mai arranged the enlarger so that the image was projected onto the wall.

"They're all dated," she said, "so I'll put them in sequence."

She went through the series of negatives, one by one, flashing them up on the wall. Above the fence could be seen flocks of birds in various formations diving, soaring, circling, descending. But it wasn't the birds Mai was referring to. It was the fence, itself.

"There's a bush on the outside of the perimeter that isn't there in the earlier photos. It just suddenly appears. If we go through the shots again in sequence," she said, "you'll see what I mean."

"Could you blow it up larger?" he asked her.

She put in another lens and then projected the shot again, doubling the magnification.

Grant walked up to the wall and studied the image. Then he turned to her. "Can you get it any bigger?" he asked.

"Not without losing contact with the real world," she said. "Anything larger would just be patterns of light and dark that have their own meaning. You'd be passing from the real world into the surreal."

"It's hard to tell for certain, but it looks like the fence might have been cut," he said. "And the bush might have been put there to hide it."

"That's what it looked like to me. I know that Vermuden got in to take soil samples."

"Let's see the overhead shots again."

She sorted through some other negatives till she found a strip that fit the bill. She loaded a negative into the enlarger and then switched it on.

It was a strange and rather awesome sight. The building loomed like a mighty fortress, rather than a laboratory – its many wings reaching out from the main trunk like tentacles. There were few windows and those that existed were simply slits in the massive walls. The entrances were secured by highly visible guard stations. The roof of several wings, however, was translucent though it was impossible to see inside from that height.

"That's not a typical laboratory," said Mai. "It looked to us like something the military would build."

"For what purpose?" asked Grant.

"The most profitable ventures are still those most suitable for war," she said. "Biotechnology opens up enormous new potential for killing people in a multitude of ways while saving things that business interests treasure most – namely property."

But it wasn't the sprawling building that Grant was looking at. It was the surroundings – the "farm" itself. Miniature fields were neatly arranged in small, rectangular shapes. Each one looked slightly different. But seen from above, it was hard to make out what was actually being grown.

"Blow that up as much as you can and print it," said Grant.

She did it in sections, dividing up the picture into quadrants and magnifying each to the maximum point before it lost all resolution.

Grant waited by her side as she went through the process of bathing the exposures in solution, watching closely in the soft glow of infrared light as the print slowly appeared, the shadows and textures and shapes emerging from a blank canvas of white. It was an old technology, but watching it happen was still like magic to him.

He inspected each print of separate quadrants as she hung them up to dry. He wasn't an expert agronomist, but he did know something about horticulture and what he saw didn't quite fit.

"What do you think those are?" he asked, pointing to a particular bush.

"Avocados," he said.

"I've never heard of growing avocados outdoors in England," she said.

"That's because it's not possible. It needs a much warmer climate."

He inspected another print hanging on the line. "And here," he said, "that looks like pineapple."

She looked where he was pointing. "So it does," she said. And she looked at him in wonder.

But it was the last photo that seemed to him the most amazing of all. "I'll be damned," he muttered to himself. "A coffee bush!"

Mai was pondering one of the overhead shots with a dreamy look on her face as the smoke from the cigarette she held in her other hand coiled into the air.

Grant had gone back to examining the series which were taken of the fence.

"How many people were involved in these observations?" he asked, putting the photo down.

"Three or four if you count the boys..."

"What boys?" he looked at her curiously.

"Thomas. Sometimes his friend Salvador came along."

"Salvador Rojas?"

She took a short puff on her cigarette. "Yes. They were quite good friends."

"Was there any rota or schedule when the people stood watch?" he asked.

"No. It was more casual."

He thought for a moment. Then he looked at her and said, "Is this all you brought me over to see?"

"No," she said, stubbing out her cigarette and getting up. "I want you to come with me."

"Where?"

"Back to Gaia's Revenge. We need to speak with Vermuden..."

~

She didn't bother to knock. She just opened the door to the cabin and let herself inside. Unused to this kind of informality and not knowing what to expect from unannounced entrances, Grant followed, reluctantly.

Vermuden was in the central area, designed as a sort of study or sitting room. A foldout desk was piled with books and papers. He was concentrating so hard on his writing that he didn't seem to notice them as they came in.

Mai wasn't bothered. She clearly felt at home. Opening the little gas powered fridge, she took out a bottle. "Beer?" she asked, looking at Grant as she spoke.

"Sure," he said. "Why not?"

Vermuden still hadn't looked up. Either his powers of concentration were enormous, thought Grant, or he felt no obligation to engage in artificial politeness. Mai cracked open the beer, poured out a glass and handed it to Grant. She kept the bottle for herself.

"Thomas is in a bad way," she said. "I stayed with him this morning. It seems to me he's sinking fast." She looked at him, hoping for a contradiction.

"You never can tell when a life is at stake," said Grant, "but I wouldn't hold out much hope unless..."

He took a drink.

"Unless what?" she asked.

"Unless we can locate the source and nature of the toxic substance. I was hoping you could be of help..."

"I told you everything I know," said Mai.

"How about him?" asked Grant, motioning to Vermuden.

Vermuden looked up and smiled. "Dr Grant. How nice to see you again. Sorry if I seemed to be ignoring you, but I had something to complete." He made a final flourish with his pen. "There now. Done!" He stood up and stretched. "So, how may I help you?"

"I'm stuck," said Grant. "I've run out of leads and out of time. I'm grasping at straws. I think you might have more to say – I hope so, anyway."

"Please, Dr Grant! To come here on bended knees is most unfitting for a man of your ... position."

The ring of sarcasm in Vermuden's voice did nothing for the nausea Grant was feeling. "There are people dying," he said. "Don't you think it's time to stop playing games?"

Vermuden's cool facade was betrayed by a muscular twitch which danced on his upper left temple. "I am not the one who poisoned them, Dr Grant."

"But maybe you could help save them," he said.

Mai was watching this verbal parrying with more and more discomfort. "Cut the crap!" she said to Vermuden. "One of those people dying is my nephew. And, frankly, I don't think you care beans about him. You're just interested in your God-damned mission to save the bloody Earth!"

A strange, heavy silence filled the cramped space of the boat when she stopped. It lasted for some time and was finally broken by Mai herself.

"Oh, shit!" she cursed, throwing her bottle across the cabin. It hit the wall, splattering into a thousand pieces.

Grant looked at her in wonder.

Vermuden who was watching Grant's expression broke out into a raucous laugh. "Maybe I was wrong about you," he said to Grant. "You're far too earnest to be in their pocket."

"Stop it!" shouted Mai, giving Vermuden a furious look. "This has gone way too far! I've had enough!"

"Cool down!" Vermuden's voice was calm, but it was easy to see from his face that he meant it as a warning.

But she was not to be bullied. "If you don't tell him, I will!"

Vermuden shrugged and sat down at his desk, pretending to go back to work. "Do what you want," he said, without looking up. "I'll just remind you that we promised not to compromise her safety. If you want to take that responsibility, then go ahead."

Mai continued to stare at Vermuden but her words were directed at Grant.

"Remember that 'shoot' you asked me about? It had to do with a research scientist we made contact with from TechnoFarm. She was pretty anxious to speak with us. We set up a meeting. This was the beginning of last week..."

"And?"

"And she never showed."

"Informants get cold feet," said Grant. "It's happened to me more times than I care to remember."

"The thing is she just up and vanished..."

"People who 'up and vanish' usually don't want to be found."

"Except this one did. She's scared as hell, but she's willing to talk..."

~

It was what Vermuden called a "safe house," but it was really another boat moored further down the river toward the lock.

They reached it by hiking through the fields thick with nettles and cow dung.

Vermuden knocked three times on a porthole – two short, one long – and then climbed aboard. The cabin door was locked. He fished for a key and opened it.

The cabin was dark. The curtains were drawn. There wasn't any light.

"Betty?" Vermuden called out. "It's Chris..."

A small lamp went on in the rear of the boat exposing a round face, childlike and fearful.

"Who's that with you?" said a very small voice, like a bird asking the whereabouts of a cat.

"A friend," said Mai. "Dr Grant..."

"Did you bring my magazines?"

Vermuden took her over a bundle of Nature and New Scientist. And a bag with several packets of crisps. "Salt and vinegar, I hope," she said, opening the bag.

"They only had cheese and onion," said Vermuden.

"Oh..."

Grant could barely see the face. But the voice sounded very disappointed.

"I still feel seasick," she said. "Salt and vinegar seems to be the only thing that helps."

"I'll try again later," Vermuden assured her. Then he said, "We're moving again this afternoon."

"Again?" she asked.

"It's for your own safety," Vermuden replied.

"I suppose," she said. And then she opened the crisps and started eating, while staring over at Grant. "Who is he?"

"I'm an epidemiologist," said Grant. "Several people in Cambridge have come down with severe toxic reactions to something we haven't been able to trace. I'm trying to find out whether it has anything to do with what's going on at TechnoFarm."

"Jesus!" said Betty. "I was afraid of that!"

"Why don't you start from the beginning," said Mai, looking at the young woman encouragingly. "Tell him what you were doing there..."

She let out a sigh, as if she had been through it quite enough already.

"I was recruited about a year ago to work on a bio-genetics team that was doing some fascinating experiments on cellular restructuring. I'd been doing research on genetic pigmentation – what genetic attributes define colorisation. Like why are some roses red and some white. Could we make them blue? The answer, of course, was 'yes.' As long as you understood the code..."

She took another mouthful of crisps and then went on. "The TechnoFarm project was very interested in that. In fact they had gathered some of the best researchers in the field. Experts in genetic agronomy. We were involved in colour. But they had teams involved with size, shape, flavour as well. That was the morphology group. There were other groups involved with metabolic factors and plant nutrition and habitat and disease resistance..." She took a deep breath. "You get the picture, don't you?"

"They were trying to create better hybrids, I suppose," said Grant.

Betty shook her head as she stuffed in more crisps. "They were going way beyond that," she said. "They were trying to develop a whole new range of agriculture. Plants that were tailored for specific markets and tastes..."

Vermuden took a notebook from the table. "Listen to this list of projects she told us about," he said. "Low calorie avocados that could be grown in Scotland. Sugar-sweet seedless oranges that could be grown in northern wastelands. Frost-resistant corn that could be farmed intensively in the tundra. Caffeine-free coffee trees that could be grown outside the tropics..."

"Sounds great, doesn't it?" said Mai. "Except in the hands of multinational combines world agriculture would be even more in their pocket than it is today. They already are patenting seeds. Now they're patenting the whole damned vegetable!"

Vermuden took up where Mai left off. "The ability to develop produce for specific tastes, grown wherever and whenever you desire, to 'own' the rights to the genetic makeup of a plant, is not only playing God; it's playing God as a robber baron! These people are gaining the power to make the lords of finance and industry, like the Rothschilds and the Vanderbilts and the Rockefellers, seem like benighted social workers in comparison. The old shackles of imperialism still gave some room for the peasant and the worker to manoeuvre. This technology is so evil that it would destroy the small farmers and peasants of the world in one enormous cataclysm of biblical proportions!"

"I don't know about that," Betty said, giving him a curious look. "The fact is, there was some great science being done. But these people were under enormous pressure to deliver. They already had their catalogues printed..."

"But they couldn't grow the vegetables as promised?" asked Grant.

"Oh, they grew them all right," said Betty. Her face darkened as if she was suddenly hit by a memory which disturbed her. "The problem is that something went terribly wrong..."

~

"We first started noticing it with the birds. Their little corpses were collected in batches every day for a month. Autopsies were done on them. But, as far as I know, there was never any reason discovered for their deaths. We were told, at the beginning, that the problem was strychnine from neighbouring farms that had been put in bait for foxes. But that didn't cut any ice. Strychnine causes voracious thirst. The bodies become bloated and swollen. These were emaciated from some sort of wastage. Some of us started questioning whether it wasn't the plants themselves that somehow had gone toxic..."

"Surely there were hot house experiments testing the safety of the plants before they were grown in fields," said Grant.

"Of course," she said. "But you have to recognise that the main thing TechnoFarm was trying to prove was viability. When Japanese businessmen came to inspect the factory, they wanted to see crops being grown in conditions that were advertised. You had to be able to show them cocoa beans grown in the open – in impossible soils and climates. Anything can be grown in a hothouse. Besides, how do you test for toxicity?"

That was a question Grant had often asked himself. Toxicity was relative to the organism. It was a factor that could only be tested through time and usage.

"How did you test for it?"

"We fed samples of all crops to laboratory animals. Any reaction was noted. But, as you know, even monkeys don't always react to the same things as squirrels or humans, for that matter. And the variation of strains was enormous. There were hundreds of seeds being tested. Most were total duds. Sometimes you'd get a beautiful looking plant that tasted terrible. Sometimes the colours were incorrect – who would buy a green carrot or a blue tomato? To get all the factors perfect – flavour, shape, size and viability – took the kind of brilliant scientific and technical teamwork that sent a rocket to the moon." For a moment she seemed to bask in the remembered glory of their remarkable successes.

"But something went wrong," Grant reminded her.

"About a month ago, word came down from management that a push was on to get a viable show. That meant having the display fields ready for inspection by agro-business executives. At least, that's what we thought. As it turned out, it was something even bigger. The company has long been after government subsidies. Research and development costs are spectacular. It's one thing to develop and grow a new crop. It's another to have it accepted for the market. The time it takes for safety studies is enormous – as well it should be. Essentially, this is a new industry. And it takes time to launch. And during that time, there's nothing coming in and a hell of a lot going out. But for all the risks, the potential for profit is enormous. With the right support, an industry like this could be competitive with silicon. We – Britain, that is – didn't do such a great job competing there. But we're on the ground floor with the biotech stuff and we could really use this as a base to get the country moving again."

She seemed suddenly to catch herself. She blushed. "I'm sorry if I sound like a flag waver. But it is – it was – so exciting. We really fucked things up here. We have great scientists, great creative potential. And what we end up doing is giving it all away due to shortsighted policies. The idea of having the government actually support an industry for a change, to accept a national challenge, was really marvellous. All of us felt that way. Until we saw what happened."

"What do you mean?" asked Grant. "Are you talking about safety limitations?"

She almost laughed. "Just the opposite. The pressure to cut corners, to get results, was greater than ever. They wanted viable products to display. Something tangible. So we gave it to them. And then maybe it was inevitable someone died. A gardener..."

"What happened?"

"We don't know. He was found in one of the experimental fields where the AVFTs were being researched..."

"AVFTs?" Grant shook his head.

"Of course," she smiled, thinly. "You wouldn't know about them, would you. Altered Venus Flytraps. It was a new hybrid that was being tested as part of the Self Sustainable Farm Project. We wanted to develop a plant that could defend against predators. The carnivorous traits of the Venus Flytrap were combined with larger species. Certain pheromones and perfumes that were sexual attractors were genetically programmed in, along with chemical beta-blockers. The idea was to seduce the predator, put it to sleep and then use the enzymes from the Altered Flytrap to recycle it..."

"You mean you were breeding plants that could eat animals?" Grant looked at her in disbelief.

"I suppose so. Yes. We were thinking of little animals though. Like mice and rats. What we didn't realise, though, was as the plants grew bigger they developed a taste for bigger things..."

"Like what?"

"Like stray dogs."

"And gardeners?"

She shook her head. "I don't know. It's pretty hard to believe..."

"What happened to the body?" asked Grant.

"They sent his body straight down to London. I never actually saw it. But people said he was half decomposed..."

Her face suddenly darkened and her eyes dampened. "Later we heard his death was listed as accidental...I knew him. He was a friend. He was really concerned at the animal deaths. He argued that experimentation should be only in enclosed conditions. That experimentation in the field could lead to disaster. He argued that position within the company. He threatened to go public unless they did something..."

"Can you give me his name?" asked Grant.

"Seamus O'Neal," she said.

Grant copied down the gardener's name. Then he asked, "What happened after that?"

"The scientists live under a reign of terror. We all had to sign contracts that forbade us to talk about anything that went on at TechnoFarm. We're all afraid for our jobs, our careers. Besides, we don't have any real evidence of anything beyond a few dead birds. But morale sunk to a new low after we heard about the break-in."

"What break-in?"

"We'd been telling them for months that the fencing was insecure. But the cost of redoing the perimeter wasn't in the budget.

"Then we heard that two kids had been spotted in the field and a hole had been cut in the fence along Girton Road. After that, the company went security crazy. They must have spent a million setting up new perimeters. They even have devices the military use – sensors that locate precisely where an intruder is standing."

"Do you know what the kids who broke in took?"

She shook her head. "No. But they do – the company, that is. They have every tree, bush and flower numbered. Every fruit is labelled while it's still on the vine. Nothing is grown that isn't inspected every single day. They know exactly what was taken. And I'll bet you anything whatever it was, they're out looking for it right now. Can you imagine what it would do to their credibility if a toxic fruit or vegetable grown at TechnoFarm had caused an epidemic?"

~

"Something was stolen from TechnoFarm," he told Pauline, stopping at a phone box to ring her. "Two kids burrowed under the security fence and took some produce from a field of genetically engineered plants. We don't know what was taken but we think we know who did it..."

"Who?"

"Salvador and Thomas."

"Salvador Rojas?" Her voice sounded her disbelief.

"I'm going up to Addenbrooke's," said Grant. "Can you try ringing him at home?"

"I can try," said Pauline. "But I just spoke to Maria. Salvador didn't come home last night. She hasn't seen him since his father was taken to jail."

He made a grunt of displeasure. "I'll see if I can talk with Thomas. Although Mai says he's in a pretty bad way. We really need Salvador..."

"I'll phone around," said Pauline. "Maybe I can trace him. Oh, by the way, Katz rang. He wants you to phone him back as soon as you can."

Grant dialled Katz's number as soon as he got off the phone with Pauline.

"I have the list you wanted," said Katz.

"Thanks," said Grant. "When can I pick it up?"

"I'll be in my office for a while if you want to stop by. But I should tell you, some strange things have been going on..."

"Like what?"

"Like practically everyone in the Chilean community has had their fridges ransacked! They've come home to find that someone's taken their food supplies!"

~

He had given Katz a rundown of what he had found out and told him he'd be there in about an hour. Then he had rung up Tracy Poon and asked her to meet him at Katz's office. Finally, he phoned Cook, the consultant at Addenbrooke's, and told him he was coming with some important information.

Cook listened carefully to everything that Grant told him, even though he was still numb from having spent the last few days struggling with a strange and malevolent syndrome that had threatened to kill off more patients in a single week than he had lost in the entire year. First they had tried to convince him it was related to a toxic oil case that had devastated Spain something that over ten years later the Spanish still weren't able to cure or even understand. And now Grant was trying to put a bug in his ear about some toxic plants that had been stolen from an experimental farm.

"What evidence do you have?" asked Cook, looking at him suspiciously.

They were sitting in the consultants' room. Grant was leaning forward in his chair, gesticulating with his hands. It was a most uncharacteristic mannerism and showed, more than anything else, the state he was in since his tone of voice remained calm and reasoned.

"Besides my anonymous informant, none. But that's why it's so important to interview Thomas."

Cook shook his head. "He's under sedation. I'm afraid I couldn't allow it..."

"Let me try..." Grant wasn't someone who found it easy to plead for favours, but this wasn't for himself. The look on his face said it all.

Getting up from his chair, Cook walked over to the window overlooking the emergency entrance to the hospital. An ambulance had just driven up. A body was being lowered onto a gurney. An oxygen mask was strapped onto the head. The gurney was wheeled quickly out of sight. It all happened in the wink of an eye.

"Five minutes," said Cook turning around. "That's all the time you've got."

~

Grant rolled back the plastic of the oxygen tent and then, sitting down in the chair, he gently rubbed the boy's arm.

Thomas's long eyelashes gave a flutter.

Grant leaned closer. "Thomas," he said, "my name is Dr Grant. I'd like to ask you a few questions..."

There was no response. The boy's eyes looked up without comprehension. Grant thought that he was in a semi-conscious state. But where he was within his mind was anyone's guess.

"Thomas," Grant said again, in a soft but determined voice, "I need your help. I'm trying to find something – something that might let us understand why you became so ill. Do you think you could help me?"

He was trying to speak. his chapped lips, cracked like the parched earth in a hot and arid land, moved painfully. They were trying to shape words but something was missing. The will was there, it seemed, but not the velocity.

"Remember the birds?" he asked. "Remember taking photographs of them over the fields when you were there with Vermuden?"

His head made a movement. A nod Grant thought.

"Remember the fence that surrounded the field? There was a hole in it, wasn't there?"

The large blue eyes seemed to be focused on Grant's face. But Grant could see nothing in those eyes except his own image staring back.

"The hole was hidden by a bush. Remember? Did you go though the hole to the other side?"

He thought he saw a nod again.

"Thomas. This is very, very important. I really need to know – did you go into those fields?"

The thin, cracked lips tried painfully to shape the words. "Bamboo..."

"Yes, the bamboo," said Grant. "On the other side of the bamboo there was something quite amazing, wasn't there?"

He nodded.

"Something strange. What was it?"

The boy's eyes seemed to sink further into a dream.

"What did you see there?"

A wonderful smile came over Thomas's face. Like a golden sunbeam. "The Garden of Eden..." he whispered.

~

Cook put a consoling arm around Grant's shoulder. "Thomas is in a different world. Even if he were more lucid, I don't think he'd make a good informant..."

"The kids were in there," said Grant. "We have to find out what they took."

They were standing in the foyer outside the Toxic Syndrome ward. "Then you'll have to get it from the Rojas boy," said Cook.

"I would if I could," Grant replied. "The trouble is, he's missing."

A young nurse had just walked up to them. "Could you take a look at Kathy Battersea?" she asked, gazing up at the consultant with undisguised admiration. "I'm a bit worried about her..."

"Right away," said Cook. Then turning to Grant, he said, "I'll see what I can get out of him later..."

"Just one other thing," said Grant, as Cook started to follow the nurse into the ward.

Cook looked back and raised his eyebrows.

"Kathy Battersea has a boyfriend. Has he been to see her lately?"

"A rather pale young man with John Lennon spectacles?" said the nurse. "He was just here."

"When?" asked Grant.

"Just two minutes ago. He must have passed you in the corridor..."

Grant turned and hurried through the foyer and then into the central corridor. No one was there. He pushed the button for the lift, but he could tell from the dial above the doors that it was already headed down.

Rushing over to the stairs, he quickly made his way to the ground floor, emerging into the central lobby gasping for breath.

Just a few elderly people were congregated by the snack bar. The rest of the place seemed deserted. He raced over to the main entry door. A security guard looked at him curiously.

"A pale young man...John Lennon specs. Did you see him?"

The security guard motioned outside where a thin young man was getting into a taxi.

Bolting out the door, Grant called out. "Pinter! Wait!"

The taxi drove off.

He saw the young man in the back seat turn around. He wasn't wearing glasses.

~

He got a coffee from the snack bar and sat down at a table. He felt a tightness in his chest. His body seemed heavy and ungainly.

Sometimes things came easily. Other times they came hard. But he had never in the past reached a state of chronic inertia so severe as this. It was like being in a hall of mirrors and constantly reaching out to touch something that wasn't there.

Taking a sip of the sickening stuff in his cup, he glanced up. The person who had sat down across from him was reading a book. Grant's eyes fixed on the title – *Being and Nothingness* by John-Paul Sartre. He almost smiled at the curious synchronisity. And then, suddenly, it struck him.

"Pinter?"

The young man put down his book and stared at him, wide-eyed, through his metal rimmed glasses. "Who are you?"

"I rang you about an hour ago, damn it! How come you didn't wait?"

Pinter's eyes grew wider still. His spotty cheeks almost glowed. "I...I was coming to see Kathy...you didn't say who you were..."

Grant closed his eyes and took a deep breath. When he opened them again he saw a pale faced young man sitting across from him, his mouth slightly agape, looking scared to death.

"I'm sorry," Grant apologised. "I'm an epidemiologist investigating the toxic syndrome cases. I wanted to speak with you because Kathy said she stayed at your place on the 17th..."

"The 17th?"

"Last Friday."

"Last Friday." He nodded. "Oh, yes..."

"Do you remember what you had to eat?"

"Eat?" Pinter looked at him, curiously.

"Eat. You know. What you put in your mouth when you're hungry..." He wondered whether Schopanhauer had anything to say about that.

"Yes. It's just that I haven't been eating much lately..."

"Actually, it's Kathy I'm concerned about."

"She just eats fruit, nuts..."

Grant nodded. "She told me. Did you give her any?" He used his hand as a prompt "Fruit, nuts..."

"She usually brings her own..."

"Usually."

"Yes."

"How about on Friday."

"Friday..." His glasses slid slightly down his nose as he looked up. "Let me think..."

A tear came rolling from his eye down his cheek.

"She's a lovely young woman," said Grant, softly.

Pinter nodded.

"We're trying to help her. But it's important to know what she ate."

The young man had closed his eyes.

"Try to imagine what you did that day. Picture it in your mind..."

"I went to the library," he said. "I always go to the library on Friday..."

"Which one?"

"The one in the Arbury Estate..."

"The Arbury Estate? Is that close to where you live?"

"It's just a few minutes away. I do my shopping there..."

"Where?"

"At the small market. I don't like the big one. It's too alienating. Besides, the veggies there are rather sickly..."

"What veggies did you buy that day?"

"On Friday?" He shook his head. "Not any, I don't think..." He closed his eyes again and tried to focus. "Just a sec..."

"Yes?"

"When I was walking back from the library, that is. I go down Alex Wood Road..."

Grant's ears perked up. "There's a hall..."

"Yes, they were having some sort of festival that day..."

"That's right!" said Grant, encouragingly. "You went in?"

"No." Pinter shook his head.

"You didn't?" Grant's voice sounded disappointed.

"No. But there was a stall set up out front..."

"Out front of the hall?"

"Yes. Near to the pavement. Two boys. They were selling tomatoes. Garden fresh, they said. The biggest tomatoes I ever saw."

Grant stared at the young man. Everything suddenly started coming together in his head. "And you bought some..."

"I had to buy one, didn't I? For her, you know. For Kathy..." A dreamlike look came over his face. "To her it was better than a bouquet of flowers..."

~

It was almost an hour and a half after he phoned that Grant arrived at the King Street office of Morris Katz.

Tracy Poon had been there for some time. But she wasn't put out.

"We've been comparing pasta recipes. He thinks the Jews invented spaghetti," she laughed.

"She still holds to that old canard about Marco Polo getting it from the Chinese! In India it was called sevika, in Arabia it was known as rishta and the Jews called it kreplach. They found it was the perfect dried food to take with them on trading expeditions when they went to China centuries before Marco Polo's little jaunt," said Katz.

Grant wasn't amused. He had no time for such nonsense. Accepting a cup of decent Italian coffee, he told them what he had found out about the theft at TechnoFarm.

"Tomatoes?" Tracy Poon looked at him as if he was off his head. "How could tomatoes cause a reaction like that?"

"We need to find out what was done to them in order to explain how. But at least we've got our vector. The boys sold them last Friday outside the hall in Alex Wood Road. So there was a general relation to the Chilean event in space and time, but not a specific one. There's no case against the Rojas family at all."

"That's why Eduardo is refusing to testify in his own defence," said Katz. "He doesn't want to implicate his son!"

"It explains a lot more than that," said Grant.

"You mean the strange food thefts in the Chilean community?" Katz slammed his fist down on his desk, making

Tracy Poon jump. "They knew, those pork-eared bastards! But they'd rather let some poor bugger die!"

"You said you have the list of people who went to the event?" Grant asked.

"Those who signed up..." Katz rummaged through a pile on his desk and pulled out a folder. "I've made a copy," he said, handing it to Grant. "But I'm not sure what good it's going to do you."

"We need to find one of those tomatoes to have it analysed. Our best hope is someone on this list might still have one."

"I wouldn't bet on it," said Katz. "What I would bet, though, is that someone else has this list and is twenty steps ahead of you."

"What else would you suggest?" he asked. "Right now, it's all we've got."

"Look," said Katz, "I was brought in by the Rojas family. First, it was a simple case of theft. Then the charge became manslaughter and the case became complicated. Now I can see that what we're dealing with is a conspiracy to frame an innocent man in order to divert attention from a major ecological catastrophe. I think we need to be aware that we've bumped into the tip of an enormous iceberg. But, whatever the extent of the conspiracy, we happen to be in a unique position of maybe being able to do something about it. We can't bring back the dead – excuse me doctor for speaking frankly – or even cure the ill. But we certainly can try to make sure that no one else has to suffer from their crimes. And that starts with Eduardo. As it stands now, that poor bastard is going down the Swanee without a bloody paddle!"

"I'm as angry as you are," said Grant. "Maybe even angrier. You're right, most of the toxic syndrome patients are probably going to die. But I'm an epidemiologist, a doctor. As long as we have the tiniest possibility of finding a cure, we have to pursue it. The only chance we have is if we can find out what's causing their reaction. And for that we need the goddamned TechnoFarm tomato so we can try to get it analysed!" He looked over at Tracy. "Will you help?"

She looked back at him. There was a lump in her throat. She felt frightened but, in a strange way, also honoured to have gained his trust. "That's what I'm here for," she replied.

~

Grant drove back to Pauline's house, parking her car in front of the Ford Transit van – the same place he had parked it before. He thought it curious that the van had remained there without having been moved. What bothered him was the parabolic communications dish connected to the roof which spoke of expensive equipment hidden inside the windowless body. He knew you didn't leave equipment like that lying around idle. He realised it was there for some reason.

Going up to the house, he let himself in and walked down the corridor to the front room. Through the doorway, he saw her stretched out on the settee, asleep.

He went over to where she was sleeping and gazed down at her. She had taken a patchwork quilt to cover herself. The bottom half had slipped onto the floor.

It was only when he reached down to cover her legs that he noticed it. She was wearing a cotton nightgown that had worked its way up to her thigh, exposing her porcelain skin. He bent down to inspect it closer, touching the strange, uneven blotches gently so as not to awaken her.

She opened her eyes. He reacted quickly by letting the quilt fall back onto her.

She looked at him curiously. "How long have you been here?" she asked.

"Just a few moments," he said.

For a while she said nothing. Then she said, simply; "I suppose you saw."

He nodded and pressed his lips together. Suddenly he was filled with an enormous sense of emptiness and loss.

"You've known for a while, haven't you?" he said.

"Yes," she replied. "But I thought you did as well..."

He shook his head. "Maybe I did. I don't know."

"It happened so fast. This morning I still thought that I might just have a touch of the flu..."

"You should have said something to me." He was aware that his voice had sounded accusing.

"What was there to say?" she asked. And then she smiled at him, weakly.

He went over to the chair opposite the settee. He sat down and stared at her. He wanted to say something. Maybe she was right. What was there to say? But why, he wondered, was the first word that came to mind "betrayal"? Why was he thinking of himself and not of her?

It was as if she had read his mind. "This is the second time I've left you, isn't it?" she said.

"You're not leaving. No one's leaving."

"I love you, Peter," she said.

He looked down at the ground, wishing so much she hadn't said that. "People do survive this, you know. The death rate in Spain was only 20%."

"This isn't Spain. This isn't Toxic Oil Syndrome."

Suddenly he felt himself grow cold inside. He ran his hand over her forehead and down her cheek. "You'll be OK," he said, getting up out of the chair.

"Where are you going, Peter?" she asked him, watching as he started to leave the room.

"I'm calling for an ambulance."

"No...please..."

He stopped and turned. There was a determined look on her face.

"Not yet..."

"The sooner you're treated the better chance there is," he said, softly.

"Treated how?" she asked. "For what? If something was ingested several days ago, it's already too late. At Addenbrooke's they're just treating the symptoms. Besides..." Her voice trailed off.

"Besides what?"

"I have some medication, myself..."

It was the most he could to do, convincing her to go back to bed. As he helped her up the stairs, he said, "The salad, the one you had when I first arrived. Where did you get the tomato?" He could still picture it in his mind; red, luscious, a true pomme d'amour he had thought, from a garden of earthly delights.

"Of course," she whispered, "the tomato..."

"Where did it come from?"

"It was a gift..."

"From?"

"An anonymous patient." She laughed. It was a soft, rasping laugh, filled more with the absurdity of life than spiteful irony.

"Weren't you suspicious?"

"Why should I have been suspicious?"

"But a tomato as gift from an unknown admirer..."

"Oh, no. We often get gifts like that. A hand-made scarf, a basket of berries. Our patients are so sweet, you know. So appreciative..."

He helped her into bed, fluffing up the pillow and smoothing down the sheet.

"Stay with me," she said, holding out her hand.

Sitting down on the edge of the bed, he took her hand. It felt soft and warm and triggered off a faint tactile memory of tenderness that almost overrode the melancholy.

"When all this is over, perhaps we could go somewhere," she whispered.

"Where would you like to go?"

"Anywhere."

"Back to Rangoon?"

"That would be nice." A tear welled up in her eye and she turned away her head.

"I still have an image of us there, like a fantasy captured in aspic."

"Yes. I know." She gave his hand a little squeeze and then let go.

He sat there till she fell asleep. He stayed a while more. Then he went downstairs to the study.

Taking the list that Katz had given him – the half that he had kept for himself, the other half went to Tracy – he began phoning around to see if anyone who signed up at the Chilean fête still had a tomato that hadn't been eaten.

It was a long and arduous process going over the reason for his call, time after time, struggling to make himself understood and midway through he began to realise the futility of it all. Why would anyone still have a tomato bought almost a week before? Either it would have been eaten or thrown away. Or, as Katz wisely foretold, vanished in a mysterious disappearance.

He went into the kitchen and fixed himself a drink from a bottle of whisky he found there. The heat of the alcohol revived him.

Glancing around, he tried to remember the way it was that evening when he had first come there. He looked at the table and recalled the row of vegetables neatly trimmed, ready to be combined into a salad. And he pictured the tomato, ripe, exotic, almost sensual, sitting like a succulent prize for a gourmet prince.

He tried to imagine each and every detail. The shape plump as a blushing Buddha. The texture silky smooth. The colour a red so deep it verged on purple, contrasted only by the green of the stem which curled up from the top like the severed cord of an umbilicus.

It was only then that it struck him. She couldn't have eaten it all! Not every little morsel! Certainly, at the very least, she must have cut around the stem!

But if she hadn't, where would the detritus be? Where did she keep her rubbish bin!?

He searched around, finally locating it underneath the sink.

Spreading some newspaper on the floor, he dumped out the contents. The mass of organic waste, as she had neatly divided up her trash, oozed like a sickly pudding.

Working through the mess like an urban archaeologist, uncovering each successive layer, he inspected the contents for any sign of tomato. What he found, eventually, was a stem and some slimy trimmings perhaps. He couldn't be certain. But that's what they seemed to be.

He found a plastic baggy in a drawer which he used to put them in, twisting it shut.

It was then that the telephone rang. Putting the bag on the table, he went to answer it.

"Is this Dr Grant?"

The voice was deep. The tone was serious.

"It is," said Grant. "What can I do for you?"

"The question is what you can do for yourself, Dr Grant. At the moment, you're in great danger..."

"Who is this?" he asked, brusquely.

"A simple warning should suffice. If not, if you persist in playing with fire, you have only yourself to blame. I think you know what I'm talking about..."

And then the caller rang off.

CHAPTER 4

~FRIDAY 24 JUNE~

THE SOFT, HEALING strains of a Mozart piano concerto filled the room and contrasted starkly with the sound of her laboured breathing.

On the night table he had found some used syringes, a catalogue of drugs which had kept her going – steroids, atropine, morphine.

The time was a little after midnight.

It was six AM when he finally called for an ambulance.

Cook was there at the ward when the ambulance arrived. His hair was a mess. His thin fingers were clutched rigidly around a paper coffee cup. His face looked fagged out and wasted.

"Thomas is gone," he said, when Grant met him in the corridor.

"When?"

"Just a few minutes ago." Cook put down his cup just long enough to light up a cigarette. He looked at Grant through eyes that were intensely bloodshot. "Three others are on the brink. Most of the rest haven't long to go."

He helped settle Pauline into the ward. He sat with her for a while. Then whispering something into her ear, he got up.

"I'm going to London," he said to the nurse on duty. "I'll be back as soon as I can. But if anything ...happens...here's my number." He scribbled the number to his office answerphone onto a slip of paper.

"I'll give it to Matron," said the nurse. And as he was about to walk away, she added, "We all know Dr Quail. She's the best there is. We'll take good care of her."

It was on his way out that Grant saw them. First, Maria Rojas. She was sitting in the waiting area, just outside the ward.

Her head was bent low, as if in prayer. He stopped for a moment, knelt down and touched her hand. She looked up. In her eyes he glimpsed something of the agony and sorrow – just an inkling of what it was like to be the mother of a dying child, whose husband was locked away and whose son was missing. He said nothing. The sympathy he felt for her was conveyed in other ways. She pressed her lips together till they just became thin lines and nodded her head, accepting his silent compassion.

Then, in the corridor, Mai Cunningham. Her arm was cradling the head of Thomas's father who wept openly. He watched as Mai, who was crying herself, tried to comfort him.

"So much for your medicine..."

The voice came from behind him. He turned and saw Vermuden. "This wasn't an act of God. It was an act of man. The ultimate achievement of Western science..."

"What do you want?" Grant felt his dislike of Vermuden transforming quickly into hatred.

"What do I want?" The muscles in Vermuden's face tensed so much that you could see the veins pulsating in his head. "What I want is simple. I want revenge." He smiled a terrible smile. The kind of smile that curdles blood. "What do you want, Dr Grant?"

~

He drove at top speed as fast as the Renault 2CV could take him down the M11, hitting London's orbital motorway before the rush hour traffic.

When he arrived, Grant went straight to his office. It was only when he was safely inside and seated at his desk that he allowed himself to relax and try to make sense of it all.

There was something he needed to know. He dialled a colleague's extension to see if he was there. The line was engaged. He got up from the desk and left his office, walking down the corridor to a larger office at the end.

Clarke was at his desk moaning over the telephone as Grant came in.

"You must be joking! The proposals have to be entirely rewritten? Why in fart's name do we hire these bloody people if they can't get it right the first bloody time around?"

He slammed down the phone, looked over at Grant and said, "Bloody hell!"

"What do you know about plant genetics?" asked Grant.

"Genetics is genetics," said Clarke clasping his hands behind his head and giving a regal stretch, like a prince relaxing in his chamber after a hard day of shouting at his minions. "That's the beauty of it. Start out with a carrot, shift a little DNA and you get a rabbit instead." He smiled. "We truly are the masters of the universe except when it comes to writing grants. Then we're the little bits of lint you find in your navel."

Grant thought he liked him better when Clarke was running on some other high octane rather than the detritus of his ego. "Are you current on new developments?"

"You mean, what's on the drawing board?" Clarke gave a shrug. "Whatever agribusiness wants. Mainly, how to get a greater yield at lower cost."

"How about patenting new plants?"

"Sure. Why not? But new foods are a marketing problem. The real business is in adapting your traditional produce – the stuff everyone eats. If, for example, you could mass-produce a tasty tomato that could be easily produced, mechanically harvested, has a long shelf-life and looks like it came from a truck farm in the south of France, my boy, you'd have the world at your feet."

"Why a tomato?" Grant asked, surprised at Clarke's choice of examples.

"Because tomatoes are the biggest conundrum. Real tomatoes, the kind you dream of – if you ever had the opportunity to taste one garden fresh – are hard to mass produce. Their skins are delicate and so they need to be harvested by hand. The mass-produced varieties have been engineered to be harvested by machine. But they taste like food for robots. To get the balance of toughness, tenderness and taste is a tricky business. The commodities market would bestow a king's fortune on the right patent."

"What would that entail?" asked Grant. "How would a company go about doing it?"

"There isn't a simple gene for 'taste'. That's a subjective quality. There isn't a single gene for 'machine harvestibility', either. All these factors are complex. You need a lot of technique, a lot of money and, most of all, a lot of time..."

"Let's say you wanted to do it fast."

"Then you'd need a great deal more money and some exceptionally brilliant scientists."

"To create a good mass-produced tomato?"

"Well the kind I would want to put on my plate..."

Grant rubbed the stubble on his chin and realised how long it was since he had shaved. "Suppose I had a tomato that was genetically engineered. Could you work backward and tell what had been done to it?"

"That's an interesting question," said Clarke. "The problem is there's quite a few varieties of tomato – what with crossbreeds and mutations, probably quite a few more. If you knew the variety that was used as a starting point, it would be a simple matter of comparing the DNA. But then you'd have to know what the changes meant. And that's a project in itself."

"How would you go about finding what the changes meant?"

"You'd have to analyse each genetic change independently. And, even then, you wouldn't be certain. You have to know what to look for. People see what they want to see, don't they? If something is staring you in the face, you can identify it. Other things aren't so visible. Especially if you're not looking for them."

"What other things would agribusiness want from engineered produce besides taste and ease of harvesting?" asked Grant.

"What any business wants," Clarke replied. "Greater yield for less cost. The two major burdens on the agricultural budget are fertiliser and pesticide. If you could engineer plants to be self-fertilising like legumes that create their own nitrates and their own intracellular pesticides, you'd revolutionise the way the farm is run and probably win a hero's reward from ecologists to boot. Of course, you'd have to make sure these intracellular pesticides are non-toxic to humans..."

"Is that kind of research being done at the present?"

"Of course. Take potatoes. There have been over ninety new breeds created over the last few years. One, for example, has a gene tacked on from a certain bacterium which is toxic to its main predator the Colorado beetle. It's been on the market for years already. You've probably eaten it yourself. "

"I hope not," Grant mumbled.

"You're not one of those bloody pure food moaners, are you?" said Clarke, looking at him with disappointment.

"It depends on what you mean by 'moan'. If you're asking me whether I'm concerned with food safety well, that's my job..."

"You're also a scientist of sorts. Progress means taking chances. Otherwise we'd still be in the stone age wielding clubs because some committee of moaners had stopped the invention of the axe for fear we'd cut our bloody thumb! Besides, you know that the chemical industry is more responsible for toxic food reactions than plant mutations. There's enough stringent controls. That's why we can't get anything bloody well done!"

"Twenty years ago you'd probably have been making the same arguments for the chemical industry," said Grant. "You'd have said the same thing about DDT..."

"And DDT probably saved more lives than were lost through overuse. Christ, you're an epidemiologist. You should bloody well know how many people were saved from malaria..."

"How many have been lost from all the new strains that have been created? The American military powdered the entire country of Vietnam with DDT and flooded it with Agent Orange. That didn't stop thousands of soldiers from coming down with malaria even though they were taking the 'proper' prophylactics everyday. The numbers game is tricky," said Grant.

"Look," said Clarke, picking up the telephone again. "I've got a lot of work to do. Let's continue our chat when I've got a little more liquor in me and some time to kill."

He turned himself off as easily as he turned himself on. That's what made him such a good administrator, Grant thought to himself as he walked out of Clarke's office. But Clarke had confirmed what Grant had thought all along. It would be a major project to analyse the tomato remnants, genetically, to find out what had been "done" to it. If he had any chance of discovering the toxic factor, it would have to be through a more straightforward approach. He'd have to be more direct.

~

The toxicology lab was staffed by Franklyn, a short, emaciated man with a face like a garden gnome. Because of his appearance, most people gave him a rather wide berth. But Franklyn was a type that took a while to know. And Grant had found that if one persevered beyond his undeniably grotesque features there was an even more grotesque mind at work.

"This rat should have died weeks ago," said Franklyn as Grant came inside the cluttered laboratory, uniquely decorated with posters of second-rate monster films like 'My Daughter Was A Teenage Vampire' affixed to the walls. Franklyn indicated a rodent that was dashing through a maze on its way to cheesy heaven. "I've fed it difenacoum, brodifacoum and bromadiolone, the most potent anticoagulants on the market, and the little bugger still won't snuff. I'm afraid we've got ourselves another super rat," he said, shaking his goulish head. Then, suddenly, a little smile appeared on his face and his eyes twinkled. "I've named it 'Heseltine'," he said. "I'm going to truly enjoy learning how it's done!"

Grant took out a plastic bag from his briefcase. "Try giving him a little of this tomato," he said.

Franklyn lifted the bag with his long, bony fingers and held it up to the light. "Looks like a botched abortion. What do you want done?"

"See if you can find anything unusual. You might try analysing it for atypical pesticides or heavy metals."

"When do you want it?"

"Now."

Franklyn scrunched up his face making it look even more inscrutable. "People want everything now. We've got to the point where we've almost eradicated the future tense. In fact, that's how the end will come. People will stop talking about the future so much that it will cease to exist. You really want it now?"

"I'd appreciate it," said Grant.

"It's a tomato, you say?" Franklyn lifted the bag to the light again.

"Of a sort."

"Looks like it's been thrown at someone."

"Just be careful with it," said Grant. "I think it may be deadly."

~

He waited for the results in his office. In the end, they came to nothing.

"The sample you gave me was contaminated with every bacteria in the world," said Franklyn. "There really wasn't enough to test for heavy metals. But I tested for organophosphates and couldn't find anything."

After he received Franklyn's report, he telephoned Katz.

Katz didn't sound happy. "The scumbags actually did it!" he seethed over the line when Grant got through to him. "I wouldn't have believed they'd have the bald-faced nerve!"

"Slow down," Grant said. "How about starting from the beginning..."

"It's that man, Solomon Ashu..."

"The cleaner who supposedly exchanged places with Eduardo?"

"Yes. They actually shipped him back to Ethiopia."

"They deported him already?"

"Early this morning. He's somewhere between Heathrow and Addis Ababa."

"Can they do that?"

"It's not a matter of can. They did! I've been on the phone to the Home Office shouting my lungs out all morning. I explained to them that Ashu was a material witness in a murder case. They admit the cockup – ha, ha."

"That's jolly good of them," said Grant, feeling almost as indignant as Katz.

"I'm trying to get authority to have the bugger met at the airport in Addis Ababa and shipped back."

"Is that possible?"

"If they don't, there will be hell to pay! I told them it would be brought up on the floor of the Commons. Their pointy ears prick up when you threaten them with things like that. But even if they do send him back to England, they haven't heard the end of this! Not by a long shot!"

"So what now?" asked Grant. "I can't get anything on the tomato."

"We need some inside information. You were talking about someone from the Department of Health who you said was involved..."

"Simon Bates." The name was painful to utter. "I knew him when I worked in the States..."

"Can you get to him?"

"I'm not sure I understand what you mean."

"Does he trust you?"

"No."

"Does he have a conscience?"

"Not unless he grew one last week. He's an Old Boy."

"And you're not?"

"Not from their perspective."

"Well, see what you can do," Katz suggested.

He wondered what had happened to all his contacts from the old days. People, he supposed, had gone their own ways just like him. Some were on assignment in a far off locale. Others had gone back to their native lands, doing more boring but less stressful jobs.

Nobody seemed to have kept in touch with Bates, especially after he had joined the ministry some years ago. Those that had gone into the upper echelons had disappeared into a different universe. It was as if they had joined a separate race and were no longer part of the same world as the others who still soldiered on in their relatively unimportant positions.

He did manage to get hold of his old professor, Paulo Levi, and arranged to meet him for a drink. Levi had worked on the original Toxic Oil case and Grant thought he might be of some help as he remembered something Levi had once said about a maverick physician in Spain who claimed to have discovered a cure.

After he spoke with Levi, he continued through his phone directory, stopping at an entry that had been written so long ago the writing was fading on the page. He hesitated a moment. Then he picked up the phone and tapped out a number.

A familiar voice answered. It sounded just as it had ten years ago.

"Conroy here."

"Hello, Jason," said Grant. "It's me. Peter."

"Peter?"

There was a silence. He considered hanging up. Maybe it really had been too long.

"How are you?" said Jason, finally. "We've wondered, Diana and I. You're back in England?"

"I've been teaching at the University," said Grant.

"How long?"

"For some time." He wondered how to phrase it. "It was hard to call..."

"I understand." There was another silence. Then Jason said, "You know, I've been thinking about her and you. It was ten years ago last week..."

"I need your help," said Grant, cutting him off.

"My help?" The voice sounded surprised.

"Do you know Simon Bates?"

"He's in a different ministry. Environment, I believe."

"Yes. We worked together in the States. Do you see him?"

"Only occasionally. I see him at the club..."

"The Carlton?"

"Yes. He has his dinner there when he's staying in the city."

"I need to talk with him. It's rather urgent. Do you think I could come as your guest?"

"I suppose. When would you like?"

"It's quite urgent, as I said. Tonight?"

"I'm afraid I couldn't make it tonight. Diana has me down for the opera. Tomorrow, perhaps?"

He knew he shouldn't have called. "I'll try someone else," he said. "Good speaking with you, Jason. Give my love to Diana..."

"Peter! Blimey! It's been ten years! Don't just hang up!"

"I'll call again. It's just that I have urgent business...you know how it is..."

"I do know how it is. Listen, I'll ring up the Carlton and tell them to put your name on the guest list. As long as I say I'm meeting you, they'll let you in."

"Thanks," he said. He fumbled around for the words. "Tell Diana I'm really sorry for not calling sooner. How is she?"

"The same. Still heartbroken over losing her only daughter."

"She never did forgive me, did she?"

"She never blamed you, Peter. You blamed yourself."

He found himself blurting out the words. "I shouldn't have let her go that night. Not like that..."

"No. You shouldn't have. But you didn't know what would happen. People have arguments all the time..."

"Not when their wife is pregnant."

"Especially when their wife is pregnant. You can't keep all that guilt locked up inside you. The world moves on..."

"That's not what you said ten years ago."

"I've changed. I suppose you've changed too. Ten years is a long time, Peter."

"To me, it's just like yesterday," he said. "Thanks again." And he hung up the phone.

~

Simon Bates was sitting in the reading room, nursing a gin and tonic, when Grant found him. He was chatting to an imposing figure of a man tall, lean and stooped with a great, flowing mane of brilliant white hair.

He couldn't have helped but notice Grant as he came up to where they were chatting, but if, he did, he chose to ignore him.

"I need to speak with you," said Grant, breaking into the conversation.

Bates continued speaking, ignoring him the way a gentleman might have ignored his inferiors in a past century. "...Galton wasn't wrong," he was saying, "it's just the way he phrased it. Even the Fabians supported eugenics in those days..."

"I need to speak with you," Grant repeated in a voice that could hardly be disregarded. The people on the other side of the large, well-appointed room, turned their heads.

Initially, the look on Bates' face was one of anger. It was quickly moderated to a more refined distaste. "Grant! I didn't know you were a member..."

"I'm Jason Conroy's guest," he said.

"Oh, of course. Your father-in-law, isn't he?" The remembrance seemed to change Bates' attitude.

"Do you know Michael Hilton? Soon to be Lord Justice, we hope."

Hilton stood up and shook hands with Grant. "How is old Conroy?" he asked. "Still at the FO? Silly question, I suppose. Civil servants never leave, do they? Not even when they pass on. Why should they? Heaven doesn't offer quite the same endowment." Hilton looked around. "Where is the old reprobate?"

"I'm meeting him later," said Grant. Then turning to Bates, he said, "We need to talk."

Bates looked at his watch. "I'm rather in a rush. Maybe next week sometime. Why don't you phone my secretary..."

"I found the tomatoes," said Grant. "I've had them analysed."

Bates, who was about to walk off, suddenly stopped. He rubbed his chin, as if quickly thinking something out.

"What's this about tomatoes?" asked Hilton. "Not been on the receiving end like some of your friends in government, I hope."

"It's nothing," said Bates, apologetically to the man with the shaggy mane. "Just a small case of contamination. Seems we need to put the matter to rest. Do you mind?"

Bates had taken him to a small meeting room toward the rear of the club. As soon as the door was closed, Bates turned on him.

"How dare you approach me in that manner? In my own club, for bloody sake!"

Grant didn't know what he expected, though it did occur to him that people like Bates were bred never to admit anything, even when caught red-handed stealing the Queen's best silver. They had an uncanny ability to restructure, rewrite and redefine any act or situation as long as they came out on top at the end.

"Come off it, Bates," he said. "You know damned well I couldn't meet you anywhere else. I could have waited from now till Doomsday to get an appointment to see you at work."

"All right," said Bates, with a patronising sigh, "what's so bloody urgent?"

Grant looked at him, unbelievingly. "What's so bloody urgent? People have died. Others are extremely ill. An innocent man is charged with murder. And you ask me what's so bloody urgent?"

"Calm down," said Bates. "You're just getting emotional. In fact, that was always your problem. You have a good mind when you're not whinging on about something. You could have gone far..."

"Coming from you," said Grant, "that's not much of a compliment."

"I wasn't complimenting you," said Bates, glancing down at his watch. "Why don't you just tell me what you want."

"I want you to contact TechnoFarm. I want you to instruct them to release the records on their biogenetic experiments..."

Bates chuckled. "You want me to do what? Ask a company to give away its investments? Do you think that's reasonable?"

"I also want you to explain why you set a Chilean refugee up as a scapegoat..."

"A scapegoat for what?"

"To divert suspicion from the true source of the toxic reactions!"

"And what was the 'true source', if I might ask."

"Tomatoes taken from TechnoFarm by two youths..."

"You're saying that two juveniles broke into a research facility and stole an experimental product..."

"What I'm saying is that two boys went through a hole in a fence and picked some tomatoes that were growing in a field..."

"And if two boys entered a bank safe, what would you say about that?"

"I'd wonder how the bloody hell they did it!"

"But you wouldn't doubt the crime. And after questioning the sorry state of security, I doubt that you'd want to blame the entire banking industry on one such fault."

"We're not talking about the banking industry or petty crimes, Bates. We're talking about a biogenetic farm where tainted food was being grown..."

"Experimental crops, you mean. And there was a fence that was signposted. I'm not sure you fully appreciate that..."

"What I appreciate is that these tomatoes were taken with full knowledge of management and that instead of coming out with an immediate admission, trying to assist in tracking them down and helping to analyse the toxic vector so that a treatment could be found – instead of that, the episode was covered up!"

"OK," said Bates, "let's go back to the beginning. You say that some experimental vegetation was most unfortunately stolen from the research fields of this organisation..."

"A number of toxic tomatoes were released into the community..."

"Allegedly toxic tomatoes. And what is the source of this information?"

"The statement of a research scientist from TechnoFarm who claims the organisation knew about the theft and was concerned..."

"You have a deposition I suppose?"

"Yes."

"Well, I'd be interested in seeing it. You also say you have one of these allegedly toxic tomatoes. Where did you find it?"

"I'd rather not say."

"How do you know that particular tomato comes from TechnoFarm?"

"I have my reasons."

"All right. I won't press you now. But, for argument's sake, let's say that tomato was one of the experimental crops from TechnoFarm. How can you be sure it was the toxic vector?"

"I told you it's being analysed."

"So, I suppose you haven't found the toxic factor. Or you wouldn't be so coy."

"I'll find it."

"If it's there, I'm sure a good scientist like yourself will find it. And if not, I'm equally sure you'll be the first to apologise for your ghastly mistake. Meanwhile, there's something perhaps you should know..."

Grant thought the little smile on Bates' face was the most stomach-wrenching smirk he'd ever seen.

"It's about that man Rojas the one who stole the toxic oil..."

"You mean the Chilean refugee who had the oil planted on him..."

"Oh, dear boy. I suppose you haven't heard. Well, how could you. It just happened today. Eduardo Rojas signed a full confession!"

~

He tried ringing Katz after leaving the Carlton, but he couldn't get through. The pub where he stopped to use the phone was loud and smoky, crammed with pin-striped City types who wanted a quick fix before leaving for home.

Grant ordered a double whisky at the bar and downed it like a medicinal dose. It calmed him only slightly, but it was enough to see him home.

~

The Coffee Gallery on Museum Street was close to Grant's flat. It was also a stone's throw away from the British Library where Levi was doing some research. It seemed a convenient place to meet and since Levi said it reminded him of a café he knew in Italy, that's where they met.

Theirs was a strange relationship. Over the years Paulo Levi had become the closest thing Grant had to family. Yet they could go for long periods of time without seeing one another or even writing.

"When was the last time we met?" Paulo asked him, ushering Grant to a little table he had reserved for them in the back.

"When I came home from Africa," Grant reminded him.

"You were debating whether to accept your position at the University. But, of course, it turned out well for you."

"I suppose."

"Nonsense! It was just what you needed at the time. A safe little sinecure. A retreat from the world. But offering some intellectual stimulation. How could you say no?"

"I didn't."

"Quite right. So what's the problem?"

"The problem?"

"Yes, the problem." Levi gave him a knowing smile. "Why else would you ask to see me?"

Grant gave him a brief rundown of the events over the past week. Levi listened with interest, letting Grant speak without volunteering any comment.

When he finished, Grant waited for a moment for Levi's response. As Levi remained silent, Grant finally said, "You must be in contact with a lot of the research that's going on in biotechnology these days. What do you think, Paulo?"

"I think biologists have yet to learn the lessons physicists had to find out the hard way."

"What do you mean?"

"You know, yourself, Peter, my friend. In the early years of the century, the physicists used to complain how little their ideas could earn them. The most they could hope for was a professorship in a university, a comfortable flat with a moderately attractive wife and maybe some fluffy kittens. They were taken far less seriously than the chemists who were fitted out in fine industrial research labs and given fancy cars to drive in from the suburbs. Then came the war and suddenly the physicists found themselves awash with funds, more money than they ever dreamt possible. But it was the classic Faustian pact, wasn't it? All they had to do to collect these new riches was to create a device capable of destroying the world."

"I don't think you'd find many biologists who would claim that's what's on offer from their end."

"Of course not. I'm being rather provocative, aren't I? But the thing about scientists, you see, is that we're people with very active imaginations. We're explorers who are loath to leave our sitting rooms. We are dreamers who prefer the fantasies of our mind rather than the reality of the ordinary world. And because we need to communicate these dreams and desires, we have developed intricate languages which allow us to reach others of like mind. But, in so doing, we have also separated ourselves from the world of the ordinary – the butcher, the baker and the woman who knits your socks. Now that in itself isn't so bad. Priests have done that. So have philosophers. We've shown an amazing diversity of ideas and given people cause to believe that there was more than one way of living out their tragic existence. The problem came when these ordinary people started bestowing on us the mantle of gods. When life becomes unbearable people naturally turn to either priests or scientists. Priests hold out hope for the life hereafter. Scientists hold out hope for the here and now. Neither of them can actually fulfil their pledge, however. But what they can do is put on a damned good show. Priests can build elaborate buildings, burn exotic incense and create words that inspire boundless faith and trust. Scientists can build things that go bang in the night and perform amazing tricks with bits of protein that are invisible to the naked eye. But that, in fact, is the essence of a magician. A magician misdirects your senses and makes you believe he has the power to do the impossible. If we believe, we believe because we wish to believe. It's nothing more."

If Grant had to say what he found difficult with his good friend and teacher, it was Levi's problem of not being able to answer a simple question with a simple response. On the other hand, there was usually something of interest in what Levi had to say. But intellectual meandering, no matter how profound, wasn't what he wanted right now.

"How can you tell the difference between a genetically engineered plant and one that has undergone spontaneous mutation?" asked Grant.

Levi shook his head. "What is the difference between the hand of man or the hand of God? Genetic mutation can be caused by an infinite number of factors. The result is either viable or not. If it is viable, the cause of its viability is essentially a question for philosophers. It's only our arrogance that leads us to believe we are capable of creating life according to a plan. We may have participated in a process, but life, all life, from the smallest molecular structure to a complex organism, has its own agenda. As I see it, genetic engineering is just another form of spontaneous mutation. We might have a purpose, from our own narrow perspective, but in the larger scheme of things it's nothing more than one possible strategy out of an infinite number of variations. In the end, it must stand the same test of all other biological forms survival. And that, my friend, is a game in which we are only observers."

Grant stared at him with an expression both anxious and weary..

"I can see you're growing impatient with me," said Levi, giving him an apologetic look. "But short answers often evade the real question. And I think the real question you wish to have answered is whether it is actually possible to engineer something biological for a specific purpose."

"Isn't it? Surely adaptation of plants has been one of the primary goals of agronomists – how to grow better crops more efficiently, how to develop disease resistant strains, how to grow them under adverse conditions. The process of controlling nature for the benefit of humankind is one of the things civilisation is all about. We can't have any problem with that – how could we?"

Levi shrugged. "Plant genetics has always been a pragmatic venture. From Mendel's time up until the recent past, it was a matter of experimenting and seeing what you came up with. If it was of value, you kept it as your stock. If not, you tried again with something else. The passage of time indicated whether the good in something outweighed the bad – from our own perspective, of course. But contemporary genetic engineering seems to have forgotten a main tenet in scientific logic – if you change something, you change everything. DNA is actually a very unstable compound. There is a real and pressing question of whether we truly know how it works or, in case of a malfunction, how it doesn't work. With respect to viruses and bacteria, for example, we're constantly surprised at how fast they modify themselves to ensure their survival against an onslaught of our best antibiotics. In Brazil they've found that a subtle mutation in the genetic makeup of a previously insignificant organism which had caused only minor eye problems has turned it into a deadly killer. You know from your own work the terrible possibilities of organic mutations causing virulent epidemics..."

"Bacteria and viruses, yes. What about plants?"

"Plants are a very sophisticated form of life. Two hundred years ago, we appreciated that more than today. Every major European city, every university town, had their botanical garden and great herbaria where plants were brought from all over the world. Botany, then, was the Queen of Science. It was the basis of medicine, chemistry and gastronomics. Skilled gardeners were scientists in their own right. They were natural historians who roamed the globe for new acquisitions, for new forms of life. Of course the idea of man creating plants for his own purposes back then was ridiculous, if not sacrilegious. They felt there were an infinite number of plants created by God that could be used for food or drugs. Somewhere on earth there was the remnants of the Garden of Eden. Along with gold and precious stones, the search for the Garden of Eden was what the great explorations were all about."

"But contemporary science has to deal with contemporary problems," said Grant. "Our society is organised in different ways. Food is controlled by massive business combines, medicinal pharmacology by giant drug companies. To them, genetic engineering is their Garden of Eden."

"Perhaps. But, as I said, it comes from a mistaken notion that we can create a plant – or any life form – that does exactly what we want from it. You know yourself from your study of toxins that organisms are all unique, all individual. Even identical twins end up having different body chemistries. That's because all life forms are constantly evolving, constantly changing, constantly adapting. I read an interesting paper the other day, for example, that was a study of plants under stress. Plants normally create natural toxins in order to repel predators. However, plants under attack can increase their production of natural pesticides to the point where edible plants can actually become toxic to humans. Some people estimate that the great majority of pesticide in human diets come from these natural toxins."

Grant listened to this last comment with interest. "The problem we're facing in Cambridge is that we're fairly certain the toxic reaction was triggered from some chemical in a genetically engineered tomato but we can't find the factor. We're not even sure of the toxic reaction. But the similarity to the toxic oil syndrome in Spain is quite remarkable."

"The fact that you've come up with such a small number of cases contained in an equally small area indicates that the toxic vector has probably been nipped in the bud," Levi responded. "The interesting thing about the toxic oil case was the enormous number of cases over such a wide area. The oil, of course, could never be shown to have been toxic – at least to everyone's satisfaction. That's because so many people ate the oil without any ill effects. On the other hand, you claim there were several dozen genetically engineered tomatoes that were circulated and everyone who ate them became ill..."

"We've run out of things to try," said Grant.

"And so you've come to search for a cure."

There was a troubled look on Grant's face as he spoke. "There isn't much time..."

"There never is," said Levi. "Especially when you're trying to save someone." He was silent for a moment. He looked concerned. "I'm worried about you, my friend," he said.

"You were always the one who spoke about the passion of learning," said Grant.

"The passion of learning, yes. The passion of saving..." Levi turned up his palms in an empty gesture. "That's something else."

"Then what's the point of being a physician?"

"What's the point of being anything? You do what you do. You provide information from your experience. You offer resources. You educate. You sympathise, you empathise, but you cannot save."

Grant knew what he meant, in a way. Though he, himself, might have expressed it differently. He always had understood the danger of getting too close to his patients. It was one of the primary reasons he had left the practice of medicine and had gone into epidemiology in the first place. But this was no longer a reasoned response. He couldn't help himself.

Levi probably realised that. It was the way he shook his head and smiled, as if giving advice to an errant youth while at the same time knowing he was going to do what he had to do.

"You once told me about a doctor in Spain who had some remarkable success in treating the toxic oil patients," Grant reminded him.

"Yes. A very interesting man named Ernesto Chu Lopez. His treatment was based on the similarity in symptoms between TOS and certain types of pesticide poisoning, if I remember correctly."

"Do you know him?" asked Grant.

"I haven't met him personally. But we corresponded about a certain matter a few years ago. He lives in Barcelona."

"Could you get me his address?" asked Grant.

"If he's still there," said Levi, taking out his address book from the inside pocket of his jacket.

~

As he climbed the stairs of his building, he could hear the telephone ringing from inside his flat. Fumbling for his keys, he opened the door too late. Whoever it was had already hung up by the time he came in.

He poured himself a drink and sat down in his easy chair. The throbbing in his head had yet to cease. He drank the whisky straight. It was a temporary measure but it seemed to work at least as well as aspirin.

He sat in his chair, comatose. His eyes were fixed on nothing in particular. Just a speck on the wall. As he stared, it seemed to him the wall was slightly trembling as if there was a tiny rumble that had shaken the building. Then he realised. It was his own body that was shaking. Not the building.

The telephone rang again. He leapt up from his chair to answer it.

"It's all over," said a voice drained of all emotion. "Eduardo is dead."

"Katz?" he said. His throat felt dry. His voice was husky.

"He hanged himself. He used his shirt to make a noose. They said it was quite expertly done. Maybe he learned it in Chile."

"Eduardo's dead?" he asked, as if refusing to comprehend the words that had electronically reformulated themselves through the line.

"He wrote a full confession. I haven't seen the original, just a typed transcript."

"He confessed to stealing the toxic oil? What language did he write it in?" It was a stupid question but the only one he thought to ask.

"English. He said he was the only one to blame. He said he used the bulk oil to fill the smaller corn oil containers. Neither Maria nor anyone else had any knowledge of what he did. That's what was written on the photocopy of the document they gave me, anyway..."

Grant rubbed his eyes. He felt the gnawing pain in his head. "He did it to save his son, didn't he?"

"Whatever," said Katz. "He's dead. Except for a few minor details, the case is finished."

~

He brought down some dusty medical books and spent the rest of the day paging through them. But soon the words stopped making sense. He rubbed his eyes and saw the colours from the pressure of his hand.

Several times he tried ringing the number Levi had given him for Chu Lopez, the doctor in Barcelona who had claimed to have cured the Toxic Oil patients. He was able to confirm that Chu Lopez was there, but he wasn't able to connect.

By late afternoon, he had made a decision.

He rang Addenbrooke's and spoke to the ward nurse.

"This is Dr Grant," he said. "Is Pauline ... is Dr Quail awake?"

"I'm sorry, Dr Grant," the nurse replied. "I don't think she'll be able to speak with you..."

"Could you give her a message?" he asked. "If she wakes up, that is..." He cleared his throat. "Would you tell her..."

"I'm sorry? I didn't hear..."

"Would you tell her that I love her..."

"Certainly, Dr Grant. I'll try."

He hung up the phone and packed a bag. Then he left for Heathrow.

~

Barcelona was a place that fascinated him. He had been there numerous times while Franco was alive, when the city simmered quietly like a slumbering volcano, and then, after his death, when the great molten lava of repressed dreams and desires flowed uncontrollably down the Rambla in a fiery wave of passion. He loved the Café Torino and the throbbing, organic designs of Gaudi and Cadafalch and the spires of the Sagrada Familia whose doors Dali likened to tender slices of calves liver. It was a city of madness, originality and vision. And it was unlike London in every possible respect.

This afternoon, however, he headed not for the great cafés and galleries in the city's centre but to a workers' barrio on the edge of town.

The barrio was just beginning to wake from its siesta when Grant's taxi left him on a main square near to the address. The bustle of traffic at this peak hour made it impossible to enter the side roads by car and the driver, raising his arms in a gesture of frustration, said he was close enough to walk.

Here, in this impoverished barrio, the odour of pungent spices lingered like an olfactory veil hiding the smell of rancid oils and unchilled meats and cheeses that were becoming overly ripe. Gypsy music mingled with harsh black tobacco and the heady mix of stale beer and cheap, red wine.

Shouting voices. Meaningless graffiti. Burnt out cars. Shirtless boys with darkened needle holes running down their arms. Men with hairy chests and cigarette burns on their lips and scars from knife slashes. Women with too much rouge. Chemical perfume turning sour on sweaty faces. Noxious smells from blocked up drains. Shit on the pavement. Spit and slime on the floor.

Gaudi wasn't here. Neither were the workers of 1835.

Poverty was never nice, thought Grant as he stepped over a drunken body. Nor was it at all romantic. Even in Barcelona.

The clinic was a white stucco building set apart from the shuttered apartment blocks. Outside, a queue of people had already started to form, waiting for the afternoon consultation session to begin.

Grant went up to the uniformed guard who was standing by the entrance and spoke to him in Spanish, asking for the office of Dr. Chu Lopez. The guard looked Grant up and down and then, deciding on his status, tipped his hat, opened the heavy door and directed him down a long, dark passageway.

It was cool inside and smelled familiar. Carbolic acid smelled the same all over the world.

Chu Lopez was seated behind his desk in the consulting room. He stood up as Grant came in. He smiled, openly, and stuck out his hand.

"Dr Grant," he said. "It is an honour to meet you."

He was a curious looking man, Grant thought as he took the offered hand and shook it. Chu Lopez was short – perhaps five foot four – and slim, but very well proportioned. He had the type of build, like many film actors, that could easily be mistaken as tall without a reference point beside it. What made him appear so curious, though, was the mixture of Spanish and Oriental which had been genetically blended into his body.

"I suppose you received my wire," said Grant. "I'm sorry for the intrusion."

Chu Lopez shook his head. "Please, Dr Grant. Do not apologise. I understand the urgency of your situation. I can speak with you only briefly now. If you stay the evening, however, we will have more time."

He got up and walked to a cabinet by the side of his desk. "Would you care for a little glass of Madeira?"

"Thank you," Grant replied. And then, getting straight to the point, he said, "Paulo – Dr Levi – told me that you had treated some of the toxic oil cases successfully. Is that correct?"

Chu Lopez handed him a small glass of the sweet, fortified wine. "Some toxic oil victims had been referred to my clinic. Most of them are improving. I hope my efforts have had some effect." He raised his glass. "Chinchin."

"Salud," Grant replied, raising his own glass. He took a drink and then he said, "I hope you'll be able to tell me your procedure."

"I will be happy to share whatever information I can with you, Dr Grant. However, I must tell you first that the authorities here in Spain do not look upon my work with favour."

"Why is that?"

"Because I have been – how shall I put it? – a thorn in their side. The toxic oil scandal has been, in my opinion, a massive fraud and a cover-up on an enormous scale. Hundreds of people have died and thousands have been condemned to a life of misery because of a government that refuses to listen." Then, as if he had said something unseemly, he made a wry smile and asked, "How much do you know of this epidemic, Dr Grant?"

"I was working for World Health when it happened," Grant replied. "So I'm familiar with the basics. But I thought the problem was located in the provinces around Madrid. How did Catalonia get involved?"

"The question is why we weren't involved more," said Chu Lopez. "The adulterated rapeseed oil was also refined and distributed here, but there was no epidemic of illness as there was in the barrios around Madrid. I personally became interested when I saw some of the victims. No one had the faintest idea how to treat them nor could they come up with a plausible theory of why these people became ill. Yet the authorities stuck to their story that the adulterated cooking oil was to blame."

"You weren't convinced of the anilide theory, I suppose."

"There were an estimated 100,000 tons of adulterated cooking oil sold door to door. In some areas thousands of people became ill. In other areas where the oil was consumed, no one became ill. The anilide theory just didn't make sense at all."

"So you think it wasn't the cooking oil?"

"If it was the cooking oil, then some of the batches were contaminated."

"With another pollutant? Like what?"

Chu Lopez shrugged his narrow shoulders. "We'll never know. Over two million litres of suspect oil was turned in. Most of it was mislabelled. The collection was so haphazard and disorganised that it became impossible to conduct any kind of serious study."

Grant looked at him in confusion. "But I thought you had worked out a cure based on some interpretation of the reaction."

"My treatment is based on the nature of the disease. I have seen this kind of reaction to a substance only once before. When I worked in Latin America some years ago I had observed a group of patients with very similar symptoms. The etiology of that occurrence was almost the same as I witnessed here. Only in Colombia, where I was working, the agricultural labourers I had been seeing suffered from paraquat poisoning."

"Paraquat," Grant muttered to himself.

"You're familiar with it?" asked Chu Lopez.

Grant nodded. "They were using it as weed killer near the coffee plantations when I was in Kenya..."

"So you've seen the effects?"

"I've seen several cases of severe poisoning. Yes." Grant remembered the ugly lesions on the skin and the respiratory paralysis. It was much more dramatic than the wasting away of the toxic oil victims he had read about.

"Of course we aren't talking about paraquat in any large dosage. The contamination, if it occurred, would have made it quite dilute."

"What evidence do you have that paraquat was the active toxin?" asked Grant.

Chu Lopez smiled faintly. "None."

Grant looked at him, confused, "I don't understand."

"I only said that it reminded me of cases that I had seen. However, because nothing else worked, I decided to treat several of my patients as if they had a toxic reaction to paraquat. The results were quite startling."

It suddenly became clear to Grant why this man had been branded a charlatan and he felt his hopes, once again, being crushed.

"I can see the disapproval in your face," said Chu Lopez. "But I assure you I am not a madman. What is medicine, after all, if not a pragmatic science? What is healing if not an art? I, myself, am a blend of the East and the West, the North and the South. My mother was Chinese. My father was Catalonian. I had one grandparent who was a Morano and another who was a Moor. I have studied the healing skills of many different cultures. I have taken for my own something from one and something from another. In the end, I have come to see disease as an imbalance in the equilibrium of life. The road to health lies in the reestablishment of that balance. This is the course a doctor must chart. But the path may lead in many directions."

"There is also such a thing as cause and effect," said Grant. "The success of medical science is its rigour. To know is more than to believe. I have seen too many people die from preventable disease in Africa..."

"Yes, but how about those who died of diseases you couldn't cure? How about the wave of epidemics sweeping through the world at this very moment? What if you were a doctor during the Middle Ages forced to contend with the plague? Perhaps you, yourself, will sometime be in that position, Dr Grant."

He had been in that position already. He was in that position now.

Chu Lopez stood up. "I am very sorry, but I have patients I must attend. However, I would be pleased to show you my findings if you would care to return this evening after the clinic has closed."

Grant got up from his chair, as well, and shook hands. "Thank you, again for your hospitality," he said. "When is your surgery finished?"

"At nine tonight we close our doors. If you wish, you could join me for dinner."

~

That evening, Chu Lopez had taken him back to his house. On the wall behind the desk in his study was an ancient woodcut of a man in a ragged cassock riding an emaciated stallion with a wild mane. The man swung an enormous, bloody scythe and looked out from the woodcut with eyes sunk back into a darkened skull. The horse had an appalling substance that ran from its mouth as it galloped angrily above the threatening clouds.

The Fourth Horseman of the Apocalypse was an image Grant was well acquainted with. It had stalked his consciousness ever since medical school in Edinburgh. He would never have thought of putting it on the wall.

Chu Lopez said he kept it there as an awesome reminder of the terrible force he had wrestled with throughout his career. It was that force which had demolished empires and conquered nations bringing fearless armies to their knees within days of hearing the dreaded hoof beats.

It was a force, Chu Lopez said, that the modern world, in its arrogance, had nearly banished from its collective mind. The rule of the technocrats had convinced an ever gullible populace that the twentieth century had provided them with the weapons to hold both plague and pestilence at bay.

Because of antibiotics and vaccines, people had been brought to feel that plagues were conquered. Who remembered the great pandemic of 1918 that took close to fifty million lives throughout the world? How many people even today took AIDS seriously?

But the history of epidemics, he said, was such that even the most cursory reading would show its tireless and most adaptive diversity. Viruses, bacteria and other forms of disease yet defined had proven themselves to be the most enduring forms of life, evolving and evolving again in a time scale that for other creatures would be just a wink of an eye.

The 20th century had deceived itself into thinking that mankind had triumphed over nature. This success was nothing but a grand illusion. We had been fortunate to have lived through a cycle where the worst of plague and pestilence was on the wane. But that cycle was ending now with the collapse of social frameworks that had temporarily held them in check.

A rather bleak view of the world, Grant had thought and he had said as much to Chu Lopez. But Chu Lopez had countered by saying that he hadn't been meaning to sound so despairing. He was a doctor, himself, after all. The problem had to do with our expectations and the way Western health care was set up.

In a "one shot cures all" society, people were led to expect that the public health ramifications of political decision-making had nothing to do with them or the way they lived their lives. Social obligations were minimal and poverty could be tolerated as long as it was kept out of sight.

This notion of social Darwinism, Chu Lopez had argued, was self-defeating because the public health consequences of such policies were a great leveller. Already, in his barrio, for example, diseases like antibiotic resistant TB and dyptheria had made their appearance. The vector of these diseases were well known and were directly related to the dire living conditions that came from abject poverty and urban decay. However, once unleashed, they knew no social boundaries – as consumptive, middle-class artists a few decades before well understood.

Of course, as a public health professional, Grant had no difficulty with those ideas. And, having observed first-hand the consequences of war and starvation on the continent of Africa, he was not about to deny the relationship between political upheaval and pandemic. However, he still believed in Western science as a major step in civilisation. To him, the god had not quite failed. It had just taken a small step backwards.

On the other hand, he wasn't blind. He saw how in England the medical system was hanging on by its thumbs. He could see the institutions unravelling if not actually falling apart. And, most importantly, he was beginning to see how easily they were abused by politicians who cynically used them for purposes of their own.

Yet he also had known marvellous surgeries and committed physicians. The General Practitioners, as the front line of the public health battle, were still struggling on, despite the enormous pressures and obstacles put in their way. But could their promises be kept? Or were they, more and more, like Grant himself, becoming voyeurs, watching with horrified fascination the collapse?

CHAPTER 5

SATURDAY 25 JUNE

GRANT RUBBED HIS eyes and looked out the porthole next to him. The sky was pitch black. He glanced at his watch. It was five AM. Soon the morning sun would start to brighten the eastern horizon. He closed his eyes again and tried to sleep while balancing the packet Chu Lopez had given him atop his lap.

The packet contained a drug that Chu Lopez had developed. He claimed it had counteracted the reaction to the suspected pesticide poisoning in a number of patients that he had treated. But, even if he was wrong about his suspicions concerning the so-called toxic oil victims, the formula still seemed to work.

Grant had lifted the vial filled with an amber-coloured powder to the light. "What is it?" he had asked.

"A combination of plant extracts and herbs," Chu Lopez had replied. "The formula is here if you care to study it."

Grant had looked through the research documents without much comprehension. As far as he was concerned, it was a witch's brew. But even witch's brews sometimes worked.

"I thought of it when I read about an experiment that was being carried out on reclaimed land," Chu Lopez had explained. "The soil was highly contaminated with various metals. Then someone came up with the idea of using certain plants with a known capacity to leech metals from the earth, like cabbages, as a sponge to soak up the contaminants. Once harvested, the metal-logged plants could then be refined, extracting the metal from its leaves while the earth would now be safe for farming. An ingenious solution, don't you think?"

It was an ingenious solution to cleanse the fields of certain contaminants. But it said nothing of the human body, even if one knew what the contaminants were. That was the point, however. The contaminants were unknown. And even if they were known, the chemical reactions had already done their damage.

"There is a very strict regimen for recovery that goes along with this," Chu Lopez had told him. "As with the recovery of the earth, it's not enough to take something out. Other things must be put back in. The Asian physicians knew that. So did the Arabs and the Greeks. The quest for health is the search for equilibrium. You can call it Yin or Yang or Fire, Water, Earth and Air. The metaphor still applies."

In Africa Grant had fought to have the aid agencies take cognisance of tribal cures. Traditional medicine had often worked where western medicine hadn't. But traditional medicine, he believed, was part of a process which, like language, had at its core an indelible tie to culture. One couldn't, he had argued, extract a certain part without understanding its relationship to the rest. A chant was just a chant unless you could link it to a shared experience. For example, who could doubt the value of a mother's song to a fevered infant? But how could that song be separated from a mother's touch or the fragrance of her breast?

The more he looked over the case histories that Chu Lopez had given him, the more he realised how much against the grain this was. He didn't doubt in the least that Chu Lopez had some remarkable successes. But who knew how these patients would have reacted with other cures? These, after all, were selected cases. People who had sought him out. They had a strong will to live, to return to health. They wanted to believe his cure would work.

Doctors were always coming up against these wonder cures. Most recently with AIDS. Every month or so someone else had claimed a drug or diet would work a miracle and bring the half-dead back to health. Most were touted by charlatans wanting to make their fortune in a manner more obscene than a hired assassin. But others were well-meaning physicians who actually had limited success with a certain formula. They were usually ignored or rejected by the medical establishment. And sometimes for good reason. Because, even if a certain procedure worked for them, their techniques just couldn't be replicated.

Grant had long wondered about this phenomena. And what he had finally decided was that, in the end, as Chu Lopez had pointed out, medicine was an art. Healing was a talent as well as a skill. Many could paint. Few could create the Mona Lisa.

The landing lights had been turned on. The plane was making its descent. Grant looked down at the packet on his lap.

Why had he accepted it? The question was unanswerable. It was no longer a question, in fact. If someone found the Holy Grail, how would they know they found what they were after?

~

Roger Cook was sacked out in the consultant's room when the wire was delivered to him.

"I'm sorry for waking you," said the nurse, "but it's marked 'Most Urgent'."

Cook sat up on the couch and ripped open the envelope. It had been the worst night of his life. Perhaps the wire would tell him it had all just been a terrible dream, he thought.

He quickly scanned the enclosure:

The dateline was Saturday, 25 June; 3:15 AM; Barcelona. The message read "Have found possible cure for TA Syndrome! Desperately need your help! Will be back at Addenbrooke's Saturday morning...Peter Grant."

Cook rubbed his weary eyes, wadded up the message, shoved it into the pocket of his smock and muttered, "Poor bloody bastard!"

~

He had left the Renault in Heathrow's short term parking and paid a king's ransom to get it out. But it had given him quick and easy access, and now, speeding along the motorway, he focused his thoughts on the only thing he cared about. He had suddenly come to realise that nothing else really mattered to him except Pauline's well-being.

When this happened or how it happened, he wasn't quite sure. But she had come to dominate his thoughts. It was as if she had always been with him since the first time they met. He had loved her then and he loved her still. And when he had finally allowed himself to admit it, the whole thing became obvious to him. They had been apart for a while, each on their own separate missions. Now they would be together again. It was as simple as that.

By the time he reached Cambridge, he had even allowed himself to think that perhaps happiness and contentment weren't such impossible ideas as he had once thought. And, as he accelerated into Addenbrooke's car park, he squeezed the vial which was resting, conspicuously, on the seat beside him like a precious amulet.

~

It struck him, as he rushed madly through the hospital corridor, that time was somehow out of sync. Both time and motion. He felt he was outside his body and could actually observe himself running through the narrow passageways.

Yet others who saw him thought he was insane. They leapt to get out of his way as if some wild animal had been let loose inside Addenbrooke's.

He was unconcerned. What others thought didn't matter. Nothing mattered except getting there fast. Faster than fast. Getting there then.

He dashed up the stairs, two at a time. And, finally at the second level, bounding through the corridor to the double doors of the TA ward.

Clutching the vial, he threw open the doors.

It was like going from darkness into light. It was blinding. He saw nothing but shadows.

"Cook!" he shouted.

The shadows danced before his eyes.

A nurse touched his arm. He turned, confused.

"Can I help you?" she asked.

"Where's Cook?" he said, pulling himself away. "I need him!"

Something was wrong. He could feel it. And then he heard it.

"Grant!"

The voice came from the other side of the ward. He was coming toward him, all dressed in white. Like an angel, resplendent.

"Cook!" he shouted, lifting the vial high in the air. "It's all right! I've got it!"

He bounded over to the figure walking toward him.

"I've got it!" he shouted again. And, reaching him, he pressed it into his hand.

"Get a grip on yourself!" said Cook, clutching Grant's shoulder firmly.

Their eyes met.

Suddenly the world came back into focus. He felt a terrible ache in his head.

He struggled to get the words out. He couldn't. All he could manage was "When...?"

"Early this morning."

Grant lowered his head.

"She went peacefully," Cook said.

~

All feeling had been drained. All emotion. It was as if someone had stuck in a hypodermic and sucked it all out.

Nothing mattered. Not to him. Not anymore.

He parked the Renault next to her house, in front of the Ford Transit van. He sat behind the wheel after he turned the engine off, unable to move. He closed his eyes. He stayed there for a while and then, finally, he got out.

Walking over to her door, he took out her keys. His hand was unsteady. It took him a moment to undo the latch.

He went inside and mechanically turned on the light. The hallway which glowed warm before, now felt colder somehow brittle and annoying.

Going into the kitchen, he found the bottle he had used the other night. He drained the leftover contents into a glass, drank it up and then went into the front room to get another bottle from the liquor collection.

He refilled his glass and took a long, deep drink.

The telephone rang.

He took another drink.

The telephone rang again.

He walked over to the study.

The telephone rang again.

He looked down at the device. He touched it with the tips of his fingers. He couldn't bring himself to lift up the receiver.

The answering machine switched on.

"Grant! This is Katz. I need to speak with you immediately. Not over the phone. You know why. Those bloody bastards!"

He went over to the window and pulled back the curtain. He looked out. The street was quiet and calm. Outside it was peaceful. Manicured gardens. Robins safe in their nests. But all he could see was the Ford Transit van. All he could think was that Pauline was dead.

He felt the heat from the whisky go to his head. It seemed to ignite his anger and his passion.

He didn't know why. It just needed to be done. And he needed to do it himself.

He took the hardwood cane the one he had bought her in Burma and gripping it so tightly in his hand that it whitened his knuckles, he marched out the front, leaving ajar the door.

His footsteps resounded heavily on the paving stones. The sound echoed in his ears – thudump, thudump, thudump. Drops of sweat appeared on the bridge of his nose and trickled down to his eyes, making them sting. What he saw was a blur. Along with the echo of his heavy feet, what he heard was a high-pitched hum.

The Transit van sparkled white in the morning sun as he stood before it. He took the hardwood cane and brought it high above his head. He held it there for an instant and then brought it down with all his might, beating it against the metal door. "Boowm!" The sound was chilling to the ear. "Boowm! Boowm!"

Three massive dents appeared on the door of the van. The crinkled paint fell like pale, white blood.

"Boowm!" He hit it again. "Boowm! Boowm!"

"What the hell...!" A voice from inside rang out.

He hit it again. "Boowm!"

"Just a bloody minute!"

The door opened. A bearded face peered from within.

Grabbing him by the collar, Grant heaved the man out. Then flinging wide the door, he entered the bowels of the electronic chamber.

"Hey, you crazy shit! You fucking can't go in there...!"

Swinging the cane like a furious batsman gone wild, he began smashing everything in sight – VDU screens, keyboards, recording equipment, mikes. Shards of glass splattered against the walls. Silicon fragmented from the force of the blows. Plastic chipped, metal cracked, wood splintered. Within seconds, years of technical genius was reduced to a useless pile of junk.

Outside, the bearded man had fled in terror, still clutching his copy of Wired magazine in his sweaty hand.

~

He went back into the house and rang Katz.

"I need to talk with you right away," Katz said.

"Talk," said Grant.

"Not over the phone."

"It doesn't matter now."

"I don't know what you're on about," said Katz. "But this concerns Tracy and something she found..."

Grant met him downstairs at the Roma. The café had just opened and the place was still empty. Even so, Katz was sitting at a table tucked into a little niche near the rear window.

"What is it you want?" asked Grant, sitting down across from him. His look was one of extreme annoyance. "I thought you said the case was finished."

"I said there were some details to finish up. Details are important..."

"Pauline's dead," said Grant. The muscles of his face went taut.

"I know," said Katz. "I'm sorry."

"I don't really care about the details...."

"Not even ones you could use to nail the bastards to the wall?"

Grant threw him a look that said he meant business. "I'll nail them anyway."

Katz motioned to the husky Italian behind the bar to bring over some coffees. Then, turning back to Grant, he said, "Listen, you can either do this smart or you can do it stupid. You have to know what you want to get out of it and then play it to get what you can."

"I know what I want." Grant narrowed his eyes. "How about you?"

The Italian brought over two freshly brewed coffees in tiny white espresso cups. Katz took one, put in a spoonful of sugar and stirred. "I want compensation for Maria Rojas. I want TechnoFarm shut down."

"You'll never do it through the courts," said Grant.

"I'm not talking about the courts. I'm talking about a deal...with your help, that is."

Grant looked at him as if he were mad. "You can't deal with people like that."

"I think I can." Katz drank his coffee down in one gulp. "I know them. They're arrogant, devious, corrupt and totally devoid of compassion but they're not idiots. England didn't become an Empire without knowing how to deal. And deal they will. They'll deal their sons and their mothers as long as they feel they can win in the end."

"And they always win in the end, don't they?"

"You want that coffee?" Katz asked, pointing to the undrunk cup.

Grant shook his head.

Katz spooned in a sugar and drank that one down as well. "It depends on what you mean by winning. What we want and what they want might be entirely different."

"But what do we have to deal with?" asked Grant.

"Solomon Ashu, for one..."

"The cleaner who they claimed switched jobs with Eduardo?"

"I had a colleague meet him at the airport. We're getting a deposition. It's not much, but it's something."

"What else?" asked Grant.

"The informant from TechnoFarm – think you can get a deposition from her as well?"

"That's up to Mai and Vermuden. She's in their care."

"Well, see what you can do."

"That's it?" Grant looked at him with disbelief. "That's what you're going to bargain with?"

There was a little smile on his lips as Katz reached down to the seat next to him and brought up a metal canister. "Oh, there's also this..."

The canister had an ornate, flowery design and was like something he might have stored his sugar in. Katz took off the lid and handed the box to Grant.

Peering inside, Grant saw a luscious, ripe tomato. On top, right beneath the stem, was a little golden sticker. The letters were quite small, but the label clearly read, "TechnoFarm Experimental Produce. X213/Tomato. No. 21."

"Where the hell did you get this?" Grant asked.

"Tracy Poon. She couldn't find you so she left it with me. It seems that when she went through the list I got for you – the one from the Chilean event – she recognised an address that was next door to someone you had interviewed – a man named Styles... "

"Morton Styles." Grant recalled the crusty old man the first of his interviews several days ago. "Cook told me his wife died."

"So I understand. Tracy checked with the woman next door who had, in fact, gone to the Chilean fête, purchased two tomatoes at the boys' stall and had given them both to her neighbour as recompense..."

"Recompense for what?"

"It seems that her cat had destroyed the tomato plants in Styles' garden. Styles told Tracy his wife ate one and the other – get this! – he put in the freezer to save for her when she returned. He thought it would be a special treat since she enjoyed the first one so much."

Despite himself, Grant couldn't help but marvel at the curious chain of events.

Katz held up the canister, looked at it admiringly and said, "This might be our tomato in the hole."

Grant rubbed the side of his face, feeling an old toothache coming back. "I've already spoken to my forensic expert at college. I gave him some scraps that I found in Pauline's trash. He couldn't find anything in it..."

"Are you sure it was a TechnoFarm tomato?"

Grant shrugged. "Pretty certain. Yes."

"This one is definite." Katz pointed to the label. "You can't get any more definite than that."

"But he has to know what to test for. If we have no idea what caused the TA reaction, how can he test for it?"

Katz stared at him hard. There was a toughness to his look. "Do you believe this tomato is toxic?"

Grant nodded his head.

"Then you bloody well can get me a piece of paper that says it!"

~

Roger Cook smelled like a sewage spill in July. He hadn't bathed in the last three days. In the last two days he hadn't slept more than several hours. But even though he had been through hell's anus and had come out the other end, he still wasn't prepared to sit back and watch the rest of them die.

The problem was that he had run out of ideas. He was at the point where the text books said "see to your patient's last comforts", suggesting intricate cocktails of opiates and analgesics.

Several times his fingers touched the vial in the pocket of his smock – the one that Grant had left him. He had taken it up to the lab to have it analysed.

"Just herbs and flowers. Vegetable stuff as far as I can determine," the woman at the lab had said. "I don't think there's anything toxic. Of course, you can never be certain."

He wouldn't have considered it for a second if it hadn't come from Grant. Certainly Grant's state of mind made it all a bit suspect but what else had he got? The stuff in the vial might possibly be toxic, he thought, but there was nothing more toxic than death, itself.

Maria Rojas was sitting next to her daughter's bed. She was mechanically knitting a shawl Felicia would use for her confirmation. Her fingers worked quickly, tirelessly. She couldn't stop. It was as if her simple act of knitting was the only thing that kept Felicia's soul from flying off to heaven.

Coming up close to her and putting a hand on her shoulder, Cook said, "Maria, there's one more thing I'd like to try..."

She looked up at him as if he were her parish priest asking for one last ounce of faith and perseverance.

"I have a new medicine – an experimental medicine. We don't know if it works..."

She gazed at him without comprehension.

"We need your permission to try it..."

~

He could have put the car on automatic pilot. It could almost have driven to his London college by itself.

Hamish saw him when he arrived, as he was walking down the corridor.

"What's up, Grant?" he asked. "I understand there are questions being asked..."

"About what?"

"About you. Vetting you, I suppose. Everyone gets vetted these days. What I don't understand is what they vet you for. I mean, who cares anymore if you're a communist? It was easy then. Little more difficult now. They don't have a name for it yet."

"Don't worry," said Grant, opening the door to his office. "They'll think of one soon."

"On that," Hamish said, continuing his stroll, "you can bet."

Inside his office, he searched the boxes for some of his ancient chemistry books. It took him a while, but he found what he wanted.

He copied down the formula on a pad and then, tearing off the slip of paper, stuffed it in his shirt pocket and then left.

Making his way to the lift, he punched the number to the floor of the chemistry lab. The lift jerked into motion, winding the rusty cables onto the spools, bringing him up to the floor he wanted.

The lift came to an abrupt halt. The door opened. He walked out into the smelly hallway reeking from the rotten egg odour of reactive sulphur and sodium.

Inside one of the smaller of the labs, the one the faculty reserved for themselves to make their little brews, he found the stuff he needed on the open shelves. He didn't even have to sign out for them.

He took a beaker and poured in the ingredients to the formula's specification. It wasn't exact. He didn't want it that way. In fact, he added a few other odds and ends, like a thief covering his tracks.

When he was finished, he closed the beaker and then put everything away, cleaning up afterward as he had taught his students but could never get them to do for themselves.

Then, re-locking the door to the lab, he brought the beaker back down to his office.

He got his case and took out a syringe and a hypodermic needle. Then he opened the metal canister and, taking the tomato out, he placed it gently on the table. He fitted the needle to the syringe and then stuck it into the beaker, sucking out about 5 millilitres of fluid.

As he jabbed the needle into the tomato, it occurred to him that what he was doing could be considered ethically questionable. But, as far as he was concerned, at this point it really didn't matter any longer.

~

It was dark by the time Grant got back. But he could tell someone had been there as soon as he opened the door. There was an aura of danger without any physical portent. He felt it nonetheless. Like an animal sniffing the wind and sensing blood.

He turned on the lights and saw that the door to the study was open. He walked over and glanced inside. Papers lay strewn on the floor. The desk drawers were empty. Even the duvet on the sofa bed was torn.

From the study, he went down the corridor to the kitchen. There, at least, they had been neater. It was as if someone had come in and boxed up all the food. The shelves were absolutely barren.

Going over to the fridge, he looked at the note she had pasted to the door of the freezer section. "Time waits for no man," it said. "Time" was written in red with little curlicues around the "T". And she had crossed out the "man" and had pencilled in "woman".

He opened the fridge. It was empty.

Nothing remained that was edible. Nothing at all. He ran his finger over the counter. Not even a crumb.

The front room had been pillaged as well. Fortunately for him they left the whisky. And the cigarettes. Perhaps they were Seventh Day Adventist burglars, he thought, as he lit up a smoke and poured himself a drink.

Searching his jacket pocket, he found the card Katz had given him. He took the glass with him to the phone and dialled the number that was written beneath the address.

The number rang and then stopped. Then, instead of the answering machine going on, the ringing started up again. Grant thought the call was being diverted somewhere else. He had been wrong so often that day, he was astonished to be proven right for once.

It was the voice of a child that answered. Somehow, Grant found that surprising. He didn't know why, but he had pictured Katz living alone.

"My little girl," Katz explained. "She just learned to talk. Now that's all she does. Mona says she gets it from her father."

"Mona's probably right," said Grant. "I have what you want. Part of it at any rate."

"Where are you?"

"Pauline's house. It's been ransacked."

"So has my office," said Katz. "Let's not talk over the phone."

"I told you not to worry about it..."

"I worry anyway. It's part of my job. Stay where you are. I'll be there in ten minutes."

~

He went upstairs while he waited for Katz. The door to Pauline's room was ajar. He went inside.

They had been here too. The dresser drawers were open. Her things were strewn around.

He picked them up – the socks, the underclothes, the blouses – folded them neatly and put them back where they had been.

Then he went into the adjoining room. The one she used as her personal study. It was a room he had never entered before and he found it odd going in.

It was a woman's room. The walls were a pastel shade of pink, the pictures were of calm maternal scenes – a woman singing to a child she was holding in her arms, a girl watching her mother brush her long, silken locks. There was a single flower on the window sill. A single violet.

On the desk he found a letter written in her pen. The letter was eight pages long and as his lifted up the sheets he saw the writing became progressively more difficult toward the end. But what she said was both clear and lucid.

The letter was to Cicely, her daughter. One of the pages read:

"I remember when you were very little and you would come to me crying in the middle of the night. The thought that the world would someday continue on without you seemed quite terrifying. Perhaps there was a time when I had these terrible anxieties that people would still be enjoying all life had to offer whilst I would cease to be. But I no longer dread mortality, nor do I believe in an afterlife, if an afterlife is set in some mythological heaven. I believe in life itself, in all its myraid qualities. I am intrigued by the transitions of birth, of development, and even the deterioration of ageing. I have loved being alive. It's the wonder of it all that still does fascinate. But life and death are part of a continuum, part of a process. One does not exist without the other. And I am comforted in the notion that you will be here with all your anger, your love and your wonderful joy of being..."

It was Cicely whose pictures, he supposed, were tacked to a corkboard on the wall by her desk. He went over and inspected them. If it wasn't for the fact that Pauline was in some of the photos, he would have thought the other woman was her younger self. She had the same look, the same bearing, the same confident smile.

There was an envelope by the letter. On it she had written Cicely's German address.

He folded the letter and put it in the envelope. Then he put the envelope in his jacket pocket and went downstairs to open the door for Katz.

~

Katz appeared a bit ruffled as he stood by the door. He was holding a brown, paper bag.

"I think I'm being followed," he said.

There was a wry look on his face even though there was nothing funny in what Katz said. For him, humour was in the grotesque. It helped ameliorate the dire condition of the human race. Katz had the ability to turn all drama into farce. Just by his appearance. Just by looking at him.

He wouldn't come into the house.

"What were you able to get?" he asked, standing outside on the door-stoop.

"A letter from the chief of forensics at the medical school..."

"Saying?"

"That the sample contained a chemical very similar to Paraquat – an extremely toxic pesticide known to trigger auto-immune reactions in humans..."

"Good!" Katz said. "What about the deposition?"

"I haven't been able to get a hold of Vermuden yet. I'll give Mai a call now if you want..."

"I need to get going," said Katz, handing Grant the brown, paper bag. "Give me a ring in about an hour and let me know..." He quickly jotted down a note on a small pad he pulled from his jacket pocket. He tore off the slip and gave it to Grant..

Back inside the house, Grant opened the bag Katz had given him. It contained a tomato rather wimpy compared to the first one Katz had passed him. He glanced at the note. Following instructions, he made the switch Katz had requested (putting the other one back into cold storage) and went outside, carrying the canister – which now contained the wimpy tomato – and an envelope.

A Morris Minor wasn't exactly what Grant expected. But that was the car he found Katz sitting in, parked before the house.

He went around to the passenger door and opened it up.

"Put the things on the seat," said Katz.

Grant complied, placing the canister and the envelope on the seat as requested.

"Now, get into your car and drive around the corner. Hopefully, they'll follow you. Then I'll take off."

He held out his hand. Grant gave it a shake and said, "Good luck."

"Good luck is for suckers," Katz replied. Then, giving Grant a wink, he reached over and pulled the passenger door shut.

Walking casually over to the Renault, Grant opened the door and got in. He started the car, revved up the engine for a minute and then pulled out.

He drove around the corner and then down Chesterton Road, stopping at the Coop to get something to drink. Then, getting back in his car, he drove to Pauline's again.

By the time he returned, Katz had gone.

~

It was growing dark as Katz drove the tiny car down the A1301 toward Duxford. The evening mist had fogged up the windscreen making it difficult to see. He had to use the sleeve of his shirt to clean a circle of vision since the defroster was on the blink.

He stopped at Shelford and made a phone call from a pub. He had a quick drink and then, going back to the car, he started off again.

A little past Shelford, he turned onto a smaller road. He noticed that a car behind him followed. The car accelerated till it was close behind. It kept flashing its lights as if signalling Katz to pull over.

Katz sped up instead. He wondered whether they thought he was an absolute idiot. He certainly wasn't about to stop. Not on this road. Not for anyone.

But he was close enough. He figured it would be all right.

There was a crossing he knew would come a half mile down the road that lead to a village. At the very least, there would be the safety of a pub.

He tried cleaning the foggy windows again. But the harsh light from behind, reflected in the rear-view mirror, blinded him.

Reaching up, he twisted the mirror out of the way. At the same time, he felt the car behind bump against his fender. He tried speeding up more but the Morris was going as fast as it could run.

The bump against his fender this time was harder. It made him swerve and he had to fight to stay on the road.

"Fungus-faced bastard!" he shouted. "Slimy son of a sodomised goat!"

The car behind seemed to have decelerated. Katz breathed a sigh of relief. The crossroads couldn't be more than another three hundred yards in front of him, he thought.

Suddenly, the car behind lurched forward again. This time, its fender locked into his. Then it started to accelerate. Katz grasped the steering wheel and watched as the needle on his odometer began moving 50, 60, 70. When it reached 80, Katz felt he no longer could keep control. Leaning against his horn, he sent a shrill blast, screaming into the night air.

The car behind slammed on its brakes.

The Morris hurtled off the road, careening into a sold oak that had been there for centuries.

A black Mercedes pulled up behind and came to a stop. A man, wearing black leather gloves got out. He walked up to the Morris, what was left of it, hissing steam and crumpled lifelessly against the mighty oak tree.

The man went back to the Mercedes, opened the boot, and fetched a crow bar. He brought it to the Morris and fitted it into the space between the mangled frame and the door. One powerful pry was enough to force it open.

Katz's twisted body, which had been crushed against the door and the shattered windscreen, rolled out. The man knelt down and took what he could from the blood-soaked pockets.

Then, searching inside the car, he took the envelope and the metal canister which were on the floor below the passenger seat.

A hand in a black leather glove opened the canister, exposing the tomato. A satisfied look came over his face as the man replaced the lid.

~

Mai wasn't in when he rang. Or she wasn't answering her telephone.

After Grant put down the receiver, he tidied the study. He picked up the papers that littered the floor, re-shelved the books and watered the plants.

When he was finished, he went into the front room, fixed himself a drink. Then he rang Mai's number once more. This time she answered.

"Things have reached a boil," he said. "We need a deposition from your source."

"That wouldn't be easy," said Mai.

"Why not? She seemed quite willing to talk yesterday."

"That was yesterday. She had a change of heart."

"Can't you convince her?"

"Perhaps. If we could find her. But the truth is, she got cold feet and did a runner..." Mai sounded anxious and uneasy. "Listen," she said, "I've got to go."

"I need to speak with Vermuden," he said.

"Then you better speak with him soon. He's going down river."

"What do you mean?"

"Forget it," she said. "Things have gone too far. You'll only get yourself hurt."

"I'm past that," he replied.

"Just forget it," she said, hanging up the phone.

After getting the dial tone again, he rang the number Katz had written for him to phone.

The man who answered sounded quite upset.

"He rang me from Shelford about an hour ago. Shelford is only ten minutes away."

"Maybe he stopped for a drink," said Grant.

"He said he was coming straight to me." The man's voice faltered. "He said he thought he was being followed."

"Did you check with his house?"

"Just before you phoned."

"He was bringing you the information on TechnoFarm, I suppose."

"Yes. He contacted me yesterday after that poor Chilean hanged himself."

"Katz didn't give me your name," said Grant.

"Thomas McFadden. I'm parliamentary secretary for our local MP. Katz and I go back a long way. If anything's happened to him..." His voice trailed off.

Grant took a pen and marked his name down on a slip of paper. "Give me your address," he said.

"My home address? I don't know if I should. You can contact me at Parliament. This thing might be more complicated than I thought..."

"I'm sure it is," said Grant, slamming down the phone, angrily.

He felt his head was splitting as he walked into the front room. He poured out the rest of the whisky into his glass and then, finding one of her cigarettes, he sat down in the easy chair, had a smoke and finished off the drink.

For a while he just sat there trying to resolve things in his mind. No matter how he tried juggling it, there was no solution he could come up with. Katz was wrong, he thought. There wasn't any deals you could make with them.

Strangely, coming to that conclusion seemed to settle him. Then he went back into the study and set himself up at the desk.

He had a very organised manner when he got down to work. He centred the Underwood typewriter on the desk, interleaved the clean sheets of paper with carbonised pages and lined up a pen, pencil and whiteout in a neat little row.

Then, winding the first page into the machine along with the carbons, he started typing. The heading, underlined and in caps, read:

REPORT ON TOXIC ALLERGIC SYNDROME
CAMBRIDGE, ENGLAND / JUNE 1994

He started working at eight. By ten he was done.

Sorting out the copies into piles, he then addressed three envelopes – one to Thomas McFadden at Parliament and the others to Roger Cook at Addenbrooke's and Paulo Levi in London. He folded the original and inserted it into the envelope to McFadden. He put one copy into the envelope addressed to Cook and another was directed to Levi. The third copy he included with the letter that Pauline had written to her daughter, Cicely.

In the one addressed to Cicely, he included a note: "I don't know you and I suspect you don't know me. But I knew your mother when she was just your age. She was quite an extraordinary woman and someone I loved very much. She died as bravely as she lived her life. If the story of what happened to her makes you angry, as well it should, then there are things you could do..."

He ended with a cryptic message. "The fruit of the Aztecs is frozen in Time."

Then, sealing the four envelopes, he stamped them and putting them in his jacket pocket, he left the house.

~

Ghia's Revenge was dark when he passed it on Stourbridge Common. Peering into a window built in the hull, he could see it was empty.

Continuing on along the river, Grant crossed the railway bridge and then came into the adjoining field. In the distance he could see the "safe house" boat where the TechnoFarm researcher had been kept. A small pickup had made its way through the grassland and was parked alongside it. As he came closer, silhouetted against the moonlit sky, he was able to make out the image of people loading things from the boat onto the open bed of the truck.

Whatever was being carried was obviously heavy. The figures, one big and the other small, seemed to lumber as they fought against the weight. The knees of the smaller one buckled and the load fell to the ground.

He was close enough now to see it was Mai who had fallen. Vermuden was helping her up as Grant walked over to them.

Vermuden didn't look pleased. He glared at Mai and then directed himself at Grant. "What are you doing here?" he asked. His arms hung stiffly by his sides. His fists were clenched.

"I want to help," Grant replied, boldly staring back at him.

They stood like two angry stags, sizing each other up prior to battle.

Mai, still on her knees, closed her eyes and said, "I told you, we can't do it ourselves."

Vermuden looked down at her with disdain. "Are you saying you don't have the strength. Not even after what happened to Thomas?"

Tears were rolling down Mai's cheeks. Her face was caked with mud. The tears made thin brown lines. "Yes, that's what I'm saying. I don't have the strength."

Grant picked up a side of the crate that had fallen. He stood there waiting for Vermuden to pick up his end.

"What do you want?" asked Vermuden, still staring at him grimly.

"What I want," said Grant, grinding his teeth, "is vengeance."

~

The four-wheel drive pickup truck spat mud from its rear tyres as it ground a path through the field and out the gate into the village of Fen Ditton. Further on they hit the highway and Vermuden steered back toward the city, veering off when he came to the Ring Road and then continuing along till he reached Girton.

It was close to midnight when they stopped at another field, pulling off the road till the truck could no longer be easily seen.

Once they were safely parked, the three left the truck and started unloading the crates and boxes.

"What is this stuff?" asked Grant, feeling his muscles tighten and quiver against the heavy load. He and Vermuden had just lifted out what seemed like two hundred pounds compressed inside a tea chest.

"You'll see soon enough," said Vermuden, going back for another crate. "Get moving. We need to have this all set up inside an hour."

Mai was using a hammer and chisel to break open the wooden boxes that had already been unloaded. At the periphery of his vision he could see her pulling out what looked to be an enormous piece of material bundled together with miles of hemp.

The last carton was especially heavy. "Be careful with this one," Vermuden warned. "We can't let it drop."

"You've got a bomb?" asked Grant.

"No," said Vermuden. "Something better or worse, depending on your perspective."

It took all the strength he had to keep it steady as Vermuden, standing above him on the truck bed, tilted it into his arms. As the centre of balance slowly shifted his way, he felt his sinews being stretched to their limit. The weight increased even more. Suddenly, he felt as if they were about to snap.

"I don't think I can hold it any longer!" he shouted.

Vermuden jumped down from the truck and grabbed the other end, just as Grant fell to his knees though still managing to hold his end up.

"Slowly...gently," Vermuden said, as they lowered it to the ground.

He felt the dirt under his hands and let go just before his fingers were crushed. The crate fell the half inch more with a thud.

Wiping the sweat which was dripping from his brow, Grant stood up and gazed at Vermuden with amazement. "You were going to do this just with her?" he asked, looking over at Mai. "Just the two of you? Alone?"

"If I had to, yes. Women half as big as her carried twice this load in Vietnam."

"Vietnam?" Grant gave him a questioning glance. "What's in here? Napalm?"

"That's quite a good guess," said Vermuden.

Grant looked over at the material, now spread out on the ground. The shape was drawn in two dimensions but it was clear what it would be with a lot of air pumped into it. He shook his head. "I'll be damned," he said.

"Not if we play our cards carefully," said Vermuden, chiselling open another crate and extracting a large metal cylinder.

"Compressed gas?" asked Grant.

"Hydrogen," Vermuden said, connecting the valve of the cylinder to a rubber hose.

"I thought these things are inflated with hot air," said Grant, watching with fascination as Vermuden extended the hose to the mouth of the balloon.

"Mostly nowadays, yes. But we don't have a crew, do we? And hydrogen works just as well."

"Except it's volatile, isn't it?"

"That is a drawback," said Vermuden, tying some cords that connected the still deflated balloon to a huge wicker basket.

Mai worked quickly alongside of him, securing various cords and ropes. They had clearly done this thing before, Grant thought.

When the basket and cords were secured, Vermuden and Mai took a brief rest. Mai went to the truck and brought out a thermos and some cups. She poured out the contents – coffee, piping hot – and handed it around.

It was only when they took a moment to drink their coffee that Grant pieced together what was going on.

"We're napalming TechnoFarm?" He stared at the two of them.

"How the hell else are you going to stop them?" said Mai.

Grant sipped at his coffee. She was right. How the hell else?

~

It was truly an amazing sight.

As the gas seeped in, the material took on life. It was as if a creature made of castoff cloth and stuffed with cotton suddenly began to breath and then, filling its lungs with lightened air, to defy gravity itself and float.

It rose. Straining at its guy lines attached to anchors hammered into the earth, it rose, stretching at its seams until Grant thought they would burst.

But how marvellous it looked! Big and black and bold, set against the moonlit sky, it took his breath away. He felt the palpitations in his chest. He could taste the excitement on his lips and deep inside his throat.

And like a mighty stallion, restless at the gate, steam, hot and wet, shooting from its nostrils this giant balloon, hissing from its infusion of cold gas, strained to be released from its hold.

Vermuden was working on the cylinder of napalm undoing the outer case with his tools. "It's been reinforced to stop accidental spillage," he explained. "Most of the weight was in the outside metal. The inner case is much lighter."

"But easier to damage, I suppose."

"Give me a hand," said Vermuden, as he tipped the basket over so the top edge met the ground. The three of them together carefully loaded the napalm inside.

Grant looked at his watch and saw it was nearing one o'clock. "When do we start?" he asked.

"We're waiting for the wind," said Vermuden. He pointed to a device Mai had planted in the ground. It was a pole with a nylon sock atop. "The only way we can drop our load onto its target is by waiting for the right air stream to slip us in. You can only navigate a balloon by going up or down. You have to find the proper current to take you where you want to go."

"And where's that?" asked Grant. "I mean how do you know where to drop it?"

"I did manage to make a plan of TechnoFarm from the overhead shots I took and from chatting with our little bird before she flew the coop."

He took Grant over to the map board and showed him the sketch. "Here's the main facility," he said, pointing to the outline of the building. "And here's the research farm." He drew his finger due west to several plots of land. "Regardless of all their blather about self-sustaining produce, they still had heaps of fertiliser that they used." He pointed to a cylindrical looking structure midway between the building and the farm land. "According to our source, the silo here is filled with nitrogenous chemicals. It has been pointed out by their safety officer that the place is a class 'A' hazard." He winked at Grant.

"The IRA knew that," said Mai. "The biggest bomb they detonated was a dump truck filled with fertiliser."

"That's a pretty tiny target," said Grant, inspecting the detailed drawings.

"You're right," Vermuden said. "But we don't have to hit it. We just need to get somewhere near. The napalm blaze will set it off. The heat it produces is like a furnace! With any luck, we'll destroy the farm and the research facility all in one go!"

~

The sensation was like nothing he had ever experienced before in his life. With a gentle evening breeze blowing in their direction, the giant balloon rose from its moorings, upward, into the sky.

They were standing in the basket. Grant was holding tight to the edge, staring out, wide-eyed at the ground below, watching as the figure of Mai became smaller.

"How will she find us when we land?" he asked, seeing Mai disappear from view.

"There's a signalling device in the instrument box. She has a receiver. All she has to do is follow the flashing light."

As the balloon rose higher, the breeze became stiffer. But it carried them in the general direction they wanted to go. Below, he could see the perimeter fence of TechnoFarm, the razor wire sparkling in the moonlight like tiny diamonds. How impenetrable it had looked from below and how innocuous from above, he mused.

Suddenly Vermuden reached up and pulled a rope that was hanging from the inflating tube that dangled above them like an elephant's trunk. There was a loud hissing sound and Grant felt it in his stomach as the balloon began to descend.

"What's going on?" Grant felt a slight bit of panic, as if things were out of control.

"Not to worry," Vermuden assured him. "Just making a slight correction." He pointed to the rope. "It's connected to the valve up top. Letting out some gas allows you to go down."

"What if you want to go up again?"

"You throw off some poundage." Vermuden grinned. "How much do you weigh, Dr Grant?"

Grant looked as if he almost believed him and Vermuden laughed. "That's what those sandbags are for. The one's hanging over the edge."

As the balloon sank down, Grant could clearly see the layout of TechnoFarm. It conformed nicely to the diagrammatic sketch. To the Northwest was the main facility, its various wings connected by narrow corridors, forming the shape of an 'H' on the ground.

Directly below them were the experimental gardens. The colours, muted in the darkness were barely visible in the light of the moon, but Grant could see the lushness and fascinating variety in the growth. Yet there was something inexplicably odd about it too. Something almost eerie. Perhaps it was his realisation of what actually was being done to those plants – what he had come to view as a monstrous evil – that made him see it as almost creepy. Or the strange growths on the periphery that seemed to dance in the moonlight like cobras being charmed by the sound of an oriental flute. Or maybe it was the curious odour that hung heavy in the air, even at their altitude – an erotic smell that had the taste of delight but also of danger and death.

"We're right on course," said Vermuden, indicating the silo where, according to his information, the volatile fertiliser was kept. "We'll only have one go, so we have to do it right. When the napalm hits the ground, I expect we'll have a few minutes before the silo is set off. In that time, we need to cut our ballast and throw our dead weight off and hope to rise quickly before we fry along with the veggie stuff..."

"How high would we go?" asked Grant.

"High enough. Once we get rid of our bomb and our ballast, we could go up to where your blood would boil and your skin would freeze..." He looked at Grant to see if he had forced the desired reaction.

"Except we could always pull the valve rope, right?"

"Correct," said Vermuden with a wink. "You catch on quickly."

Saying that, Vermuden got down on his knees, took a tool out of his shirt pocket and began fiddling with the nose cone of the napalm cylinder.

"What are you doing?" asked Grant.

"The cone has a small detonator device. I'm setting the timer on it. It's not a very large explosion but the napalm is packed under extreme pressure. When the device explodes, the napalm will be sprayed for a good hundred yards." He looked up at Grant. "You know what this stuff is, of course..."

He knew it only too well, having been sent to Vietnam by World Health during the war. "A mixture of naphthenic and palmitic acids – it forms a sort of jellied petrol. It caused the most horrible effects I've ever seen. It sticks to anything, including skin. You can't get it off. It just keeps burning..." Even now he still remembered the sickening smell of burning flesh, children running in the streets, napalm covered bodies rolling in the dirt, screaming, trying to smoother the unquenchable flames.

"It's time," said Vermuden, bending down to get the cylinder.

And that's when he saw it. Why he hadn't thought of it earlier, he didn't know. But it was the wee hours of the morning. Why would anyone be there now?

"The near wing of the building over there," said Grant, pointing to the part of the main facility closest to them. "There's some lights..."

"So someone left the lights on," said Vermuden lifting up his end. "Grant, I need your help..."

"I saw a shadow of something moving. Someone's in there..." He looked down at Vermuden and repeated, in case he hadn't heard, "Someone's in there!"

Vermuden stood up and took Grant by the collar and pulled him close so close, Grant could see the spittle on the corner of his lips and the fire in his eyes. "Of course there's someone in there, you fool! It's Blumgarten! I know his every movements! He comes here when everyone's asleep so he can create more of his monstrosities! Why do you think we've chosen this time? We're going to kill Dr Frankenstein and all of his creations!"

Grant shoved him away. "You didn't say anything about killing people!"

"Blumgarten isn't a person! He's not human! He's worse than the abortions he created!" Vermuden bent down again. "We haven't much time. Help me, Grant!"

"How the hell do you know he's alone? How do you know there isn't someone there with him? How about the security staff?"

"Was Pauline alone?" shouted Vermuden. "Was Thomas? Were all the others?"

"I'm not killing people!" Grant shouted back. "I'm not going to be their judge, their juror and their executioner!"

Vermuden stood up again. His muscles tightened. A facial nerve twitched and his tight muscles trembled. "You bloody wimp! All your talk! All your feigned anger! When it comes to action, you're all the same, aren't you? You're slime! You're lower than slime! Even slime has more dignity than you!"

His long, think fingers undid the sheath attached to his belt. He withdrew his knife and held it out in Grant's direction. The blade glistened in the moonlight. "You can't stop this, Grant! This place is evil! It has to be destroyed! Even at the cost of ourselves!"

Vermuden looked down. The silo was behind them.

"This is your last chance, Grant! Will you help?"

Grant shook his head. "Not this way..."

"It's up to you," Vermuden said. He took his knife and with one might swing he cut a rope that fixed the passenger basket to the balloon's suspension hoop.

The basket lurched down at an angle. The napalm cylinder rolled and slammed against the side. Grant lost his footing, but managed to cling to the edge.

"The choice is yours, Grant!" Vermuden said, holding his knife out again.

"Vermuden! You're crazy! Don't be an idiot."

He slashed at the second rope. The passenger basket lurched down again and the napalm cylinder rolled further to the edge, now tilted 45 degrees toward earth.

"We can settle this some other way!" Grant shouted. "We don't have to be like them!"

Vermuden's knife struck out again. The basket lurched down another 10 degrees. The napalm crashed against the basket's rim and teetered on the edge. Grant, clinging to one of the uncut lines, heard a hissing sound and saw the lethal jelly start oozing from the sides.

Using every bit of strength he could muster, Grant pulled himself up the rope till he could grab the suspension hoop of the balloon, about six feet above the basket.

It wasn't a moment too soon. The basket, set ablaze by the leaking napalm, broke from its last mooring and fell to earth. Vermuden, clinging to a line, was burning.

Grant reached out. "Grab my hand!" he shouted.

It was too late. The flames from the napalm on Vermuden's leg was licking at the rope. It broke.

There was a smile on Vermuden's lips, a chilling, incomprehensible smile, just before he fell. It etched itself into Grant's head like a graven image he had seen before. The fourth horseman at the house of Chu Lopez. The horseman called "Death".

The napalm bomb exploded sending its lethal substance hurtling over the farm. Then, seconds later, the silo erupted.

It was like the beginning of the universe. First there was nothing. Then space seemed to quiver and the nothingness shook. At the nanosecond just before the explosion, he could feel it suck him back. The balloon seemed to be drawn back to earth. Closer and closer to the fire. And then...

The force of the explosion sent forth a blast mightier than a hurricane, shooting the balloon straight up into the air. Below, the ripples of sight and sound seemed to be in slow motion. He saw the ground erupt and the buildings collapse in a terrifying vision of apocalyptic horror.

Perched on the metal rim of the suspension hoop, clinging to the balloon's guy lines, he watched, his mouth agape. Like Lazarus, he witnessed the world engulfed in flames as he rose skyward.

And rise he did. Higher and higher into the sky. There was nothing to do. No line to pull – it had burnt and snapped from the spillage of napalm.

But, as he ascended into the heavens, he saw a marvellous sight. The ravages of TechnoFarm grew smaller and then faded from sight. Then the city of Cambridge, its ivory towered colleges, slowly disappeared from view. And then, in the dawning of the new day's light, he saw the green of the countryside and the gentle rolling hills. And then the seas and the mountains. And finally, he saw the curve of the earth, shimmering in the heat of the resurgent sun. And he heard a strange and wonderful sound. And he wondered where it was coming from.

EPILOGUE

EPILOGUE

~MONDAY 27 JULY, 2015~

CICELY SAT AT her mother's desk in the Cambridge house where nothing had changed in the last 21 years. Even the fridge still wore its ancient sign – 'Time waits for no woman'. She was finishing up her presentation notes for an event which was to be held that afternoon at the Mai Cunningham Institute for Investigative Journalism in celebration of a forthcoming book entitled *TechnoFarm – A Cautionary Tale.*

Pausing a moment to glance up at a photo she had fixed to the wall above the writing table - a picture of a woman who looked very much like herself – she ended by writing:

"Most likely we will never know the complete story of what happened over two decades ago when a secret research centre was mysteriously engulfed in flames and burned to the ground. Nor can we be certain about the mystifying disappearance of Dr Peter Grant – one of the country's foremost epidemiologists. Or the strange death of Morris Katz, the lawyer representing Eduardo Rojas, a Chilean refugee who himself died under curious circumstances. But with the help of Thomas McFadden, a courageous parliamentary secretary who has worked tirelessly to unearth some crucial documents and our team of investigators – Dr Tracy Poon, Felicia Rojas (one of the lucky survivors of the so-called 'Toxic Oil Scare') and Rachel Katz – we have managed to shed some critical light on that unholy alliance between government and agribusiness which worshiped Mammon, the god of gluttony, rather than Demeter, the all-nourishing mother of the soil.

"Together we came to understand that TechnoFarm was not a place but a state of mind where the dream of bountiful produce and freedom from hunger became a nightmare of corporate greed and governmental collusion. TechnoFarm, the place, may have been destroyed but TechnoFarm, the idea, continues on.

"We hope that, perhaps, this tragic story retold can inspire a new generation of people - brave youth like Felicia Rojas and Rachel Katz - who are fighting for a world where humanity triumphs over avarice. But what is the alternative?"

With that question hanging in the air, Cicely put down her pen, folded the sheet of paper on which she had been writing and stood up. Looking once more at the photo on the wall, she blew it a kiss. And then she bounded out the door.

www.ingramcontent.com/pod-product-compliance
Lightning Source LLC
Chambersburg PA
CBHW020329030826
48979CB00021B/498
* 9 7 8 1 9 0 0 3 5 5 1 0 0 *